**Triple Crown Publications
presents**

Contagious

By Quentin Carter

Compilation and Introduction copyright © 2007 by
Triple Crown Publications
PO Box 6888
Columbus, Ohio 43205
www.TripleCrownPublications.com

Library of Congress Control Number: 2006902055
ISBN: 0-9767894-8-5
ISBN 13: 978-0-9767894-8-2
Cover Design/Graphics: www.MarionDesigns.com
Author: Quentin Carter
Typesetting: Holscher Type and Design
Associate Editor: Cynthia Parker, Lisa Williams
Editorial Assistant: Elizabeth Zaleski
Editor-in-Chief: Mia McPherson
Consulting: Vickie M. Stringer

First Trade Paperback Edition Printing March 2007

10 9 8 7 6 5 4 3 2 1

Printed in the United States of America

Acknowledgements

First, I would like to thank God as always for coming into my life at a time when I needed Him most, and for allowing me to make the best out of the seven years I've lost out of my life.

A special thank you to my mother and father, Lois and Charles Williams. And to my brothers and sisters who have been there through it all, Christopher, Brad, Dewayne, Joey, Cheron and Niecy.

My family who continues to show me their unconditional love, Barbara Jones, Willie Carter, June and Ruby Carter, Vickie Reeder, TT, Micheal, Darryl Leggs, Stevie Jones, Lillian White, Nettie Melson, Grandma Lucy Acklin, Macoshia Williams, D-Loc and Rocky. Anybody that I forgot to mention probably didn't deserve to be mentioned.

My children, Quentez, Mikel, Breanna, Brianna, Micheal and Brandis. Ya'll are the very reasons that I have to be successful in whatever I do.

And the women, even though y'all piss me off more than a little, y'all have still done a lot more than I feel that I really deserved. Danika Acklin, Keosha, Lady, Kiria, Kelly, Lakisha, Mauri and Erin.

The group that made it all possible, Vickie Stringer, Mia McPherson, Tammy and the entire TCP family.

I mustn't forget those who stayed up late nights reading and giving me their ideas for the manuscript, Teko, Big Hamp, Chris, Jarrett Jackson, Derrick McDonald, Monie, J. Juice, Ray Duck, Big Geno, Big Corn, Shorty Reed, Chris Lamon and Keith Haliburton.

To my good friend, typist and editor, Cynthia Parker. You do a lot more for me than you have to, and if I ever make it big in this game, I won't forget you.

My regards to my fellow authors who share the same pain that I do. Leo Sullivan, Darrell DeBrew, Darrell King, Jason Poole and Victor L. Martin. Even locked up, we refuse to be held down.

And last but not least, my fans. You people spent your precious money purchasing my book and took the time out to either write me about it or post your comments online. To T. Styles, author of *Black & Ugly*, I didn't even know you were a fan. Katrina McClain (KC), Lisa Aquilar (Brooklyn, NY), Unique C. (Virginia), Tiara Carmen (Norfolk, VA), Nicki Duckch (Federick, MD), My girl Lady Scorpio (Coast to Coast Readers), Shyste, Chocolate Girl, C. Price (DC), Mzadie (Oakland, CA), Brooke Love, Sexy Love (LA), Jewelz81 (Jersey). All of your comments are welcome and very much appreciated.

Hopefully you'll enjoy all of my books just as well as you did the first.

Every story has been told, it's just the way I tell it that keeps the reader turning pages.

- King Author -

All comments, good or bad, can be addressed to:

Quentin Carter 13685-045
K-Unit
F.C.I.
P.O. Box 1000
Sandstone, MN 55072

Dedication

To the man who stepped up to the plate after my daddy struck out. Charles, this book's for you.

Chapter 1

Maurice Jones sat comfortably behind his huge, solid oak desk with his feet propped up, staring out of his office window. He sipped on a tall glass of lemonade while he watched a pretty young woman browse through the rows of cars. She seemed to be giving most of her attention to a white Chrysler Sebring.

The dropped top was what grabbed her attention. That, he was sure of. That's why he let it down when he got to work that morning. He knew that convertibles were young women's first choice. With the top down, they could be seen while they paraded up and down the streets going nowhere. He also knew that it was income tax time and they would be flocking in, trying to spend their tax returns before they even got them.

It was only his third year working at the dealership, and he had already been promoted to top salesman. He was good at what he did and took pride in his work. Maurice hustled cars like a dope man hustled dope. He was young, tall and extremely handsome. A highly intelligent young man, most would say. That, along with his charm and wit, helped him earn an enormous commission check every month.

He could wheel and deal anybody, but he preferred doing business with women. They were just as easy to talk out of their money as they were their panties.

He wasn't a star but he was very well known around Kansas

City. His name was brought up in every beauty salon, nail shop, club and everywhere else females hung out in the city. He was a player at heart and they all knew it. But yet and still, they couldn't get enough of the young stud. He could trick them into doing damn near anything he wanted, without effort. His friends tried to mock his style, but couldn't come close. Like he informed them a long time ago, he was a pimp by nature, not by choice. And that, he truly believed.

Maurice hated the way men were today. They bought pussy. They constantly wined and dined women, making it bad for all the real players out there. He thought God made woman for a man, not man for a woman, and it was man around whom the world revolved.

If women could get paid just by lying down and opening up their legs, then surely a man could get paid for doing all the work. In his book, there wasn't a pussy out there that was worth more than his dick.

There was a knock on the door.

"Come in," Maurice said without taking his eyes off the young woman out front. For a second, he got a brief peek at her underwear as she bent over to pick up something she dropped.

His co-worker and closest friend, Derrick, came through the door carrying two boxes of Kentucky Fried Chicken. He tossed one of the boxes onto Maurice's desk. Maurice picked the box up and opened it. He frowned at its contents.

"What the fuck is this?" Maurice asked. "I told you to bring me two legs, a breast and a pepper. I see two legs and a damn thigh."

Derrick frowned. "Why every time you speak to me, you have to yell and shit? You ain't got to talk to me like I'm stupid."

"The hell I don't," Maurice snapped. "You've got to start paying more attention to shit, Derrick, man." He shook his head in disgust. He hated thighs, and he couldn't eat nobody's chicken without a pepper.

"Nigga, you act like you my damn daddy or something."

Derrick was twenty-one, three years younger than Maurice.

"Sometimes I feel like I am your daddy, nigga." He took a leg out of the box, placing it on a napkin. He reached over, opening up Derrick's box. Without asking, he took out his pepper. "Since you forgot mine, I'm taking yours."

Derrick brushed it off. Arguing with Maurice could turn into an all day thing if he let it. Derrick was a light-skinned dude with short, wavy, reddish hair and big brown eyes. He used to fall in love quick and was easily suckered by girls, until he and Maurice started hanging out. Maurice made him tighten up his game and realize how much of a stud he could be. He already had the body and the brown eyes, he just needed the game.

Finally, Derrick sat down in one of the two chairs in front of Maurice's desk. "You got a fucked up attitude, Reece. You know that? Next time, just go get the shit yourself. That way you ain't got to worry about me fuckin' up your order." He took a piece of chicken out of his box. "You act like people can't make mistakes."

"You said that like it was your first time or something," Maurice responded. Maurice noticed that Derrick had sat down. "Who the fuck said you could eat in my office?"

Derrick stared at him in disbelief. Maurice could be an asshole sometimes over the pettiest shit. "Man, fuck you," Derrick stated. "I can eat in here if I want to."

"*I can eat in here if I want to,*" Maurice mocked him. "You sound like a little bitch."

"Yeah, whatever."

Maurice chewed on a leg while focusing his attention back on the girl outside. Now she was sitting behind the wheel inside the Sebring, pretending to be driving. Derrick said, "Why don't you take your cranky ass out there and sell a car or something."

Maurice shook his head. "She ain't ready yet," he said evenly. He seemed to have calmed down.

"So what happened with that bitch you left the club with last night?" Derrick asked, changing the subject.

"I fucked her," he replied nonchalantly. "Fuck you think happened?"

"That bitch was bad. Pussy was good, wasn't it?"

Maurice shrugged. "You've fucked one, you've fucked them all."

"That reminds me," Derrick said, unclipping his cell phone from his hip. "Melissa's supposed to buy me this watch on Friday." He showed him a picture he had stored in his phone. "She says she wants me to have something to remind me of her. She got one just like it."

Maurice shot accusing eyes at him. "Y'all been spending an awful lot of time together lately," he complained. "You sure you ain't falling in love with that bitch?" He said "bitch" just to see how Derrick would react.

"Hell naw. She just cool," he said weakly. He knew why Maurice had called her a bitch. He wasn't gonna give him the satisfaction by commenting on it.

"Good." Maurice sat up in his chair. "Let the bitch fall for you, man. Every woman is a fool for pretty niggas like us. They'd suck our shit through a straw if they could." He pointed a finger at him. "Take advantage while you can. You'll be having to buy pussy after you turn fifty."

"I thought you said you would never buy no pussy."

"I ain't. That's why I said *you'll* have to."

Derrick wiped his hands with a napkin. "If I got to buy it, then I don't need it."

Maurice smiled as he stood up, stretching his long frame. Once again, Derrick had passed his verbal test. He patted him on top of his head. "Just making sure you're still on point, bro," he said on his way out the door.

The thought of a woman tricking for Derrick tickled Maurice. He could remember when Derrick was too scared to ask a girl for some pussy, let alone some money.

Maurice walked outside to approach the young lady. "How are you today?" he asked, thrusting his hand forward. "My name is

Maurice Jones."

"I'm fine," she replied sweetly. She was still sitting behind the wheel of the car.

"Yes, you are," he flirted. "What can I do for you today?" He put his hands inside his pockets and leaned up against the car.

She looked up at him through soft, worried green eyes. He knew right away what that look meant: *I want this car, but I don't have enough credit.* He had a remedy for women in her situation.

"I am so in love with this car." She toyed with the wheel like a child. "But the price is—"

"Too high, huh?" he said, cutting her off.

"Mmm hmm," she grunted.

"What's your name?"

"Pasha," she said with a smile. Her mother taught her to always keep a flirtatious smile on her face when buying anything from a man. Sometimes it worked, sometimes it didn't.

"Pasha," he repeated. "Have you had a credit check done?"

"Yes, but they only approved me for a twenty-thousand-dollar loan, and I only have a thousand to put down."

"Hmm?" Maurice took a moment to think to himself. "There might be something that I can do for you. Follow me inside."

"Okay," she said happily. He opened the car door for her.

The smell of his cologne and the way he looked in his Armani suit turned her on. She knew he had a way with women. She had heard about Maurice Jones long before she met him. He was real smooth. The kind of guy she would like to get next to. It would be refreshing to date someone different than the drug dealing thugs she was used to.

Maurice rid his office of Derrick and told Pasha to have a seat.

"Do you mind if I call you Reece?" she asked. She shot him a seductive look. "That's what all the girls down at the shop call you. I think that's a sexy-ass name."

She's trying to run game on me, he thought. *I know she don't think that lame shit is gonna work on me. I can't get mad at her for trying, though.*

He took a seat behind his desk, trying to suppress his smile. "Call me whatever makes you feel comfortable." He stared into her eyes.

She blushed, wanting to look away, but couldn't seem to take her eyes off of him. He was fine as a muthafucka. She thought she was being admired, but she wasn't. He was searching her face for weakness and vulnerability.

Satisfied with what he saw, he pulled out a tan folder from his file cabinet.

"It says here that the Sebring is going for twenty-six thousand dollars." He closed the folder, setting it down on the desk. "And you say that the bank only approved you for a twenty-thousand-dollar loan?"

"Mm hmm," she said nervously.

He leaned back in his leather chair. "Well, I do have a special program for women in your situation. But it's—"

"I know all about your program," she blurted out.

Now he knew why she was wearing that short skirt.

"Aw, yeah? How you know about that?" he asked suspiciously.

"My friend, Cashunda," she replied proudly. "She works at the beauty shop down on Gregory. She told me what you did for her. That's why I came to see you."

Cashunda, he thought to himself. Yes, he remembered her well. After selling her a new Dodge Intrepid, he ended up spending the whole weekend with her. They had checked into a hotel that Friday and didn't come out until Monday morning. Her pussy was just that damn good, and the head was fire. She was well worth what he had done for her.

"Reece," Pasha called out, bringing him back to reality.

"Huh? Yeah, I remember Cashunda. She's the one with the tongue ring, right?"

She nodded. "Yeah, that's her."

"Alright, then." He took a sheet of paper from his desk drawer. It was a contract. He handed it to her.

It read:

*I, _____, agree to pay Maurice Jones the amount of
five thousand dollars in twenty-five monthly payments
of two hundred dollars.*

Her face balled up after she finished reading it.

"What's this for?" she quizzed. "Why do I have to pay after we do what we're gonna do?"

His eyebrows shot up. "Look here, baby. I mean, I'm sure your pussy is gold and all, but it ain't worth no five grand."

"Cashunda said that all I had to do was fuck you, and you'd hook me up."

"Cashunda told you right." He sat up in his chair. "Look at it this way, baby. I'ma give you a pre-approved five-thousand-dollar loan, with only a shot of pussy as an interest fee. You can't beat that."

"Just a shot of pussy," she repeated. "You said that like I'm a ho or something. I ain't no damn ho, nigga."

He sighed. "Look here. I didn't call you no ho, but if you want this car bad enough, you're gonna have to temporarily stoop to the level of a ho to get it." He turned around, pointing out the window. "I've got a whole selection of Dodge Neons out there that you could easily get approved for."

She pictured herself pulling up to the beauty shop in her sporty new drop top. All them hoes would hate on her. And don't let her put some 17-inch chrome rims on it. Suddenly, she didn't care what she had to do to get it.

"Fine," she said hastily. "Let's get this over with."

He got up, slowly walked over to the door, and opened it up.

"What are you doing?" she asked curiously.

"I've changed my mind," he said calmly.

"Why?"

"'Cause your attitude is not acceptable up in here. I'd rather just say fuck it, altogether."

She stood up and walked toward the door. She placed her hand on top of his, removing it from around the doorknob. She closed the door. "I'm sorry," she pleaded, still holding his hand.

"Cashunda just didn't tell me all of the details. I'm cool with it."

"You sure?"

"Mm hmm." She leaned forward, kissing him and backing him up toward his desk.

He broke away from her so he could pull the shades on the windows. Then he took a Magnum condom out of his desk drawer. He pulled her close to him and started kissing on her neck. Carefully, he slid her skirt down to the floor while she fumbled with his zipper.

While he put on the rubber, Pasha bent over and placed her hands flat on his desk. Reaching back behind her butt, she pulled her panties to the side.

"Fuck that shit," Maurice said when he saw what she was doing. He pulled her panties down to her ankles, spread her butt cheeks, and then entered her.

"Ummmph," she moaned as her lips parted.

He started with slow, shallow strokes until she loosened up. After a while she began to meet him pound for pound. He proceeded to punish her, banging her head against his computer.

Derrick and one of his white co-workers, Roger, were walking past Maurice's office when they heard Pasha's muffled moans coming from the other side of the door.

"You hear that, man?" Roger asked, stopping in his tracks.

"Hear what?" Derrick replied, playing stupid.

"That moaning sound coming from Maurice's office?" He walked up to the door.

"Why don't you mind your own damn business sometime? That's the problem with white people today. They always got their noses in somebody else's business."

"Chill, man." Roger put his ear up against the door. "Sounds like he's in there fuckin'."

Derrick grabbed him by the arm. "Mind your business. Now come on, we've got customers outside."

"Maurice is a fuckin' black stud, man," Roger said on their way outside.

Derrick shook his head, thinking about how careless Maurice was getting. He was in his office, fucking her hard like he was at home. He was gonna fuck around and get them both fired and thrown in jail.

Maurice's mouth dropped open when he began to ejaculate. Grabbing her ass, he continued to thrust harder, until the last drop was expelled. He carefully pulled off the rubber and tossed it into the trash. After he pulled up his pants, he dropped down in his chair, panting and sweating. They were both out of breath. "Goddamn, girl! You a beast," he managed to say in between breaths.

She smiled, feeling proud of herself. *You wasn't a bad fuck yourself,* she thought as she slipped back into her skirt. After that, the thought of her degrading herself for the car disappeared from her mind.

Finally, he collected himself. He called the service manager and told him that the white convertible Sebring in the front row was sold. He watched as the car was being driven away to be washed and gassed up. It was time to get down to business. He notarized the contract after she signed it. Then he finished the remaining paperwork.

"Can I have my keys now?" She was brushing wrinkles out of her skirt.

"Just a minute." He was busy writing. "I'm gonna need your down payment and proof of insurance." He looked up at her.

She reached into her purse and pulled out a Geico insurance card. "All I have to do is call this number after I get your approval. This is the same company that insures my mama's car." Taking out her wallet, she pulled out a stack of bills, counted out one thousand dollars, then handed it to him.

He counted it twice before pocketing it. "What's the name of your bank and loan officer?" She gave it to him, then he made the necessary calls and things were done.

He grabbed a set of keys off a rack on the wall and handed them to her, along with a receipt.

"That'll do it," he said, clapping his hands together. "Take the paperwork over to your bank. Oh, yeah," he reached into his shirt pocket, took out his business card and handed it to her. "Send my payments to that address." The card had his home address on it.

Pasha twirled the keys around in her hand like an anxious child. "Okay. Is that it?"

"Yep."

She was headed out the door when the service manager returned with the car. She stopped and turned back around. "Can I call you sometime?"

"Please do."

She smiled. "I think I will. Don't let this little episode taint what we could probably become in the future. Okay? Because I'm really a good girl."

"I promise I won't."

"Bye," she said with a short wave of her small hand.

Maurice was standing in the parking lot, waving her off, when his boss walked up. "Mr. Copeland. How you doing?" he said with a smile.

Mr. Copeland was old and tall with a headful of white hair. He was about his business and rich, but he was still a down-to-earth kind of guy. He pointed a crooked finger at the trunk of the leaving Sebring.

"I see you've sold that thing already."

"Yeah. I had to let her go for twenty-one thousand," he lied. Being that he was the head salesman, he was authorized to make such deals. Derrick didn't have the authority to knock more than two grand off of a price.

"That's good," Copeland said, patting him on the back. "That's real good. Keep up the good work."

Chapter 2

Maurice clocked out at six o'clock sharp. He hopped in his new Corvette and let the top down. It was a warm May day, so he removed his shirt and tie, revealing a white tank top that displayed his cuts. The big engine roared as it came to life. He spun his wheels on his way out of the lot.

When he pulled into the driveway of his Grandview home, he noticed that his garage window had been busted out.

"It had to be that bitch Neosha," he said out loud.

Neosha was his ghetto girl who loved to cause trouble when things weren't going her way. She paid well, so he didn't mind the lightweight drama.

He shook his head as he stepped over all the broken glass on his way inside. He turned off the alarm, threw his keys on the table, then pushed the play button on the answering machine. After he fixed himself a glass of Rémy XO, he relaxed in his favorite recliner.

Message one: "Reece, this is Yvonne. I know you haven't forgotten about me already, playa. Anyway, I still want to take you out this weekend. Bye bye."

Message two: "Maur-reece, this is Neosha." She snickered. "I hope you're not mad about your broken window. You sho' don't mind breakin' hearts. Bye, pussy."

He looked at the recorder, shaking his head.

Message three: "What's up, nigga? This yo' boy, Freak. I hate to tell you this, but your bitch didn't make your car payment this month. Get with me so we can settle this matter."

Freak was a long time friend of his who owned his own loan company. He gave Maurice the loan for his Corvette, after he promised not to miss a payment. Freak was his friend, but business was business. Maurice knew that if he didn't make the payment right away, it would be repossessed. Freak didn't play games about his money, friend or no friend.

His business not being taken care of pissed Maurice off. One of his women, Michelle, was supposed to have paid his bill two days ago. She knew that it was an every month thing. *What the hell is she tripping on?* he wondered.

He dialed her number on his cordless phone.

She picked up after two rings. "Hello?"

"Michelle," he said calmly. "How did you forget to make my car payment?"

For a moment she was silent. "Hold on," she finally whispered.

He assumed that her wealthy lawyer husband was nearby. Ordinarily, he wouldn't have called her at home, but he wanted her to know how important this phone call was.

Maurice had been dating Michelle for over a year now. Secretly, he really liked her, but would never confess it even to himself. She was older, but still sexy, and cooler than any girl he had ever been with. She loved to lay up and spend time at his house, even though she had a husband at home. Maurice made her feel good, young and still full of life, unlike her old stuck-up husband, Larry. She wasn't but thirty-five, but old in comparison to Maurice.

Over time she had made a hobby out of buying Maurice nice things. She loved to see him in the best, which is why she bought him the best. Michelle didn't have to fantasize about those sexy models on TV and in GQ magazine. She had Maurice. She made the payment on his car so he could look as good riding as he did walking. What did she care? It was Larry's money anyway.

"I'm back," she whispered into the phone. "I'm sorry baby. I—"

"Sorry don't pay my bills, baby," he said harshly. "You're the one who had me buy the damn car, now you don't want to make the payments."

"Baby, I said—"

"If you can't commit to your promise about a simple thing like this, how are you gonna commit to me one day?" He hung up the phone.

He laughed as he sipped on the cognac. She'd call back. She knew she had done wrong by not paying the bill on time.

Maurice picked up his remote, turning on the flat screen TV that hung above the mantel. He was flipping through the channels when the phone rang.

"Yeah."

"Maurice," Michelle pleaded.

"What?"

"I'm gonna take care of that first thing tomorrow, baby. I promise. I couldn't do it because Larry has been home sick all week. What kind of wife would I be if I weren't there for him?"

He laughed. "What kind of wife cheats on her husband?"

"That's not fair, Maurice. How could you talk to me like that?" Her voice was weakening.

He didn't let up. "If I'm the one you love, then I should be your first priority. I love you, but it's obviously a one way street."

"I love you, too," she whispered. "And I'm sorry I let you down."

"Don't be sorry. Just take care of it," he demanded. "I'll talk to you later."

"You still mad at me?"

"How could I stay mad at you?" he said smoothly. "You're my boo. Now go take care of your sick husband."

"Bye, silly."

They hung up.

Later he'd check up on his other investors. He hoped that

none of the others were late on their payments as well. Kim was in charge of his water bill, Neosha took care of the gas and Tamisha paid his light bill. The phone, cable and rent he could handle on his own.

His mother told him years ago that all women would be a fool for a fine man, in one way or another. At first, he thought she was just speaking of her own experience. However, as he got older, he believed what she told him was absolutely correct. But the one who wouldn't play the fool would be the one to consume his thoughts and actions. She would also be the one he craved daily, and would be the one he would want without a doubt.

Chapter 3

Nekole Mitchell sat at the bar, sipping on a glass of Bacardi Limón. She bobbed her head slowly to the beat of the club's mixed jams. Men hovered around her, trying to get a close up of her big hazel eyes. She didn't bite; instead, she played it cool, ignoring the lustful stares and corny pick-up lines that came at her.

She was there with the man she wanted to be with. In fact, he was one of the biggest ballers in Los Angeles. Even though she had only known him for three weeks, he had already told her most of his personal business. She knew how many bricks he was copping and that he had a house where he kept a half million stashed, in case he was ever kidnapped. All it took for her to get him talking was a couple of glasses of vodka mixed with cranberry juice. He hadn't even gotten the pussy yet.

He walked out of the restroom, wiping his hands with a paper towel. Her eyes were focused on him when he looked in her direction, meeting his gaze. With a nod of his head, he motioned for her to come over to him. She took a second to finish her drink. Flinging her curly black hair over her shoulders, she strutted over to where he was standing. Her blue spaghetti-strapped cami and low cut Capri jeans hugged her curves like they had been painted on.

Nekole was tall with smooth, honey-colored skin. She was slender, with a plump booty and shapely thighs and hips. She was all black, but had the face of an Asian, which earned her the nickname "*Chinky*" when she was a little girl.

Her hips swayed from side to side with the rhythm of the music as she neared him. He stood there with a player's grin on his face, checking out his young piece of game. Out of all the fish in the sea, he landed a whale when he caught her.

"What's up, Chris?" she said in a low, sexy voice. She had a smile on her face that lit up the room. They were now standing body to body. Against her leg, she could feel a huge hump bulging out of his slacks.

"Hmm," she grunted, staring into his eyes. "Feels like you're workin' with a little somethin'."

"Not a little somethin'," he corrected her. He took her by the hand. "So, are we gonna finally get down or what?"

"Do you really want to?"

He let go of her hand and grabbed her waist, pulling her closer to him. "I want you to go to the hotel with me tonight," he said hopefully.

Nekole frowned. "No. My first name ain't 'ho,' and my last name ain't 'tel.'" She started rubbing her crotch up against his leg. "You got to take me to your crib if you want to get your groove on with me." She shot him a seductive look with her hazels to soften him up a bit. "If you don't trust me enough to take me to your house, that's cool," she said, flipping the script on him. "Trust me, I want to fuck just as bad as you do, but we can wait."

"It ain't that," he lied. "I just thought you'd like it better if I took you to an expensive suite."

She began nibbling on his ear. "I want to see your bed," she whispered. She started caressing his zipper. "I want you to remember it every time you walk into your bedroom." She put his hand in between her legs.

"I guess we can do that," he agreed. His dick was hard, and he needed to release. What harm would it cause if he let her spend the night at his other house? He wouldn't take her where he laid his head, but he would take her to one of his stash houses to fuck the shit out of her.

They held hands while she followed him outside to his Navigator. He helped her into the passenger side, then quickly ran around to the driver's seat. Gently, she rubbed his leg and nibbled on his earlobe all the way to his house.

As soon as they got there, Chris jumped into the shower while Nekole made herself at home. The second she heard the shower come on, she immediately started snooping around the place. This was the house where he kept the ransom money stashed – she was sure of it.

Carefully and quietly, she rummaged through his bedroom drawers and closet and checked behind every closed door in the house. She came up with nothing but a gun, jewelry and expensive clothing. She gave up her search upstairs and went to the basement door. It was locked with a padlock. Right then, she confirmed what she had already suspected. There was money in the house.

Nekole flinched when she heard the running water stop flowing. Quickly, she hurried back to his bedroom and out of her clothes. When Chris walked into the room, she was stretched out naked across his bed. Her small, honey-colored breasts were pointing straight up at the ceiling. He took a moment to admire her beauty. She motioned with her index finger for him to "come here." Slowly, he ran his eyes up her smooth legs all the way up to her chiseled stomach. Never in his life had he been with a girl who had abs.

Automatically, her legs parted, inviting him inside her womb. With the skill of a man who'd slept with many women, Chris stroked her gently while she slipped into a world of ecstasy.

x   x   x

Nekole woke the next morning to the sounds of Chris talking on the phone. The code talk that he was speaking let her know that he was handling business. Some of it she understood. Her knowledge came from years of dealing with guys who did illegal business for a living.

Goose bumps immediately covered her skin when she removed

the covers from her naked body. Her eyes roamed the floor until she spotted her thong sitting on top of her jeans. She grabbed the rest of her clothes, pretending not to be listening to his conversation. He glanced over at her after he heard the bed springs squeak. Lowering his voice, he left the room, closing the door behind him.

Nigga, ain't nobody trying to listen to your conversation, she wanted to say, knowing that she was. She shook her head in disgust. After she finished showering and dressing, she went into the living room. Chris was leaning up against his bar with the phone up to his ear. Now that there was light, Nekole could see his slender, muscular physique. His abs flexed with each breath he took.

Chris hung up the phone. "Morning, baby," he said, placing his hands on her waist. "What's up for today?" He was in a cheerful mood.

"I've got to take my aunt somewhere," she lied. "So I won't be free until later on tonight."

He looked surprised. "Don't she got her own car?"

"Yeah, but she wants me to go with her." She removed his hands from her waist. "Don't worry, baby. We gon' hook up later." She gave him a peck on his lips. "Just be patient."

"I love fuckin' you," he said seriously.

Nekole smiled. "Boy, don't talk to me like that." She smacked him gently on his shoulder. "You act like you been fuckin' me for years."

"I know. It was just so good last night, that ... I can't explain it. You'll never know the feeling of fuckin' a fine-ass woman like you."

"I should hope not," she replied. "You ready to take me home now?"

"Yep. Let me get my keys." He picked up his keys off the bar.

Her watchful eye noticed a small key on the ring that stood out from the rest. She figured it to be the key to the padlock that secured the basement door.

"What's that little key for?" She pointed to it.

Chris held the key ring up to his eyes. "It goes to a lock," he replied.

"What lock?"

The look he gave her told her that it was not something he wanted to discuss with her.

"Baby," she said, "you act like you got to keep everything a secret from me." She fixed her hazels on him. "I'm down for you."

"You down for me?"

"Yeah. If a nigga try to get at you, he gon' have to go through me first."

That seemed to do the trick. "It goes to a lock on my basement door."

"Aww. You don't want nobody gettin' down there to your stash. I see." She put that out there just to see if he was gonna confirm or deny it.

"Somethin' like that," he told her, without leaking too much information. "You ready?"

"Yes."

When Chris pulled up in front of Nekole's aunt's house, he noticed some dude sitting in a new Mustang, parked across the street. The guy was just sitting there, like he was waiting for somebody.

"Who dat?" he asked with a tinge of jealously in his voice. *That must be the reason why she needed to get home so fast,* he thought.

"Who?" Nekole said, looking at the car. "Oh, that's my cousin. He's smoking a blunt, probably. Auntie don't play that shit around her kids."

"Oh yeah?" He continued to watch the Mustang.

"Come here," she said, pulling him toward her. "Give Nicky a kiss." She could see the unmistakably jealous look in his eyes.

He finally shook it off, thinking that he was just paranoid. *If that nigga is there for her, she wouldn't be trying to kiss me,* he rationalized. He threw his arm around her neck, kissing her softly, for a long time.

She placed her hand on his chest, pushing him away. "I gotta go now, baby." She grabbed her purse. "I'll see you later."

"Fo' sho."

She blew him a kiss after she exited the vehicle. Chris sat there until she walked her sexy ass into the house. Turning around, she gave him one last wave before she disappeared inside. He smirked as he put the SUV in gear. When he pulled off, he turned up the radio, blasting rap music from his high-dollar sound system.

Nekole stood in the window, peeping through the mini blinds until Chris was gone. After he was no longer in sight, she hurriedly jogged out the front door to the Mustang parked across the street. She hopped into the passenger side, smiling from ear to ear.

"Hey, love. I missed you," she said happily, hugging her boyfriend.

"Yeah, yeah, yeah," he grumbled. "You didn't miss me when he was nine inches up in you last night. Did you?"

Her smile faded. She regarded him curiously. "I did it for you," she reminded him. "Why you trippin'?" He didn't respond. "Sirron, you know I had to do that in order to get him to trust me." With her arms folded across her chest, she shook her head and stared out the window. "I can't believe you, man."

Sirron could hear the sincerity in her voice and realized he was tripping. The girl sitting next to him loved him more than his own mother did.

"I'm sorry, baby," he said in a sweet voice. He was trying to butter her up. Reaching out for her, he said, "Come here."

Nekole resisted.

"No! Get away from me!" she demanded, pushing him away. "You're a piece of shit. I'm out here risking catching AIDS, fuckin' all these niggas so we can have some money, and you worried about petty shit."

Sirron loved how pretty she looked when she was angry. Her high arched eyebrows pointed down at her cute little nose, like a devil. And he knew everything she said was true. He just wished there was a better way for her to trap their victims other than fucking them. It just wasn't right that half of the ballers in LA were getting some of his pussy.

"I said I was sorry, baby, damn," he pleaded. "You know how I am about you." He took a freshly-rolled blunt out of the ashtray then fired it up. "So what's up with this nigga?" he asked with smoke flowing out of his nostrils.

She took the blunt out of his hand and hit it a few times. "He's a buster," she said, holding back a cough. She took another long hit, held it for a few seconds, then released the smoke into the air. "He's ready for the takin'."

"Cool," Sirron said. He then put the car into drive and pulled off. Nekole rode in silence while Sirron contemplated their next move inside his head. "We gon' hit him tonight."

"Okay," she said humbly. Whatever he wanted to do, she went along with. He was the man and he knew best.

× × ×

Chris walked out of the liquor store carrying a bottle of Rémy Martin in one hand and a plastic cup full of ice in the other. He got into his truck, setting the bottle on the seat. His cell phone rang.

"Hello?" he said coolly.

"What's up, daddy?" Nekole said. "When are you coming by? I'm feeling a little kinky right now."

Chris popped the cork on the bottle, then slowly poured it over the ice. He took a sip before responding to her question. "I've got to make a quick stop somewhere first." He started his truck.

"Well, pick me up. I wanna ride, too." She sounded like a begging child. "Please don't leave me over my aunt's with all these bad-ass kids."

He thought about it as he pulled out of the parking lot into traffic. "Aw'ight. I'm on my way," he said with a big grin on his face.

He'd been with plenty of women, but something about this girl was different. He was happy to have her fine ass jocking him like she was. But he made a promise to himself that he wouldn't let it go to his head.

Chapter 4

Nekole sat patiently, waiting on her aunt's front steps, enjoying the cool breeze that was blowing through her hair. Her eyes were fixed on a bird sitting on a tree branch making whistling noises, but her mind was on something else. She was hoping this would be a big enough score that she wouldn't have to go through this again.

Her plan was to get enough capital to open her own beauty shop, marry Sirron and live happily, but somewhere other than California. She had had enough of the state and all the people who lived in it.

The loud thump of Chris' music could be heard a block away. Nekole snapped out of her trance and focused on what lay ahead of her. A dark blue Yukon Denali came creeping down the street. It came to a stop in front of her house.

She smiled as she got up, dusting herself off. Slowly, she walked down the steps letting him get a good look at what she had to offer. She knew that she was eye candy. Her short sundress and matching bag went well with the color of her eyes. The leather sandals she wore showed off her white gold toe ring, which matched the choker around her neck. The soft wind blew her hair into her doll face. She stood there smiling coquettishly.

Chris gazed at her candidly. They exchanged scorching looks. Finally, he got out of the truck and opened the passenger door to let her in.

"What's up, playa?" she said, getting into his truck.

"You, that's what's up." He got a gander of her pretty brown legs. "You lookin' good," he said lustfully.

"Thank you," she said shyly.

Chris hopped into the driver's seat. She eyed the inside of the Denali, impressed with its accommodations. It was fully loaded with soft, gray leather interior, a wooden steering wheel and a navigation system. He had a total of six TV screens inside the truck, including two in the headrests.

"Damn, your car is tight," she complimented. "How much all of this cost?"

He smiled arrogantly. "I got over sixty-five grand into it," he said proudly.

"I wish I could afford something like this." She stroked his ego.

"That ain't no money for real. You should see the Hummer I got coming out this summer. I'm putting fourteen TV screens in that bitch."

"The H2? You rollin' like that?"

"And then some," he bragged.

Chris whipped the Denali into the parking lot of a McDonald's. He pulled over at a pay phone where a man was sitting parked in an old Monte Carlo SS. Chris dug into his console and pulled out a Crown Royal bag. He glanced at his surroundings before he got out of the truck. Nekole watched him get into the SS. From what she could see, it looked like they exchanged something. Five minutes hadn't gone by before he was back inside his own ride. She could see the lump of money that bulged out of his pocket.

That evening, they enjoyed a seven-course meal at a Japanese restaurant on the Plaza. Afterward, they rode arm in arm on a horse and carriage. They spent the rest of the day enjoying each other's company. Chris was a player. That, she couldn't deny.

It was getting late, they were feeling good and he was ready to feel her insides. He remembered how tight her pussy felt the night before and wondered how many men she had been with. She didn't seem like the type who slept around, but he could tell that she was experienced. No first-timer could work her pussy on a man like she worked hers on him.

He was used to having fine women around him, but Nekole was in a class of her own. She was cool and real laid back, kind of like one of his partners or girlfriends. He wanted to tell Nekole that he wanted her to be his "main thang," but he was afraid he would push her away by moving too fast.

Chris cut off his headlights when he pulled into his driveway. With his hand on his gun, he eyed his surroundings carefully for anything suspicious. Shrubs, trees and darkness were all that he saw.

"What's wrong, baby?" Nekole asked nervously. She was standing in front of the truck with her arms folded across her chest.

"Nothin'," he said, still looking around. "Just makin' sure ain't no punk-ass niggas waitin' around to jack me."

"Ain't nobody gonna try to jack you while you're with me." She grabbed hold of his arm. "Let's go inside."

They were barely in the house when she dropped her bag onto the floor and attacked him. She kissed him roughly while she pulled the gun out of his pocket. He hadn't gotten a chance to lock the door before she was pulling him toward the bedroom. She pulled her dress over her head, then jumped into his arms. Chris fell back onto the bed with her on top of him.

"Wait a minute, baby!" he said between their kisses. He pushed her off of him. "I gotta go lock the front door."

"In a minute, baby." She unbuttoned his jeans and pulled them down. He stepped out of them.

"I've got to do this now," he said seriously. He left the room. Nekole sighed.

She needed the front door to be unlocked so Sirron could get in. Somehow, she'd have to get away from him so she could unlock the door again. Otherwise, she would have to wait until he fell asleep.

Chris came back into the room and slapped his hands together. "Now, where were we?" He pulled her up close to him.

She pushed him on the bed. Kneeling down, she licked him from his feet, all the way up to his navel. She stopped suddenly.

He sat up frowning. "Wha' sup?" He had expected her to go down on him.

She put her finger up to her lips. "Shhhh. I'll be back after I get some ice."

"Hurry up," he said impatiently.

Nekole tiptoed to the front door while looking around to make sure he hadn't followed her. Quietly, she turned the lock until she heard it click. Opening the curtain, she peeked out for any sign of Sirron. He wasn't in sight. She picked up her bag off the floor and took out a small flashlight. She flashed it on and off in the window. Her body began to relax after she saw him flash his light back at her.

She put the flashlight back into her bag on her way to the kitchen. Chris would be suspicious if she didn't come back with the ice. When she returned, he was still lying naked across the bed with his eyes closed. She grabbed hold of his organ and began to stroke it gently.

"Mmm … Did you get the ice, baby?" he asked without opening his eyes.

"Mm hmm." She tossed a piece into her mouth. "Just relax and let Nicky do all the work."

While his eyes remained closed, she eased a nickel-plated .38 out of her bag. She wanted him naked before she made her move. Men seemed to get shy when they were naked. She wanted that advantage on him in case he tried to resist.

Chris' eyes immediately popped open when he heard the hammer cock back. His mouth fell open as his eyes focused on the gun in her hand. Her arm twitched.

"Don't kill yourself," she said coldly.

"Kill myself? Bitch, you think I'm just gonna let you—" His voice trailed off after he saw Sirron enter the room. He fingered the trigger of the chrome Desert Eagle in his hand.

"Finish yo' sentence, nigga," Sirron said. He had a devilish grin on his face.

Chris could tell by Sirron's composure that he'd done this before. Provoking him was not something that he was about to do.

Sirron reached down and grabbed Chris' braided hair, snatching him off the bed. "Get yo' ass up!" Chris got to his feet. Sirron looked at Nekole. "Which way?"

She led them to the basement door. It was secured with the same lock she'd seen the day before. Sirron violently shoved Chris into the door, telling him to open it. Chris just stood there nervously, pretending that he didn't know what Sirron wanted him to do.

Whack! The side of the Desert Eagle came crashing down on Chris' head. He fell up against the door, hollering, as blood ran down his face.

"Don't play dumb, muthafucka!" Sirron yelled at him. "Open this muthafucka up!"

Nekole stepped back out of the way, letting Sirron handle the situation. Chris looked up at her with hate-filled eyes. *How did I let this bitch make a fool out of me?* he thought. Nekole returned her own hateful stare back at him, unmoved by his cold look.

"I need the key," Chris said, his eyes still fixed on Nekole.

Why didn't I think of that before? Nekole thought. She ran to the bedroom. Her hands were shaking while she searched his pants' pockets for the keys. She was ready to get the whole thing over with. She found them in his front pocket.

When she returned, Chris was on his knees, shaking, as he was up close and personal with the barrel of Sirron's gun.

"I got 'em," she said, holding up the keys. She unlocked it herself.

Nekole opened the door and Sirron shoved Chris toward the steps. "Lead the way."

It was dark and clammy down there. It wasn't clean like the upstairs. Chris pulled a string and the room instantly lit up. A rat ran for cover behind the furnace. Chris continued on, leading them behind the staircase.

Bolted into the concrete floor was a fireproof Sentry safe with an electronic lock. Chris stood there like he didn't know what to do next.

"Fuck you waiting on? Open it up," Sirron demanded.

Chris looked pleadingly at Nekole again.

"What the fuck you keep looking at me for?" she yelled, irritated by his continued eye contact. She knew that he was looking for her to sympathize with him.

Chris' stomach was in knots. He wasn't really tripping on the money. He had plenty of that stashed in houses all over town. His main concern was what was going to happen after he opened the safe.

Sirron became fed up with Chris' stalling. He put the barrel flush up against the side of Chris' head. "You gon' stand there, play games and end up dead? Or are you gonna open the damn safe? Last chance."

Chris reluctantly pushed the correct numbers on the keypad. A green light flashed and the door popped open.

Sirron kicked Chris out of the way. The sight of all that cash brought a tear to his eye. For years now they had searched for the perfect lick, and now Baby had finally struck gold. *She humped our way to the top,* Sirron thought greedily.

Chris could tell by the crazed look in Sirron's eyes that he wasn't gonna let him live. He had to make a move soon if he wanted to get out of there with his life.

Sirron took a trash bag out of his pocket. Eyes shining with pleasure, he said to Chris, "I bet when you was stacking all of this money, you didn't know it was for me, did you?"

Chris said nothing in return. He just stared at him. He watched Sirron stick his gun into his waistline. Nekole had her gun drawn, but she was in striking distance. At the moment, she was keeping an eye on Sirron as he filled the bag.

While Nekole was busy watching Sirron, Chris made his move. He threw a quick, hard jab, hitting Nekole in the side of her face. The gun flew out of her hand as she fell to the floor. Sirron turned from the safe, meeting a jab to his eye, then another to the side of his head. The bag dropped to the floor. He fell to his knees, trying desperately to get his gun out.

Chris jumped on him in an attempt to stop him. Sirron tried to poke his finger through Chris' eye socket. Opening his mouth, Chris bit down on the side of Sirron's hand until he tasted blood.

Out of the corner of his eye, Chris saw Nekole recovering. She staggered over to her gun and picked it up off the floor. He let go of Sirron's hand and tried to rush her. The barrel of her gun was aimed toward his head. At that moment, he realized his life was over. His basement would be the last thing he would ever see.

Bam! Bam! Bam!

Nekole fired three shots at his body. Blood splattered the safe, Sirron and the bag of money. She swallowed. Her stomach contracted into a tight ball as she realized what she had done. Usually, it was Sirron who carried out the killing part of their robberies. This time, the blood had been shed by her hands.

Sirron pushed the lifeless, bloody body off to the side. He stood up and slowly reached for the gun in her hand. She released it without incident.

"You did what you had to do, baby," he assured her. "Remember that."

Nekole stared at the body like she had never seen one before.

"Come on, baby," he said. "Help me finish bagging the money."

After they finished, he ordered her to go to the police. They had a pre-fabricated story ready for the cops. Each of the robberies was carefully planned before it was put into effect. Sirron made sure that all angles were covered.

Or so he thought.

Nekole ran up the stairs. On her way to the front door, her

memory flashed back to the money that Chris had gotten from the dude at the McDonald's. She made a quick detour to his bedroom. Inside his pants' pocket, opposite where she found the keys, she found the wad of money. She saw it when she was looking for his keys, but had been in too much of a hurry to grab it then.

She stuffed it inside her bag on the floor, then dashed out of the house. Intentionally, she ran through the shrubs so that she would get scratched up, so it would look as though she hurt herself trying to get away. That, along with the knot that Chris put above her eye, she thought should be convincing enough.

Searching for a way to dispose of the body, Sirron found a can of gasoline over by a riding lawn mower. He doused Chris' body with the gas and ran a trail up the steps, all the way to the front door. He tossed the moneybag over his shoulder, struck a match, threw it on the gasoline trail, then shut the door.

Chris' nosey white neighbor, Mrs. Dunn, saw Sirron running from the house. When he was long gone, she tiptoed over to Chris' yard. That's when she saw the flames through a window.

"Jesus, Mary and Joseph!" she exclaimed. She turned and ran back to her house to call the police.

Damn near out of breath, Nekole ran nonstop to the police station. She was huffing and puffing by the time she entered the building. "Help me! Somebody, please help me!" she hollered as she fell to the floor.

A heavyset black woman came running from behind the front desk. She kneeled down next to her. "Miss, are you alright?" she asked, helping Nekole to her feet.

Nekole took a second to catch her breath. "No. Some man just tried to kill me and my boyfriend."

The heavyset officer turned toward another uniformed officer who had just walked up. "Go get me Detective Thomas. Now!" The officer quickly ran to carry out the order.

Minutes later, she found herself sitting alone in a small room with a long conference table and six chairs. The heavyset officer had gotten her a blanket and a cup of coffee while she waited to speak to the detective.

Sirron should have made it home safely by now, she thought. *All of the evidence will be burned up, and we'll get off scot-free.* She hoped this would be the last time she had to go through this, but if shit ever got back bad for them, she would gladly do it all over again.

She looked up nervously when the detective walked his tall frame through the door. He was black as a human being could be with more gray hair on his head than black. Detective Thomas looked well over his forty-seven years.

He looked down at her through a set of old, experienced brown eyes. Still watching her carefully, he took out a pack of Kools and fired up a cigarette. She glanced over at the "No Smoking" sign on the wall, next to the door. She could already tell that he was a defiant asshole.

Thomas took a seat directly in front of her. Not a word was spoken. He just sat there, puffing on his cigarette.

"Why don't you tell me what you told Officer Smith," he finally said. He had a suspicious look in his eyes. Years of experience taught him to not always believe the first person's side of a story, especially when it was a woman telling it.

Nekole wiped the fake tears from under her eyes.

"Me and my boyfriend were in bed, about to have ... to have ..."

"To have what?" Thomas interrupted.

"Sex," she said timidly.

"Umm hmm."

"Then somebody knocked on the door, and Chris ... Chris got up to see who it was." She stopped, taking a moment to sob.

She was shocked that the detective never offered her a tissue or something to wipe her face with.

"... Well," she continued, "I heard him in the doorway arguing with some guy about a girl or something. Anyway, I got up, slipped my dress back on, then went to see what was happening. That's when I saw Chris strike the man in his face."

"What did you do then?" He was reading her eyes for a sign. If she looked to the left, then she was making up the story as she went along. If she looked to the right, then she was searching her memory bank.

Her eyes unexpectedly shifted to the right. She was searching her memory bank for the lie that she and Sirron had made up earlier that day. She continued. "I, umm, I ran toward them. That was when the guy kicked Chris in the stomach and threw him against the wall. Then—"

"Where is your boyfriend now?" Thomas cut in.

Nekole stood up, slamming her hand down hard on the table. "That's what I'm trying to tell you!" she yelled. "I barely escaped. For all I know, that guy is still in the house. Chris is probably ... dead by now." She took deep, heaving breaths in between her sobs, making her words barely audible. She continued. "In the meantime, you're sitting here questioning me like—"

Thomas held his hand up for her to calm down. "We sent a car over to your boyfriend's. As soon as I—"

A short, white officer barged in, interrupting them. "Excuse me, sir," he said. "We just received a call from car number 210. He reported that the fire department was at her boyfriend's address when he arrived at the scene. It seems they think they might have found a body in the basement."

"Nooooo!" Nekole cried out.

Thomas jumped up from the table. "You keep an eye on her," he ordered. "I'm going over to that address."

Chapter 5

"Let me speak to Big Geno," Maurice said into his cell phone. The sun was out and he had the top down on his Corvette, rolling down Prospect Boulevard.

"Who dis?" Big Geno asked, answering the phone.

"This Reece, nigga. How many heads you got up there?" He hit his signal and changed lanes, pressing the gas to pass a slow-moving minivan.

"One, two." He could hear Geno counting heads in the background. "I've got about two people in front of you," Geno said. "What you gon' do?"

"I'm on my way down there now. All I need is a fresh taper with a razor line."

"Bring ya ass, trick daddy." Geno laughed at his own humor.

"On my way." He turned up the volume on his radio, bumping Nelly's "*Air Force Ones.*"

Big Geno's Barber & Beauty was located on the south end of Kansas City. For his skills, you had to pay twenty dollars for a regular haircut and twenty-five for a style. Geno honestly felt that he belonged in Beverly Hills or on the East Coast, cutting stars' heads, like Steve Harvey. He felt everybody in Kansas City whose hair he cut should consider themselves privileged to have him at their disposal for only twenty-five dollars. They could always go to Honey Cutt's down the street and only pay fifteen.

All of the latest news, like who's got the dope, who's fucking who and even who shot who, could be found out there. All you had to do was sit for a while.

Maurice liked it there because of the fine-ass hoes who hung out in the beauty shop. The place was decked out with a pool table in the back, two TVs with a PlayStation 2 and an Xbox.

Geno looked up from cutting some dark-skinned dude's head just as Maurice walked in. He wore heavy, starched Jenn shorts, a white Stafford T-shirt and black Air Maxes.

"Trick, what's up?" Geno cut off the clippers and shook Maurice's hand.

Geno stood just as tall as Maurice, but with a wider frame. He wore a white sun visor, cocked to the left over his braided hair. Geno was a shit-talking muthafucka. Everybody was a trick to Geno, except for Geno. He was cool with everybody, but if he was ever crossed, he could be as treacherous as a bitch with a broken heart.

"Y'all packed up in here," Maurice said, glancing around the room at the crowd of women looking through magazines and sitting with their heads under dryers.

He caught a glimpse of one of the beauticians, Tish, eyeing him. He winked at her as he took a seat in front of Geno's chair.

Geno started cutting on Dark Skin's hair again. Big E was the barber whose chair was next to Geno's. Peeping through his gold-framed spectacles, Big E masterfully cut away on a brown-skinned guy's head.

"What you been up to, Reece?" Big E asked without taking his eye off of his customer.

"Not a damn thing," Maurice said, picking up a *GQ* magazine.

Brown Skin said, "Like I was saying, E. So I'm fuckin' this bitch, right? She's screamin' and hollering like a muh-fucker. I spit the first nut out quick. Like bam!" He snapped his fingers.

"Uh huh," Big E said, lining up the back of his head.

"So I keep on humping like I haven't cum yet. Man, you know

what the ho said to me?"

"What's that, playa?"

"Nigga, get that limp thing outta me," he said, imitating a woman's voice. "And the bitch got up, too. I was embarrassed like a muh-fucker."

Everybody inside the shop laughed.

Tish stopped rinsing some girl's head and said, "You should have popped a Viagra." She laughed along with everybody else.

Geno said, "Man, I'm so sick of you and these stories about yo' ole no-good-ass tramps."

Big E smiled showing four solid gold teeth. "Me too. They don't even be funny." He snatched the cape off of the dude. "Get yo' dry-joke-tellin' ass up."

Maurice waited until Geno finished with Dark Skin's head, then he got into the chair.

"Nigga, sometimes I swear you're sellin' dope." Geno popped the cape in the air, knocking the hair off. He was referring to the huge diamond earrings that were in Maurice's ears.

"Sellin' a lot of cars, man," Maurice said proudly.

"Yeah, I heard about that scam you and Derrick got going on up there."

Maurice just smiled.

He remained still while Geno went to work on his wavy head. An older man was standing over his son in Big E's chair, telling the boy to hold still. For a minute, Maurice wished that he had a son to take to the barber with him. But for him, there was just too much that came along with being a father. All the baby mama drama and whatnot.

A slim girl with French-braided hair walked into the door. "What's up y'all. Hi, Maurice." She had on a too-big Nike T-shirt and baby blue jean shorts. She carried her barber's bag over to her chair and began setting up her clippers.

"Hey, babe," Maurice mumbled, barely moving his lips, while Geno trimmed his goatee.

Lucki was what a dyke would call a "stud." She was the dominant female in her lesbian relationships. Maurice often wondered what it would feel like to be inside of her tight womb gate. She was a butch, but a fine one, with her Bratz-looking features.

"Lucki!" a tall redbone chick with long, burgundy-colored hair yelled from the doorway. "You forgot your cell phone, baby."

Her ass jiggled as she swayed over to where Lucki was standing. Lucki took the phone and gave her a wet "thank you" kiss on the lips. All she was doing was putting on a show for the people inside the shop.

"Thank you, baby," Lucki said smoothly.

"I'll be back to get you 'round six," Redbone said as she turned to leave.

Geno's oldest customer, Old Man Ed, stopped reading his newspaper just to get a good look at the young tender.

"Lawd have mercy." He shook his head. "If I was twenty years younger, I'd have to have me a taste of that."

Geno chuckled. "Ed, you say that about every broad who comes through that door, and I ain't seen you pull up on one of them hoes yet."

"He scared," Big E added.

Old Man Ed frowned. "I bet you I pull mo' hoes in that eighty-three Fleetwood I got outside than you do in yo' new Blazer," he said defensively.

"Shiiid!" Big E retorted. "You see how many different hoes I got running in and out of here?" He moved his short, thick frame to the front of his chair, dusting the excess hair off the boy's head.

A man with a box-style haircut stood up and looked out the window, stalking Redbone as she walked to her car.

"I know Lucki's suckin' the shit outta that pussy," he said a little too loudly.

"What you say?" Lucki said angrily. She set down her scissors.

The man glanced around the room like he didn't know who she was talking to. "Huh? I didn't say nothin' to you."

"Yes, you did, nigga," she said, moving closer to him. She put a finger up in his face. "Yo' bitch ass probably want me to suck yo' pussy. Pussy."

"Bitch, you got me fucked up," he said defensively. His bumpy face hardened. "Better get the fuck outta my face."

Her eyes sharpened. She looked at him like she was about to swing on him at any second.

"Greg," Geno called out. "Sit your ass down."

Greg's face balled up. "Naw, man. She ain't gonna get away with calling me no pussy up in here."

Geno cut off his clippers and walked over to Greg. "I promise you don't wanna start no trouble up in here. Better yet, get yo' ass up outta here. Come back tomorrow."

Greg grimaced. "Yeah, okay," he said, inching toward the door. Geno walked back over to his station, shaking his head. "Lucki, you gotta stop gettin' into it with everybody. Damn. I know you're a tough-ass Crip and all, but sometimes you have to let shit go. You gettin' bad for business."

"He started it, Geno," she whined, watching Geno dust the hair off of Maurice's neck.

Geno ignored her.

Maurice heard loud music coming from outside, shaking the windows. He waved to everybody as he headed for the door.

"Hold on a minute, Reece, I'ma walk out with you." Geno took off his apron.

Old Man Ed looked up at Big E. "Just for the record," he said, "them girls you got runnin' in and out of here - don't none of 'em look like shit, except for your woman."

Big E smirked. "Go 'head on, Ed."

A black Escalade pulled up behind Maurice's Corvette. Freak hopped his short, muscular frame out of the SUV. He sported a white tank top, Rocawear jeans and red and black Air Force 1's.

They all shook hands. "I knew I'd find yo' ass up here," Freak said to Maurice. "Wha' sup wit' it, Geno?"

"Shit. What you got up in there beatin' like that?" Geno inquired.

"Shid ... a gorilla," he bragged. "Aw, yeah. I saw yo' bitch

Michelle today."

"Where at?"

"She was up at Swamp Man's." He was referring to a local fish joint. "Bitch was lookin' good as a muthafucka."

"She get that money to you?"

"Mm hm. I started to get on her fine ass. See how tight your game really is." Freak backed away from him smiling. Six platinum and diamond teeth blinged between his lips.

Maurice looked at him doubtfully. "It wouldn't have did you no good. When I got a bitch, I *got* a bitch," he said arrogantly.

Geno brushed him off. "Ole trick-ass nigga, please. If you was paying me, I wouldn't fuck with nobody else either." He and Freak chuckled.

"You better ask Freak about me, man. Maurice Jones ain't never paid a ho."

"Damn, Freak. You ain't got no greens?" Geno asked.

"Unt unh."

Missy Elliot's "*The Rain*" was beating out of a yellow drop-top Mustang. They watched lustfully as the caramel-colored, blond-headed woman parked in front of the shop.

She stepped out, sporting yellow shades and a short, tight yellow tennis skirt. She slung her Coach bag over her shoulder as she headed toward them.

"Who's that?" Maurice asked, licking his lips.

The tall, leggy woman walked past Freak and Maurice both, stopping in front of Geno.

"Hey, daddy," she said sweetly.

Geno remained in player mode while his boys were around. "Wha' sup baby? You should've been here an hour ago." He glanced at his watch. "My lunch break is over now," he complained.

"Baby, you know I had to get my nails done." She held them up to the sun. "Ming had this new color that she wanted to try out. See." She put the florid-colored nails up to his face.

Geno saw Freak and Maurice eyeing him accusingly. He took

her by the hand and said, "Let's go inside. We don't need our business all out in the streets."

"Take your trick ass inside then," Freak teased. "I bet' not ever hear you call nobody else a trick again."

"I ain't tryin' to hear it," he said, opening the door for her.

"We going to the Ep tonight or what?"

Maurice shrugged. "I'm tired of fuckin' with the same run-down-ass hoes, man. We need to go where some fresh fish gon' be at. I'm tired of the same passive-ass bitches. I want to be where a bitch gon' shoot game right back at me."

"Call me and let me know what's up."

Freak watched Geno disappear into the shop.

"That bitch got Geno by the balls," Freak commented.

"I don't think so," Maurice said doubtfully. "He's just kickin' it."

"What you about to do?"

"I'ma shoot around to mom's crib and check on them for a minute or two."

"Aw'ight. I'ma get up with you later."

They headed in different directions.

Chapter 6

Marijuana smoke clouded the living room at Maurice's mother's house. His daddy was sitting on the couch, dumping ashes into the ashtray, when Maurice walked through the door. His daddy's friend, Hamp, was sitting on the love seat watching an old karate movie on TV.

"Hey, pops." Maurice smacked him on top of his shoulder. His daddy looked at him like he was crazy through low, red eyes.

"How many times do I have to tell you to call me *Steve*, nigga? You can go on somewhere with that pops shit."

Steve was forty-four but looked and acted ten years younger. At least once a week, Steve had to curse Maurice out about calling him "pops." Steve didn't take aging too well. There was no way that you could get him to believe that he wasn't still the shit.

Maurice ignored Steve. "What's up, Hamp?"

"Shit," Hamp said in his loud, high-pitched voice.

Hamp was five feet, eleven inches tall and weighed over three hundred pounds. He had been Steve's closest friend since grade school. His only fault was that he told too many lies.

"I get any mail?" Maurice shuffled through some mail on top of the fireplace.

"Mm hm," Steve said, holding in the weed smoke.

He stopped shuffling when he read the name Raymond Moye on an envelope. Ray was his cousin who got caught up trying to rob a Burger King three years ago. He was sentenced to fifteen years in prison with no one to look out for him.

After hearing all the stories about his uncle's experiences in the joint, Maurice couldn't let his cousin be in there doing badly, so he made sure that he set aside two hundred dollars a month to send to Ray and visited him when he could.

Maurice stood there reading the letter from Ray, which told him about everything that was going on on the inside. And of course, he needed some more money. *As fast as Ray's going through money, he has to be gambling,* Maurice thought. Ray had a nasty gambling habit, but never won as long as Maurice had known him.

Back when they were in high school, they used to shoot dice in the boys' restroom. Ray would lose his money quickly, before the late bell rang. Still, you would see him back the next day trying his luck. Maurice suggested that Ray stop rolling the dice and start betting on whoever was winning. When he tried that, the boy who was winning, stopped winning. Talk about bad luck.

Maurice balled up the letter on the way to the kitchen where his mother was. She was standing over a pot of greens cooking on the stove.

"Mmm," Maurice said, sniffing the aroma. "What you cookin', baby?"

"Collard greens and ham hocks." She gave him a confused look. "Since when did greens start smelling good to you?"

"When I grew up." He kissed her on her forehead.

"Grew up?"

"That's what I said."

She shook her head. "You could've fooled me. Grown men have families and kids running around the house. Go to Cub Scout meetings and stuff like that. They don't run the streets, chasing whores all day."

"Whores?"

"Yes, whores." She turned down the fire on the stove, then faced him. With one hand on her hip, she said, "I know you don't call those tramps that you run around with *women?* I can't stand none of 'em. Especially Neosha's ghetto ass. Always trying to break up your shit." Her voice lowered. "I like Michelle though. I think you should be with her. She has a lot going for herself."

"Got a lot going for herself? Mama, that's her husband's money. If you gon' call anybody a whore, it should be her."

She opened her mouth to say something, but words never came out. She was speechless.

"I guess she forgot to tell you that she was married during one of y'alls talks, huh?"

"Yes she did, but that's not my point." She was determined to hold her ground. "You need to slow your ass down, Maurice. I don't want to wake up in the middle of the night to no phone call saying that somebody's husband done killed my baby." Her voice had taken on a seriousness that he understood completely.

They stared at each other in silence.

Finally, he cracked a smile, then gave her a hug.

Mama was almost as tall as Maurice and very attractive. Like her husband, she too thought that she was still young and the shit. She had been through a lot in her forty-three years, and she'd seen what jealous boyfriends and husbands did to guys like her son. Maurice being her only child, she would do anything to protect him.

"I'm gonna slow down, mama. I promise," he lied. "Just as soon as you stop going out to clubs," he said, then quickly left the kitchen.

"I go out with my husband, thank you," she hollered at his back.

Maurice took a seat next to Steve on the couch. He was thinking about what his mother had just told him. *What if some hating-ass nigga did try to kill me over they girl? Would Michelle's husband try some shit like that? You never can tell. I've got to be more careful and tighten up my game before some shit like that does happen.*

Steve saw the distant look on his son's face.

"What's up, son? Some girl got you feeling down or something?" Steve giggled. "Look like you done lost your best friend."

"I know," Hamp agreed. He noticed the distant look on Maurice's face also. "You alright, little nigga?"

Maurice frowned. "Ain't nothing wrong with me. I'm just thinking."

"Well go somewhere else and think," Steve said. "Don't come up in here blowin' my high." He thumped ashes into the tray. "Hamp, man, I wouldn't want to be twenty-four again for nothing in the world," he chuckled.

"I know my dog ain't stressing over no broad," Hamp said.

"Yes he is. Young punk."

"Come on with all that shit, pops," Maurice said. "Y'all know I'ma playa. Ain't nothing changed." He coughed from inhaling the weed smoke. "I was just thinking about something that mama said."

"Aw, shit," Steve said, passing the joint to Hamp. "Keep on listening to your mama, and you gon' always be fucked up." He fired up a Newport. "I used to keep your mama chasing me back when we were going to school."

"Sho' did," Hamp confirmed. "All the girls used to be on Steve. Remember when I fucked Rachel Parker in that Johnny on the Spot, when we skipped school at Swope Park?"

"No. Hamp, why is you lying, man? You ain't never fucked Rachel."

"Bullshit!" Hamp hollered. "That was the day we got that fifth of Night Train."

Steve shook his head while he puffed on the cigarette. "I remember the Night Train, but I don't remember you fucking nobody that day."

Maurice laughed. He loved to hear his daddy talk shit to his friends. Sometimes he would talk about them so badly, they would get up and leave. But they would always return for the same treatment, and also to smoke up his weed.

Maurice took out his wallet and counted out two hundred dollars. He placed it on top of the table. "Tell mama to send Ray this money for me."

Steve asked, "How's he doing?"

Maurice shrugged. "Same ole, same ole." He stood up. "I'ma holla at y'all later."

x x x

"I want to spend the night with you, baby. Please!" Tamisha pleaded over the phone.

"I don't know, Misha," Maurice replied. He rubbed lotion on his upper body. He had just stepped out of the shower and was preparing for the club. "I've gotta see what Derrick and Freak is gonna do."

"So you're fuckin' Derrick and Freak, now?" she said hotly.

"Come on with that bullshit." He sighed and shook his head in disgust while he slipped on a pair of slacks. "Check this out. You can meet me at my crib around three forty-five, or so. I'ma leave the key under the mat. You already know my alarm code. If I'm not here when you get here, make me some breakfast."

"Okay, daddy," she said excitedly. He could imagine the smile on her face. "I'll be naked and ready to serve you."

"Aw'ight. Peace."

"And please be drunk when you come home. Ya know how I like that drunk dick."

"Okay, but do me a favor."

"What?"

"Don't beg next time. Put your foot down."

"I'll never be too proud to beg for some of your dick, baby," she said proudly.

"I'll see you later." He hung up.

Admiring the way he looked in the full-length mirror, he could understand why Tamisha was feenin' so. "You's a sexy muthafucka, boy," he said to himself. "I don't know a bitch in her right mind who wouldn't want to be with you." The Armani suit hung just right on his muscular frame.

Reaching into his bottom drawer, he shuffled through four gold-framed portraits of each of his girls. He took out the one of

Tamisha, then carried it to the living room and hung it up on the wall.

Satisfied, he picked up his phone and keys, set the alarm, then left the house.

Chapter 7

"Mmmm. Mmmm," Nekole moaned softly while she was still asleep. She could feel a tingling sensation in between her legs. Slowly, her eyes fluttered open. Looking down, she saw the top of Sirron's wavy head. He was nibbling away at her pearl tongue.

"Unt unh. Baby, stop," she said softly, half enjoying it. She closed her legs in on his head. "We ain't got ... mmm ... time baby. I gotta go to work."

"Fuck work!" he said, trying to hold her legs open. "You don't have to work no more."

"Yes, I do. Now stop," she demanded, but it was no use.

Nekole relaxed for a minute when she felt his tongue waggling around inside of her. She could feel herself becoming wetter by the second. Her legs went limp as she lay there in submission, waiting for him to let down his guard. Releasing the grip he had on her legs, he eased two fingers into her crevice. Then she made her move. In a swift motion, she swung her right leg over his head, rolled off the bed and stood up.

Sirron frowned at her with pussy juice around his mouth.

"What you doing?" he said hotly. He had been under the impression that she was enjoying it.

"I said *no!*" she hollered over her shoulder on her way to the bathroom.

His nature swelled as he watched her walk gracefully out of the room. She looked like a model going down the runway, naked. He sighed and sat up on the bed. The news was on TV. The anchorwoman was reporting a string of robberies that had taken place in the Watts area. He had to laugh to himself, thinking about all the robberies he and Nekole had gotten away with.

It was a shame how she could get so close to their victims so quickly. All it took was a pretty face and an hour in the sack. He couldn't figure out how some of them lasted in the game as long as they did when they were so gullible. He knew that he was damn lucky to have her like he did. She could've been with anybody she wanted. Sirron could see that by the way she worked their victims.

He got up and headed for the bathroom. Butt naked, she stood in front of the mirror and wrapped her hair into a bun. It went well with her doll face and slanted eyes.

Sirron eyed her curves lustfully. He wanted to stick dick to her bad to satisfy his morning hard-on, but he knew that she wouldn't go for it. It was already after eight and she had to get to the beauty shop before her customers started showing up. Nekole wasn't one to miss money. She had plans to open up her own shop one day soon. After the lick they pulled on Chris, they had enough to do it now, if they wanted to.

Expensive trips to Jamaica, Mexico and Florida, and major shopping sprees in the Big Apple kept them from being able to keep any money in the past. Not to mention gambling in Vegas and dining in the fanciest restaurants in Hollywood. They treated themselves to the best, at other people's expense. This time it would be different. They'd invest their money into a legitimate business before their luck came to an end.

Nekole cut her eyes at him. "You can lust, but you can't touch."

"I know," he said. "I can get off just by watching yo' fine ass."

"Well, that's what you're gonna have to do. Excuse me," she said, walking past him back into the bedroom.

She rubbed herself down with cocoa butter lotion. Then she squeezed into a pair of tight-fitting jeans and a white blouse. She wrinkled up her nose, smelling a foul odor in the air. She tried to ignore it, but the smell was getting worse.

"Sirron," she called out, "you shittin'?"

"Yeah," he grunted. "That shit you cooked last night got my stomach fucked up."

Her lips curled up. "Aw, yeah? Well next time don't eat that *shit*." She shook her head. "Damn, you can say some hurtful shit sometimes," she said angrily.

Hearing the toilet flush, she grabbed her keys and purse, then stormed out of the room before he had a chance to apologize. She knew that he meant every word that he said. She had just opened the front door when he came running down the stairs.

"Hold on, boo boo," he pleaded. He reached around her, pushing the door closed.

She folded her arms across her chest. "What, boy?"

"What you mean, *what*? Girl, you know I was just talkin' shit. You gettin' mad over nothin'."

"Because you always sayin' shit to put me down. Then you try to apologize. You know damn well that I'm sensitive about my cookin'." She grunted. "I don't say nothin' about you droolin' all over the pillows and shit at night."

"I don't say nothing about you being a ho," he said defensively, "'round here fuckin' everybody but me."

"I have to ho around so *we* can have some money around this muthafucka," she said, bobbing her head. "Something your trifling ass can't seem to get on your own."

He looked at her furtively. "Don't act like you don't enjoy it."

She reached around him and opened the door. "That's it. I ain't got to take this shit." She faced him. "And don't try to apologize later." She stormed out the door. *Impotent muthafucka*, she thought to herself.

"Leave then, bitch," he mumbled under his breath. "I got all the money."

x x x

Nekole arrived at the beauty shop fifteen minutes late.

Ramonda and Angie were sitting in the waiting area, flipping through magazines, looking pissed off. They had other things to do besides wait on her all day.

"I know Nekole Mitchell ain't late for work," Ramonda said sarcastically. "Miss Thang ain't never late."

Angie had no time for games that morning. "Nekole, you know that I gotta be at the airport by one," Angie complained while she followed Nekole to the bowl.

Nekole sighed. She put her hand on her temple, feeling a headache coming on. "Girl, I know, I know. Please! Just bear with me. Sirron's been driving me crazy all morning." She put the cape around Angie's neck and leaned her head back into the sink. "Lately he's been gettin' on my fuckin' nerves."

"Whaaat? I thought you said Sirron was all that."

"I didn't say he wasn't." She squirted shampoo into her hand. "He just be trippin' on bullshit." She shook her head while lathering Angie's. "So where you going?" She changed the subject.

Angie looked relaxed as Nekole massaged her scalp on the second shampoo. "Me and my man are going to Kansas City for a few days."

"Kansas City?" Nekole said. "What the hell is in Kansas City?"

"He got some family down there. One of his cousins, Geno, is supposed to own a barber and beauty shop. Anyway, he's gonna kick it with him since they haven't seen each other in years."

"And what are you supposed to do while they're getting reacquainted?"

"He's got a girlfriend. We gon' kick it while the dogs run the streets."

Nekole wrapped a towel around Angie's head. "Well, I hope you have fun."

"I plan on it."

x x x

Detective Al Thomas sat in the lobby of the Coroner's Office smoking on his third cigarette in less than thirty minutes. He ignored the "No Smoking" signs posted on the office walls, just like he did at the police station.

The slim blond woman behind the front desk grew tired of repeatedly telling him to stop. With a spasm of irritation on her face, she stared at the tall detective as he put the cigarette out in one of the flowerpots.

Dr. McIntosh, the Medical Examiner, came walking through the double doors, snatching off his surgical mask, to greet the detective.

"Mr. Thomas," the doc said, shaking his hand.

"Doc. What you got for me?"

He took a deep breath. "Well, the victim's name is Christopher Lamon. Twenty-three years of age. I—"

"Spare me the bullshit and give me what I need to build a case. I don't have time for a full analysis."

"Okay. I found pieces of flesh stuck between the victim's front teeth."

"Really?" Detective Thomas said anxiously.

"Yes. We believe it belongs to the killer."

Thomas had his thumb and index finger resting on his chin, thinking. "So what you're saying is there was a tussle and the victim bit the killer?"

"That's exactly what I'm saying," the doctor replied. "Although we won't know for sure until the test results come back from the lab."

Thomas headed for the door. "Get me those results, ASAP," he said over his shoulder. "There's a good chance the suspect has been down before, and we'll already have his DNA on file."

As Detective Thomas left the building, he thought about the story that Nekole had told him. She said she saw Chris attacking the man while she was standing in the doorway watching. There was some truth to what she was saying, so far, he thought. Yet, he still had a gut feeling that she had a connection to the killer.

During a search of what was left of Chris' burned house, nothing seemed to look out of place. A set up and robbery was what he suspected; however, proving that Nekole was involved was another problem.

Thomas hopped inside of his unmarked Crown Victoria, fired up a cigarette, then drove back to headquarters.

x x x

A week had passed. The California sun shone down on Sirron and Nekole's heads while they cruised down Compton Avenue in their new convertible Jaguar. They wore matching outfits and Cartier sunglasses.

Nekole arrogantly turned up her nose at all the pretty girls walking down the streets, half naked, in search of a baller. She felt better than she had in a long time. In less than twenty minutes she would be downtown, signing the lease papers for her soon-to-be beauty shop. All of her dreams were becoming reality. She was on top of the world, and nothing could bring her down.

So she thought.

The street light turned red, bringing the Jag to a halt at the intersection. Sirron was too busy feeling himself to notice the unmarked police car behind him. Another unmarked car skidded to a stop in front of him as it crossed the intersection. Sirron and Nekole sat stunned as they looked around, realizing that they were being surrounded by police.

Detective Thomas was the first to jump out with his Glock drawn. "Let me see some hands. Now!" he yelled with authority.

"Hands in the air, Miss," a short, young detective yelled, approaching Nekole's side of the car.

They put up their hands slowly. Nekole's heart was beating so rapidly, she thought it was about to jump out of her chest.

Thomas snatched open the door, immediately pulling Sirron out by his neck. Sirron's reflexes caused him to jerk away defensively.

Thomas pointed the gun at his face. "Think about this," he warned. "Think about this good, before I bust your ass. Be smart, not a smart ass."

Seeing the seriousness in the detective's eyes, Sirron backed down, placing his hands on the hood of the car. Detective Thomas searched and relieved him of the chrome Desert Eagle that was tucked in his pants. Then he escorted him to the police car.

"Out of the car, Miss," the short detective ordered. "Nice and slow."

"What's this all about?" Nekole asked as she got out of the car. "We ain't done noth—"

Her voice trailed off when she saw Thomas approaching her.

"Miss Mitchell," he said, flashing a superior grin. "Good seeing you again."

"We didn't do nothing."

"Sure you didn't." Thomas looked to his short partner. "Cuff her."

Chapter 8

Nekole found herself sitting inside the same small room she had been in the day of the robbery. Nervously she sat with her legs trembling. Trying to calm herself down, she had already bitten off three of her manicured fingernails.

Conspiracy to murder was the charge. She wondered how much she could trust Sirron, now that they had been caught. Would he hold up or would he let her go down for the murder alone?

Finally, Detective Thomas entered the room in a cloud of smoke. Surprisingly, her legs had stopped shaking. She pulled herself together, preparing for whatever questions he had for her to answer.

Thomas spent almost an hour in the room, drilling her with questions about the night of the robbery. But it was useless. She was sticking to the same story that she had already told him. She never saw the face of Chris' attacker, and if it were Sirron who killed him, she knew nothing about it.

Frustrated with getting nowhere with her, Thomas jumped up and slammed the steel door behind him as he left the room. He walked down the hall a few feet, then entered another room. Sirron was slumped down in a chair with a mean look on his face when Thomas walked in.

"I want to talk to my lawyer," Sirron said to him. Thomas sat on the edge of the table, right next to Sirron.

"Okay, but first let me ask you this. You know you done fucked up, don't you?" He chuckled. "Aw, man. I've always wanted to say that."

"I ain't did nothin', homie," Sirron replied confidently.

"Yeah? Well, do you care to explain how pieces of your flesh ... got stuck ... in between the teeth ... of Christopher Lamon?" Thomas asked slowly.

Sirron looked confused. "Who?"

Thomas yelled, "Christopher Lamon! The man that you robbed and killed." He really wasn't sure about the robbery part. He only said that to see if Sirron would tell on himself. Thomas shrugged. "Of course, we only think you did it. We'll leave it up to a jury to decide if you're really guilty or not. Then maybe we can get something to stick on your girl, too." Thomas took out a Kool and lit it. He took a drag, then slowly blew the smoke into Sirron's face. "You still need a lawyer?"

Sirron sat there with a lost look on his face. The bad news struck him like a blow from a sledgehammer. He knew just what Thomas was getting at – *either plead guilty to the charge, or we're gonna take your girl down with you.* He thought about Nekole, and how long it would be before he felt her tender touch again.

Since it was his slip-up that had gotten them caught, he decided to take the weight by himself. He figured that there was no sense in both of them going down for the same crime. Plus, with her on the street, he wouldn't have to worry about money while he was locked down. He had faith in her that she would be down with him until the end.

"Nah, I don't need a lawyer," he replied in a low voice.

"Good." Thomas reached for the tape recorder that sat in the middle of the table. He pushed the record button. "State your full name for the record."

Basically, Sirron told him the same story that Nekole had told them. Only he added that he was the guy who showed up at the door, arguing with Chris. He admitted to shooting Chris after being attacked by him. Even though it was Chris' home, he still had the right to defend himself. He didn't come there to kill him. Things just turned out that way.

Afterward, Sirron decided that he might as well hit the safe. While Chris was still breathing, he dragged him down into the basement and forced him to open it. Then, he got a burst of energy from somewhere and tried to attack him again. That's when Chris bit Sirron. Two more shots were fired, knocking the life out of him. It would've been foolish to have killed him and not gotten anything out of it.

Thomas' eyes narrowed on Sirron. "What were you two arguing about?"

Sirron took a deep breath. "I found out that Nekole was cheating on me with some drug dealer who drove a Denali. So I chilled out down the street from her aunt's house, saw them together, then followed them to his house. When he answered the door naked, I knew that I interrupted something. I confronted him, things got out of hand and you know the rest."

Thomas thought back to Nekole's statement. She had told him that she heard the man at the door asking about some girl. So far, their stories were adding up.

He started pacing the floor. "So that's the reason she was able to escape. You never intended to hurt her?"

Sirron shook his head.

Thomas shut off the recorder. "Zubriski," he hollered.

A tall, red-haired white man peeked his head into the room. "Yeah?"

Thomas buttoned his navy blue blazer. "Book him, then cut the broad loose," he said evenly. He exited the room without another word.

Sirron had a wounded look on his face when Zubriski escorted him out of the room. As they inched down the hallway, Sirron caught a glimpse of Nekole's face through an open door. Thomas was standing over her, probably breaking the bad news. Her face was scarlet and eyes swollen from crying. Sirron stopped suddenly. He looked at her as if it would be the last time he saw her. Now he wished that he could be at home, eating her terrible cooking.

"Move!" Zubriski said harshly. "Pretty girls like that don't wait around for murderers like you to get out the can." He chuckled. "You're looking at ... at least twenty-five years, stud."

"You just mad you won't ever get the chance to bone a pretty girl like mine, cracker," Sirron said defensively.

Zubriski frowned. "Get your smart ass down the hall!" He pushed Sirron in the back. "Let's go."

× × ×

Tears flowed down Nekole's face while she sat in the back seat of a cab. Her man was in jail, probably for life, which left her alone. She never knew her mother, and her father was killed by some Crips back before the peace treaty. She had her aunt, but she was too busy chasing the rock to even fool with her own kids, let alone Nekole.

Everything happened so fast. One minute they were riding in luxury, about to handle some business. The next, her whole life had been ruined. In the blink of an eye, and without warning, Sirron had been taken away from her.

The beefy-faced cab driver kept staring at her through his rearview mirror. He wondered if the sad look on her face was because of money troubles. He'd give up his whole take-home for a taste of that butter pecan. He hurriedly shifted his eyes to the front window when she looked up, catching him staring for the hundredth time.

It was just her luck that she was being stalked by an ugly, perverted cab driver. All she wanted to do was get to Sirron's house. Then she could pack her things and split with all the money.

Her cell phone rang.

She searched her purse until she found it. "Hello," she said with a crack in her voice.

"Nekole, this is Angie." She was back in town.

"Hey, girl." She wiped the tears from her eyes.

"The police kicked in Sirron's house," Angie said excitedly.

"Girl, they took everything but the kitchen sink. What's going on?"

Nekole tried to remain calm while she told Angie everything that had gone down. She left out a few details. It wasn't hard for Angie to figure out, because she knew what she and Sirron were into. The cab driver was all ears, trying to hear what was being said. To his disappointment, money wasn't what was troubling her.

"What you gonna do now?" Angie asked, concerned about her friend. "You can't go back there."

"I don't know, girl," Nekole said distantly. "I wish I could get out of town, start all over. Ya know?"

They sat quietly on the phone for what seemed like forever. Angie wanted to speak, but had nothing encouraging to say to her friend. They had experienced some rough times together, but Nekole was the one who usually knew what to do.

"Ooh, ooh, I know," Angie finally said. "Why don't you move to Kansas City? You could hook up with Mack's cousin, Geno. He can hook you up with a job at his beauty shop and help you find a place to stay."

"What about Sirron? I've got to be there for him. It's because of me that he's in that place."

"No it ain't," Angie disagreed. "You said yourself that it was his DNA they found. Plus, he can't do you no good sitting in jail for twenty-five years. It's an ugly thing to say, but it's the truth."

"You're right about that. It sounds good, but how am I supposed to leave town with no money?"

Hearing those last two words caught the cabby's attention. He focused his gaze back into the rearview mirror. This time he didn't avert his eyes when they met with Nekole's. He tried hard to suppress an all too incriminating smile.

Nekole said, "On second thought, I think I've just found the money for my plane ticket." She flashed the driver a knowing smile.

"Good!" Angie exclaimed. "I'll have Mack call Geno and set things up. You can spend the night here, then leave tomorrow."

"See you in a little while
"Hey, sexy."

"Huh?" the driver sai'
seductive look in her h?

"Why don't you p⌐
some fun?" She reached ove

The cabby happily drove a
small park. He pulled over by an o⌐
hadn't been used in years. He shut off th⌐
at her.

"Come sit back here," she said, patting the ⌐
She watched him eagerly hop out of the car and ru⌐
front of the car to the back.

She eased her small pocketknife out of her purse, stuffi⌐
into her bra. Her mind wasn't made up about how she was gonna
do it yet. If she made the wrong move, the big man might take her
knife and have his way with her.

Sliding in next to her, he removed his hat, revealing a half
bald, gray head. He reeked of tequila and cheap cologne. She tried
her best not to vomit all over the stinking, pudgy man.

"How much?" he said huskily.

"That depends on what you're trying to do, daddy," she said,
imitating one of the whores that she had seen on TV. "How much
you trying to spend?"

"Whatever it takes." Subconsciously he massaged his crotch.
"What do you wanna do?"

"Hmm? What do I want to do? I want my cat licked. Can you
do that for me, daddy?"

He flashed a devilish grin. "Sure, I could do that." He put his
hand on her thigh.

"Unt unh," she said, removing his liver-spotted hand. "Money
first." She stuck out her small hand.

He pulled a roll of money out of his breast pocket. He counted out two hundred dollars, then handed it to her. She didn't care
how much he gave her. She was gonna take it all anyway.

57

...ck, butt and head," he said strongly.

...s shot up. *Butt and head? Who the fuck does he* ... thought. It didn't matter. She would get the money ...g up anything. She watched closely while he stuck ...he bills into his sock. Nekole lay back against the door. ... slobbering all over her stomach. Savagely, he kissed her ... roughly undid her zipper. Carefully, she eased the knife ... her bra. The clicking sound of the knife being opened ...d his beefy face to look up. He shrieked out in pain as the ...fe came down on his shoulder.

"You crazy bitch!" he screamed. "Gimme that knife!" He tried to grab it, only to get stuck again and again.

Nekole was careful not to hit a main artery. She had killed once because she had to. It was an experience that she didn't want to go through a second time if she could avoid it.

The pudgy man lay against the back seat, bleeding like a slaughtered hog. She could see him taking slow, deep breaths and knew that he was still alive. She held the knife tight inside her hand while she took the rest of the money out of his sock. He held his wounds while she relieved him of his earnings. The pain was too great for him to risk being stuck again.

Nekole climbed into the front seat. After ripping the wires out of the CB radio, she took his car keys and ran off. Once she was out of his sight, she stopped beside an oak tree. Tired and gasping for air, she called Angie on her cell phone to pick her up.

x   x   x

The next day, Angie and Nekole stood outside of the airport, embracing one another. They had been up all night talking about the past, when times were better. They were friends to the end, but it was time for Nekole to move on. Although Los Angeles was a big city, Angie also thought it was a good idea for Nekole to get away. She had either done, or been involved in, too many robberies of too many different people.

Nekole grabbed her bag and left to board her plane. Angie waved goodbye, wishing her friend a safe journey. She wasn't worried about her surviving. If anybody could start a new life in a strange place, with only a couple of hundred dollars to start with, it was Nekole. She was smart, tough and could handle her own.

After a bumpy plane ride to Kansas City International Airport, Nekole thanked God that she made it safely. Inside the airport, she found the bar where she was told that Geno would meet her. It was nearly empty. She took a seat at the bar and ordered a Crown and Coke while she waited for Geno to show.

Toni, Geno's girlfriend, stood in the doorway, eyeing the dimly lit bar. She scoped the room until she came across a doll-faced woman sitting all alone at the end of the bar. She could tell by the lonely look on her face that she was the woman she had been sent to get. Toni strutted her slim frame over to where Nekole was sitting.

"You Nekole?" Toni asked smartly. Now that she was up close, she could see that Nekole's face had a fading bruise on the side. Other than that, there wasn't a blemish or a mark on it, and she wasn't even wearing makeup. Instantly, Toni became jealous, knowing that Geno would find her very attractive.

"Yes," she answered defensively. She could tell by the evil glare in Toni's eyes that she didn't like what she saw.

"My man, Geno, told me to come pick you up." Toni made damn sure she knew that Geno was her man.

They got into Toni's yellow Mustang. She put the top down and put on her yellow-framed Gucci glasses. She gave Nekole a quick glance to see if she was impressed.

She wasn't.

"There's no smoking, eating or drinking in my car," Toni informed her. She had no idea what type of woman she was dealing with.

"I don't smoke," Nekole replied. She faced Toni. "Let's get something straight, right now, bitch." Toni's mouth fell open. "You ain't got no reason to be mean to me. I don't want your man or nothing else you have. Now, if there's another problem, we can get out and handle it right now."

Toni's eyes widened with alarm. She sat there in stunned silence, not knowing what to say. Without a word, she put her car into drive and pulled away.

✗   ✗   ✗

Geno stepped his blubbery body out of the tub, drying off with a green Polo towel. Admiring himself in the mirror, he applied cocoa butter to the dark area where his beard hairs had been cut. He couldn't wait until Toni showed up with their new house guest. If she was as fine as Angie said she was, he was definitely gonna hit it.

The house looked empty when the two women walked into the living room. Maxwell was playing softly out of the stereo, and they could smell incense burning. Toni dropped her purse and keys on the table on her way out to the patio to look for Geno.

Nekole stopped her. "Which way is the bathroom?"

Toni pointed a freshly manicured nail. "Down the hall, first door on the right."

Assuming it was unoccupied, Nekole walked into the bathroom without knocking. To her surprise, Geno was standing in front of the sink, naked. She couldn't help but look down to catch a glimpse of what he was working with.

"Who you?" Geno asked, unashamed of being naked in front of her.

Nekole flinched, covering her mouth with her hand. "I'm sorry. I didn't mean to—"

"Don't trip on it. You must be Nekole."

"Yes." She started to back away. "Excuse me."

"Nah. Excuse me." He stepped around her. "Go ahead. My house is your house."

Nekole stepped inside, closing the door behind her. She took a deep breath and shook her head. She couldn't believe what just happened. She hadn't been there for five minutes and had already seen him naked. If Toni got wind of that, they would be fighting for real.

She pulled down her pants and sat on the toilet. Soon after, she heard Geno and Toni arguing. She leaned closer to the door trying to hear what was being said.

"I thought that you had an apartment already set up for her!" she heard Toni yelling.

"I thought I did, too," Geno said, lying as usual. "But Larry changed his mind."

"So, what you're telling me is that tramp has to live under my roof until God knows when? I don't think so," Toni snapped. Her eyes narrowed on Geno suspiciously. "Wait a minute. I know you, Geno. You done that shit on purpose. Didn't you?"

"I didn't do shi—"

"Yes you did, nigga. Your fat ass think you're slick. Let me catch you in the bed with that ho and I'm gonna stab the shit outta both of y'all's asses."

Geno closed the bedroom door so Nekole couldn't hear them talking about her.

Nekole stared at her reflection in the mirror while she washed her hands. "Girl, what have you gotten yourself into?"

Chapter 9

The annoying sound of Michelle's cell phone ringing woke Maurice. He rolled to the left, then to the right, trying to get comfortable. He looked over at Michelle who was sleeping peacefully. He shook his head. He was about to get up and answer it himself, but it stopped ringing.

Getting up out of the bed, he threw his hands up, stretching his long chiseled frame. After doing a hundred push-ups and crunches, he jumped into the shower. He started singing. "We belong together, hmmm. And you knoooow that I'm right. How could you love me and leave me and never ... say goodbye." He loved that song by Boyz II Men.

Michelle woke up to the sound of Maurice's lovely singing voice. Even though he skipped parts of the song, it still sounded good. Her long sorrel-colored hair hung down over her face. It went well with her strawberry-and-cream skin tone. His singing was beginning to make her moist between the legs.

She had come over drunk last night, expecting to get fucked real good. Her plans were spoiled when Maurice said that he was too tired from working all day. She knew the truth. What he really meant was that he was too tired from fucking one of his younger bitches.

What is it gonna take to hook this young nigga? Michelle wondered. She fucked him good, bought him things and paid his car note. *What else can I do?*

She removed the covers from her body after she heard the shower cut off. She lay on her back, spread eagle, waiting on him to come out of the bathroom. She could see her nipples swelling in front of her eyes. Her hormones were on fire.

The bathroom door opened. Maurice appeared in the doorway, toweling himself dry. "Goddamn!" he exclaimed, seeing her lying naked across his bed. Her almond-shaped gray eyes watched him seductively. Slowly, her eyelids shut and she bit down on her bottom lip, pretending that he was deep inside of her. She rubbed her clit and jammed three fingers in and out of herself. She stared at her sorrel-colored sex nest that matched the hair on her head, probably inherited from her mother, who was Dutch.

Maurice picked up his watch off the dresser. It was seven thirty in the morning, and he had to be at work by eight. He cleared his throat to get her attention.

"Huh?" she said in a strangled voice. She had almost reached her climax.

He pointed to the sign over his door. *Check out time is seven thirty a.m.*, she read to herself. "That sign ain't for me. That's for them other hoes that you be creeping around with. I hope you use protection."

"Michelle, that sign is for anyone who don't live here," he corrected her. "Now get your thick ass up. I've got to get ready for work."

Her cell phone started ringing again. She got up, stomping her long, busty body over to the dresser. Maurice couldn't help but check out her big, jiggly ass as she stepped. She caught him staring and rolled her eyes at him.

"Hello," she said into the phone. "Oh, hey, Larry baby." She looked at Maurice, putting her index finger up to her lips, signaling him to be quiet.

How the fuck can she make me be quiet in my own house? he thought. *Bitch has got a lot of nerve.*

"Un huh," she said. "You're at the barbershop getting your

hair cut? Okay. I'll be home in a few. You know I was at work last night. Come on Larry, don't start." She sighed and put her hand on her forehead. She was tired of Larry's bitching. "Well, you should've called me at work if you didn't believe me. Bye, Larry." She pushed the end button, disconnecting him.

By the time she got off the phone, Maurice was already dressed. He had on a pair of Calvin Klein slacks, a Tommy Hilfiger shirt and tie and black square-toed dress shoes. She watched lustfully, as he brushed his wavy hair and goatee. He was thinking that he should've been a model for *GQ*. Unknown to him, Michelle was thinking the exact same thing.

In the dresser mirror, he noticed that Michelle had gotten back into his bed. She looked so sexy sitting up naked and mad, but she had to obey the rules just like all the others.

"Michelle, it's seven forty," he said harshly.

"And? What's that supposed to mean?"

He nodded his head toward the check-out sign.

"I ain't no ho," she snapped. "How are you just gonna kick me out? You know what? Fuck it!" She began putting on her clothes.

He watched her pull her pink panties over her backside.

"I come over here expecting to make love and end up playing with myself. You ain't all that. I could've stayed at home with the old man if I wanted to get finger fucked. Shit!" she pouted.

She finished dressing, grabbed her purse, and then headed for the door. On her way out, she stopped to glance at her watch. "Seven forty-four. You happy?"

"Michelle, don't act like that, baby," he said, trying to comfort her. "You knew the rules when you came over last night."

"You're right," she agreed. "Since I have to obey them, you don't have to worry about my fine ass lying in your bed no more." She left, slamming the door behind her.

"Good, you lazy-ass bitch," he said to himself. He smirked as he looked out of his front window and watched her bolt down the street in her Land Rover.

Had he looked to his right, he would've seen her husband

parked down the street, sitting low in his BMW. He waited until he saw Maurice's curtain close before he pulled off.

✗   ✗   ✗

The dealership was filled with customers when Maurice pulled up and parked in his reserved parking spot. He spotted Derrick showing a tall, big-boned girl a new Dodge Stratus. The cool look on his face made it seem more like he was macking than trying to sell a car. Maurice strolled past them into the building. While he was unlocking his office door, he saw Roger out of the corner of his eye. "Hey, my favorite white boy," Maurice said jokingly. "What's up with ya?"

"Chillin'," he replied, trying to sound black. "I need to talk to you for a minute, homie."

"Aw'ight." Maurice led Roger into his office. He flipped on the lights. "Have a seat." He made himself comfortable in the high-back leather chair behind his desk. "Talk to me."

Roger took a deep breath. "Man, yo, like I got this problem with gettin' girls. Right? And since I know you're a player, I was hoping that you could give me some pointers, or somethin' like that." Roger looked at him through serious eyes.

Maurice was aware that Roger thought of himself as black. He didn't like it, but he dealt with it because he knew that Roger was a good dude. Plus, Roger looked up to him. Every time he had a problem, he would go to Maurice for answers instead of his father, Mr. Copeland, who was the owner of Midwestern Chrysler and Dodge dealership.

"What kinda game can I give a white boy, Roger? I don't have one white broad in my stable of whores, man."

Roger jumped to his feet. "Man, cut the bullshit, Reece, man," he snapped. "I know what be going on up in this office. I ain't no damn fool. I hear the girls that come in here making moaning sounds and shit. You a stud, man. That's why I came to you."

An incriminating smile flashed across Maurice's face. "First off, Roger, with you being white, you could never possess the game that I have. So don't think that you're ever gonna be on my level, no matter how much I teach you," Maurice said arrogantly.

"I'm not trying to compete with you," he explained. "All I need you to do is gimme some game that'll make me feel more confident about myself."

"The game is to be sold, not told, Roger. How much money do you have on you?"

Roger searched his pockets. He placed a wad of crumpled bills on top of Maurice's desk, then counted them. "I've got two hundred and ten, no, eleven dollars."

"Give me the two hundred." Maurice leaned forward, snatching it out of his hand. Roger watched him stuff the money into his pocket. "Now, here's what I want you to do. Change your dress code. Go with the casual look instead of the wannabe Eminem look. You ain't no damn rapper. Imagine how silly I would look if I walked around dressed like Andre 3000 from OutKast. You think my women would respect me dressed like that?"

"Nah," Roger replied, feeling what he was saying.

Maurice pressed on. "Next, you've got to be aggressive with a woman. Talk to her with authority. Tell me what you say when you walk up to a woman that you're attracted to? Pretend that she's a black girl."

Roger thought for a moment. "Aw'ight. I'll walk up to her and say, 'Didn't I see you in a Jay-Z video?'" He smiled, thinking he had said something fly. He frowned after seeing the unimpressed look on Maurice's face. "What's wrong with that?"

Maurice sighed. "That's the lamest shit I've ever heard in my life. Any real broad would've slapped the shit out of your ass."

Roger looked dumbfounded. Maurice stood up and walked over to his file cabinet. He searched through the files until he found the one he was looking for. "Let me show you how this shit's done, boy."

"What you doing?" Roger quizzed.

Maurice sat back down in his chair. "Remember that little green-eyed girl that I sold the Sebring to a few weeks ago?"

"The one that was in here moaning?" Roger said.

"Yeah, smart ass," Maurice replied. He punched her number into the office phone, then turned on the speaker. "Take notes."

Roger made himself comfortable in order to watch the mack in action. Her phone rang twice before she picked up. "I sent your check, Reece," she said, answering the phone. Obviously she had seen the number come up on the caller ID.

Maurice looked cautiously at Roger to see if he was paying attention to what she had said. The last thing he wanted was for the cover to be blown off his scam. Roger didn't flinch; he was too busy waiting on Maurice to put his mack down.

"I ain't on that right now," Maurice said smoothly. "I called to see how you was doing." He leaned back in his chair.

"Really?" she said. "I'm sorry. I thought this was a business call."

"Unt unh. So, how's your car holding up?"

"It's cool, I'm happy. I get a lot of attention in it. Especially when I've got the top down," she bragged.

"That's good. I love a satisfied customer. Look, Pasha. I've been thinking about you ever since that day. I finally built up the nerve to call you."

"Yeah, right," she said doubtfully. "Since when did you start having to build up the nerve to talk to a woman? You know, I heard about you long before I met you."

Maurice shifted in his seat. "See, that's the thing. Something's different about you. I don't know what it is, but I get a queasy feeling in my stomach just talking to you."

She laughed softly. "Boy, you are something else. So tell me, to what do I owe the pleasure of you calling lil' ole me?"

"Umm ... how about you buying me dinner?" He winked his eye at Roger. "Is this Sunday cool?"

"Yeah, that's cool," she agreed. "What time?"

"Probably around eight. Call me. You got my number."

"I sure will. Bye, sexy."

He hung up. "That's how easy it is," he explained. "I came at her like she was all that. Then she came at me with the same game." He pointed his long finger at him. "That right there gave me the go ahead to be aggressive with her. You see how I told her what she was gonna do? Even after I taxed her for that bullshit-ass car, she's still gonna take me out to dinner." He shrugged. "It's as simple as that."

Roger looked at Maurice like he was his savior. He stood up. "Damn, bro. You a cold piece, man. I'ma do it exactly like you did, since it's that easy." Roger walked to the door. He stopped suddenly, turning around. "What about my money?" he asked curiously.

A dirty grin appeared on Maurice's face. "Like I said before, the game is to be sold, not told."

Finally, Roger got the message. He left, closing the door behind him.

Maurice called Freak on the phone. It rang for what seemed like forever before he answered.

"Hello."

"Meet me for lunch 'round," he glanced at his watch, "twelve o'clock. I gotta holla at you about something."

"That's cool. Let's go to Darryl's this time, I'm tired of TGI's," Freak complained.

"It don't make no difference to me. See you in a few." Maurice hung up.

Stepping around his huge desk, he walked over to the big window that overlooked the many rows of new cars. Derrick was leading an attractive but healthy female customer inside. He smiled, knowing that Derrick was probably gonna offer her a loan from his personal bank. He could just imagine what she would look like bent over Derrick's small desk.

Chapter 10

The mid-afternoon traffic was heavy when Maurice hopped onto the freeway. The Corvette's big engine roared as he weaved through traffic. Derrick sat on the passenger side, holding on for his life. He wanted to say something, but he knew it wouldn't do any good. Maurice turned into another person when he was behind the wheel.

Their exit was coming up. He quickly whipped the Corvette to the right, barely missing the back end of a Honda Prelude. He didn't bother slowing down as he got onto the 87th Street exit. Ignoring the red light, he made a left, spinning his tires like he was racing.

Derrick had enough. "Man, slow this muh-fucka down," he hollered. "Kill yo'self, but don't take me with you."

Maurice slowed down. "Man, I swear you act like a bitch sometimes. I'ma start callin' you little bitch instead of little Derrick." Maurice shook his head in disgust. "Get behind the wheel of this muthafucka and you'll see why I drive like this."

"Mmm hm. You gon' see too after you end up wrapped around a damn pole."

Maurice laughed, easing to a stop at a red light. It felt good to be a young player. The summer was approaching and he couldn't wait to see what new bitches would be coming out of hibernation this year.

He faced Derrick, "Man, did you—" Something caught his attention.

The baddest bitch that he had ever seen pulled up next to him in a black Excursion. He could hear Beyoncé and Jay-Z's "*Bonnie and Clyde*" belting out of it. She was in her own little world as she sang along, bobbing her head to the beat.

She sang, "If I was your girlfriend, I would be there for you." Her long, silky mane blew in the wind.

Even from a distance, he could see her shiny, honey-colored skin. She must have felt him watching her, because she turned her head and looked in his direction.

Her mouth fell open when she saw Maurice's face. *Damn, that nigga looks just like Sirron,* she thought. It was kind of scary looking at him, knowing that Sirron was all the way in California, locked up. She took off her dark shades, revealing her slanted hazel eyes. They exchanged predatory looks.

Derrick noticed the look on Maurice's face. He turned, following Maurice's eyes, to see what had his attention. Derrick's face took on the same look after he saw her.

"Man, what you waiting on?" he said, nudging Maurice. "You better get on that." He knew that she was out of his league.

When the light turned green, Nekole winked at him salaciously, then pulled off. He felt a dark cloud over his head after he saw her license plates. They read: GENO.

"Ain't that Big G's truck?" Derrick asked.

Maurice sat with a gloomy look on his face. He could tell by her eyes that she had game for a nigga. She was exactly the type he was looking for. Out of all the dudes in Kansas City who were eligible, Geno had gotten to her first.

People cursing and blowing their horns behind him brought him back to reality. He was about to drive off, but the light had turned red again. "Move, Goddamn it! Are you color blind? Get some fuckin' glasses!" he heard people yelling from their cars.

"I reminded her of somebody," Maurice said to no one in particular. "She thought she recognized me from somewhere."

Derrick looked at his watch. "*You'd* better recognize and hurry the fuck up. We gotta be back at the office at one."

The light turned green again. Maurice pulled off. "Shut the fuck up, nigga."

"Aw, you tough now, right." Derrick laughed. "Nigga, you been exposed."

Maurice looked confused. "What are you talking about?"

"You being scared to holla at that bitch. I just wanna put that on record." Derrick laughed. "First time I ever saw you freeze up."

Maurice bit down on his bottom lip, kind of embarrassed by Derrick's comment. He had to admit, the sight of Nekole did stun him for a moment, though he would never admit it out loud. "Laugh now," Maurice said. "I guess I'ma have to get at her just to show you that she ain't no different than the rest." He said that to save face. "I treat bad bitches like shit, too."

"Aw'ight, Too Short."

"Watch and see, sucka. I'ma make that ho bust her feet and her wallet," he said with confidence. "Geno gon' have to be mad at me."

Darryl's was crowded with working people from various jobs on their lunch breaks. Waiters and waitresses bumped back and forth, trying to satisfy the impatient customers. Today's special was the Riblet Platter. Derrick and Maurice entered the dimly lit place, scanning the room for Freak. They had seen his black Escalade parked out front.

They spotted his wavy, peanut head sitting at a booth near the back. Derrick pointed in his direction. Freak had a big grin on his face while he talked into his cell phone. He glanced up at the two sitting down at the table.

"I'll see you on Friday," Freak said into the phone. "You too. Bye." He hung up. He looked back and forth between the two, who were looking at him accusingly. "What?"

"You trick-ass nigga," Derrick said jokingly. "We know what 'you too' means."

"Yeah," Maurice said. "You should've just said, 'I love you

too'."

"Fuck both of you niggas," Freak said defensively. He folded up his menu. "I already ordered three samplers."

"Works for me," Maurice agreed, along with Derrick.

The waitress brought over three oval-shaped plates full of chicken, pork, beef and three side dishes. Quietly, they all sat scarfing down the delicious combination of food.

While they were eating, Maurice noticed a very attractive young black woman dining alone across the room. He kept staring at her, hoping to get her attention. His heart almost leaped out of his chest when he saw a man that he knew too well come out of nowhere and join her at her table. It was Steve.

Maurice watched the young girl feed Steve off of his plate like he didn't have a wife at home. They laughed, giggled and played footsy under the table. After they finished, Steve left an enormous tip on the table. He never saw his son sitting in the booth across the room.

Maurice had always suspected Steve of cheating on his mama, but actually seeing it was something different. He decided to keep it to himself for the time being. He didn't intend to bring chaos to his mother's home, but he would check Steve about it later.

"Man, what you over there daydreaming about?" Freak asked, bringing him back to reality.

"Yeah, nigga. Where the fuck yo' mind at?" Derrick asked.

Maurice wiped his mouth with a paper napkin. "I was thinking about something," he lied. "Derrick, what the hell did you do with that fat-ass girl that I saw you taking to your office?"

"Aw, man." Derrick paused to wipe his mouth. "I fucked the shit out of her big pretty ass. Pussy was wet as a muthafucka. I made her pay a big down payment. After wrestling with her big-ass thighs, I thought I deserved a little extra."

"You niggas is silly," Freak stated. "Y'all gon' fuck around and get fired and put up under the jail."

Derrick took a sip of his Coke. "Man, we're doing them bitches a favor. Ain't nobody gonna tell. You should see how eager those girls be to give it up. They want them new cars as bad as fiends want crack. The fucked up thing is, they think they're getting over."

Maurice nodded his head in agreement. "I didn't think it would work out this well, either. But it does. I can remember when a bitch would come in qualified for a ten thousand dollar loan, but wanted a twelve thousand dollar car and didn't have a dime in her pocket. Eventually, we'd end up knocking off the two grand to fit her budget. That's why the cars are all over-priced anyway. So we started charging extra, then tell the boss that we knocked it off the price. And I must say, my bank account has been looking pretty good ever since."

Freak said, "Don't call me to bail y'all asses out, and don't write me from county, because I ain't gon' be coming up to visit you niggas." He paused. "Now what was it that you wanted to talk to me about? I gotta be somewhere in a minute."

"Aw, yeah," Maurice said. He glanced around the room to see if anybody was listening before he whispered, "I need you to get me a gun."

Freak sat back and sucked his teeth while he pondered the request. Actually, he knew where to get one, he just wasn't sure if he should tell Maurice or not. Maurice was a player who didn't know much about the street life except how to chase hoes. If Maurice fucked around and did something stupid with it, it would be on his conscience.

"What a nigga like you need a gun for?" Freak quizzed.

"Because. You never know when one of them ole hating-ass niggas is gonna want to trip over some broad," Maurice explained. "If one of 'em find out that they girl is paying my bills, ain't no telling what they might try." He paused, realizing what Freak said. "What you mean? What a nigga like *me* need with a gun? You saying I'm a bitch or something?"

Freak put his hands up. "Hold on, Reece. I know you ain't no bitch. I was just saying. How many niggas that wear John Varvatos suits walk around carrying guns?" Freak's voice softened. "That ain't your style. That's all I'm saying."

"I can see where ya coming from," Maurice said. "But I still want one."

Freak took a deep breath. "Aw'ight. Let's go outside." He wiped his mouth and threw the napkin on his plate. Maurice picked up the tab, then followed Freak out to his truck. He reached into his glove compartment and pulled out a brand new Glock. He wiped his prints off with the sleeve of his shirt and handed it to Maurice.

"You can have this," Freak offered. "If you have to use it, get rid of it."

Maurice held the gun like it was a newborn baby. He aimed it at a parked car. "I like this."

Freak got into his truck. "Just remember what I said."

Maurice and Derrick got back inside the Corvette. He tucked it away inside the console then cautiously headed back to work.

x   x   x

This time it wasn't the garage door window that was broken when he got home. It was the living room window. Pissed off, Maurice hopped out, hit the alarm, and flew into the house. He picked up the phone, dialing Neosha's number.

"Hello," she answered, trying to sound innocent.

"Bitch! I know it was you who busted out my damn window. You're gonna keep fuckin' with me and I'ma end up poppin' the shit out yo' ass."

"With what?" She laughed. "Nigga, you don't even own a gun."

"You gon' find out with what, bitch," he retorted. "Keep on fuckin' with my shit."

"Is that how you talk to me?" Her voice was serious now. "I help pay bills around that muthafucka and I don't even get to spend the night." Her voice cracked as she began to cry. "The least you could do is drop by and say hi or something. Act like you care about me a little bit, damn."

He fixed himself a glass of cognac while she sniffled in his ear. The silence would settle her down.

She sniffed. "Hello?"

"I'm here. I'm just letting you get it all off your chest."

"I've said all I have to say."

He took a sip of his drink. "I know I have been neglecting you lately." His voice was calm. "I promise I'ma make all of this up to you." Maurice walked over to the fireplace and began going through yesterday's mail.

"See how easy that was? I know I be overreacting. I just want some attention. And don't worry, I'm going to get your window fixed."

"You didn't have to tell me that."

"When am I gonna see you?"

"Tonight. I'm feeling a little tense and need of one of your massages. Bring the baby oil."

"Cool. I'm gonna pick up some motion lotion on my way over there. It heats up when you blow on it."

"Neosha."

"Yes, baby?"

"You don't have no boyfriends that I should know about, do you?" he asked curiously.

"Naw, boy. You know that I'm too in love with your scandalous ass to fuck around with anybody else. I ain't nasty like that."

"I was just askin'. I'll see you in a minute." He hung up.

He opened the mail he received from his loan customers and placed the checks inside his wallet. He smiled when he saw the money order with Pasha's name on it.

After taking Michelle's portrait down, he replaced it with Neosha's. Then he jumped into the shower to freshen up. Since Neosha didn't have a man, the gun could remain in the car for tonight.

Like a pimp, he wasn't too fond of fucking his broads on a regular basis. That made them lose focus and could cause tender dick—a serious disease that made a man develop feelings for a broad. But Neosha was long overdue for a good fucking. Tonight he would give her enough dick to satisfy her for a month.

Chapter 11

Things were beginning to look up for Nekole. Geno had given her a booth at the beauty shop and secretly bought her a whole new wardrobe. She also got to drive his truck until she could save enough money to buy her own car.

Supposedly, Geno was still trying to find her a place to stay, but he hadn't found anything. Too bad, because she couldn't stand living under the same roof as Toni.

Already they had gotten into two catfights and had countless arguments with each other. Toni did everything she could to annoy Nekole. Especially when she and Geno had sex. Toni would moan and scream at the top of her lungs, just to try to make Nekole jealous. What she didn't know was that she was doing just the opposite. She made Nekole wonder how the big man would feel between her thighs, humping her like a savage beast. She already knew that he was a potential trick. But since Geno was Angie's man's cousin, she decided to try to keep from breaking up their happy home. She'd use them to help her get back on her feet, then bounce.

To Toni's satisfaction, Nekole had befriended a girl who had just started working at Geno's shop also. Pasha and Nekole hung out every day after work. By the time Nekole got home, she was too tired to do anything except take a shower and go to bed.

Nekole hadn't had sex in nearly a month, and her pussy was

on fire. Those late night rubs in the shower weren't cutting it. She
needed some sex, and bad. Even if she had to get it from that cute
dyke girl they call Lucki, up at the shop. She hadn't been with
another woman before, but she was horny enough to fuck a mule.

Nekole took the wrap from around her freshly done head. It
was eight, and she had to be at work within the next thirty minutes. Pasha had called ten minutes ago saying that she was on her
way.

After she finished taking care of her hygiene, she squeezed into
a pair of tight blue jeans, a T-shirt and a pair of black Reeboks. She
wanted to be comfortable standing on her feet all day. She reminded herself to stop by the mall after work so she could pick up
something skimpy to walk around the house in. That would really set Toni on fire. Nekole often wondered why she was so devious.

She was standing in the bathroom mirror applying eye shad-
ow when the doorbell rang. "Geno!" she yelled. "Could you open
up the front door for Pasha, please?"

"Open it yourself," Toni replied for him.

Nekole smiled devilishly. She checked her face in the mirror
one last time before she went to get the door.

Pasha was standing there, looking green-eyed and fine in a pair
of tight stretch pants and a T-shirt. She was very pretty and had a
nice shape, but was of no comparison to Nekole. On a regular day,
Nekole's doll face looked as if she had been to Glamour Shots for
a photo shoot. She could've easily had a career as a top model with
her tall and curvy frame. Her ass was fat, but her waist was as small
as a twelve-year-old's.

Pasha stepped her short, thick frame into the living room.
"Girl, you ready?"

"Yep. Let me grab my purse." Nekole ran down the hall to her
bedroom.

                              x   x   x

On their way to work, Pasha decided to tell Nekole about her
new friend, Maurice. "Girl, I met somebody," Pasha said excited-

ly.

Nekole knew that she had detected a new glow in Pasha's green eyes. "Really? Is he fine?"

"Fine ain't the word, girl. His face belongs on TV."

"I ain't mad at you. I'll be glad when I find me somebody."

"You and me both." She chuckled. "Girl, yo' pussy is so hot, I can feel steam coming out from between your legs." They shared a laugh. Pasha pulled over to drop her top. "Ooh, that reminds me, girl."

"What?" Nekole quizzed.

"He sells cars. He can probably help you get one." Pasha had temporarily forgotten about Maurice's loan program, and the possibility of Nekole ending up bent over his desk.

"Talk to him and see what he says."

"I will."

"*Don't Mess With My Man*" came on the radio. Pasha turned it up. She and Nekole sang along all the way to the shop.

x x x

Nelly was performing live on "*The Jenny Jones Show*," and Nekole stood in front of the TV, shaking her ass to the music. Nobody but the girls complained about her blocking the forty-five-inch TV. To the guys in the barbershop, watching her dance was more exciting than watching Nelly rap about his "*Air Force Ones.*"

Pasha was putting a relaxer on an older woman's hair and trying to see Nelly at the same time. "Girl, yo' daddy wasn't no glass maker," Pasha said to Nekole. "Get yo' big butt out from in front of the TV. We trying to see Nelly."

"Speak for yourself, girl," Tish, one of the other beauticians, said. "I'm trying to see Murphy Lee."

Lucki was finishing up on a young kid's plain haircut. "Do your thang, Nekole," she encouraged her. "Matter of fact, you can come over here and shake that thang in front of me and Big E."

Everybody on the barber's side cheered, while the women in the beauty shop all looked at each other. "Unt unh."

Nekole spun around, narrowing her hazels on Lucki. "Yours ain't big enough to handle this." She grabbed her crotch.

Old Man Ed's paper fell out of his hand. "Lawd have mercy. It's gettin' hot in here."

Nekole looked down at him. "What you babbling about, Ed? If I gave you a whiff of this, you'd probably cum in your pants."

"I don't have a problem with that," he said, matter-of-factly.

A ten-year-old sat in Geno's chair, getting his braided hair lined up. "I like coming up in here, Geno. Where did you get her from?" he asked, referring to Nekole.

Geno popped him on the ear. "Shut up and cover your ears. Ay, y'all hold that filth down. We got kids up in here."

"I ain't no kid," the boy said angrily. "I'm almost eleven."

"Eleven," Geno repeated. "Boy, your little dick ain't even big enough to hold while you pee."

The boy became embarrassed when he saw everybody, including Nekole, laughing at him. *Geno is always showing out*, he thought. He sat with his lips stuck out for the rest of the time that he was in the chair.

Nekole strutted back over to her booth to her waiting customer to finish twisting his dreadlocks. The light-skinned man was sitting in the chair, waiting patiently. "Girl, you off the chain," he said, flashing his gold-toothed smile. "'Round here gettin' everybody aroused and shit."

"Shut up, Joker," she said, hitting him on his shoulder. "I'm just having fun."

Geno dusted the hair off of the little boy's neck and helped him down off the booster seat. Geno dug into his pocket, pulled out some change, and handed it to the boy.

"Here. Buy you a bag of chips and a soda. Sit down over there until your mother gets back." He pointed to a chair that sat in front of the TV that had the PlayStation 2 connected to it. Though his lips were still poked out and he was angry, he did as he was told.

Joker wet his lips, watching Nekole's breasts dangle in front of him while she twisted his hair. He never even thought about getting his hair locked up until Nekole told him that he had the face for it. She said that they would bring out the color of his eyes. From then on, he stopped letting her braid his hair and switched to dreads.

Joker had been building up the nerve to ask her out for two weeks. He finally decided to go for it. "So, umm ... who you fuckin' with? I don't ever hear you talking about a man or nothing."

"If you're trying to ask me out," she looked him in the eye, "don't beat around the bush. Just be a man and come on out with it. All I can say is no." She paused. "Or yes."

"Aw'ight then," he said, building confidence. "Can I take you out?"

"Mmmm, no," she replied. "I don't go out with dudes unless I plan on fuckin' 'em. And I don't fuck my clients." She continued to twist his locks.

He stroked his bearded chin, making an imploring smile. "I can't be an exception?"

She finished the last lock, then took the cape from around his neck. "I would make an exception," she smiled, "but I don't like dudes who wear dreads. Pay up at the counter." She walked away to the restroom, leaving him dumbfounded.

"Dirty bitch," he said to himself.

Old Man Ed laughed. "She's a beast, ain't she?"

Lucki saw Nekole heading toward the back. It was time for her to make her move. She stopped sweeping so she could catch up with her. Nekole was opening the door when she felt a presence behind her. Startled, she turned around quickly, thinking that Joker had come after her. To her surprise, Lucki was standing there with a naughty grin on her face. She nodded her head toward the restroom, inviting Nekole inside.

Nekole stepped back, putting some distance between them. "What do you want?"

"You know what I want." She reached for Nekole's hair. "I

want to show you how much of a man I can be."

Nekole pushed her hand away. "I don't get down like that."

"Come on, girl," Lucki pleaded. "You might not have got down like that before, but you will." Lucki stepped closer to her. Her light brown eyes met Nekole's hazels. "Just as I thought, you got a look in your eye like you haven't been fucked in a while." She sniffed. "I can smell the backed-up cum through your jeans."

Lucki was attractive to Nekole. Up close, she looked like a pretty-ass boy. Of course, that could've been Nekole's hormones talking. Lucki licked her lips, focusing her attention on Nekole's crotch. Nekole could feel the moisture in her panties.

They exchanged scorching looks. All of a sudden, Nekole found herself inching into the restroom. By the time Lucki had locked the door, Nekole already had her pants off. They attacked each other, kissing wildly in the middle of the floor. Nekole panted and moaned softly while Lucki skillfully kissed her ears and neck. She stuck her fingers inside of Nekole's mouth to muffle the moaning sounds.

"Mmm. Do something to make me cum," Nekole begged. She removed her panties, hopped up on the sink and gaped her legs wide so Lucki could go down on her.

Lucki turned her ball cap to the back and squatted down between her legs. Starting out slow, she slid her tongue into her crevice, wiggling it around inside of her. Nekole let out a high pitched howl, then quickly caught herself. While Lucki expertly nibbled and sucked on her clitoris, she worked two fingers in and out of her. Nekole grabbed the back of Lucki's head, encouraging her to go on.

Lucki sucked harder when she felt Nekole's legs begin to tremble. Nekole held her breath when she felt herself cumming. "Here it ... comes," she grunted.

"Mm hmm," Lucki moaned, sucking all of the cum juice out of her. When she finished, she gave it one last kiss before she stood up.

Nekole fell back against the mirror with her eyes closed,

breathing rapidly. After her breathing slowed, she opened her eyes. Now that she had an orgasm, the thrill was gone. Realizing that it was another woman standing in front of her, she got down and put her panties back on. Lucki no longer looked like a pretty-ass boy to her. She was a woman, standing there with pussy juice drying around her mouth. Without a word, she put her clothes back on, fixed herself in the mirror, then left Lucki standing in the restroom. Alone.

Geno flipped the channel to BET and had the volume up loud. Nekole could hear P. Diddy rapping as she crept over to her booth.

Pasha looked up from styling the older lady's hair. She looked at Nekole curiously, noticing the odd look on her face. Being nosey, she glanced down the hall just in time to catch Lucki leaving the restroom with a sneaky grin on her face.

"Awww," Pasha said, covering her mouth with her free hand. She put her comb down and stormed over to where Nekole was. "What were you," Pasha said, nodding her head in Lucki's direction, "and her doing in the restroom for all that time?"

Nekole whispered in her ear, "I let her suck my pussy."

Pasha's eyes almost popped out of their sockets. "Girl, are you crazy?!"

Nekole hit her for talking too loud. "Girl, keep your damn voice down." She took Pasha by the arm, leading her to the back room. "Girl, I needed to bust a nut, bad," she explained. "I was about to explode." She paused while Jamisha, the nail technician, walked past them to the restroom. "So what it had to be with a girl," she continued. "It ain't never gonna happen again."

"I hope not, because that bitch is trifling."

"Trifling? You've only known her for two weeks, Pasha."

"And?" Pasha said smartly. "I've seen her around. And I've gathered enough to know that she'll fuck anybody who opens their legs."

Nekole sighed. "Well, whatever. Just keep this between us. Geno would probably kick me out the house if he found out."

"Nekole, Pasha," they heard Old Man Ed yell, "I'm about to order some fish. Y'all want some?"

"Yes, please," Pasha replied. "Don't forget that I like extra hot sauce on mine." Pasha turned back to Nekole. "I ain't gonna say nothing. Just don't do it again. Please."

"Cross my heart and hope to die," Nekole said, making a cross on her heart with her index finger.

Chapter 12

Sirron's legs shook nervously and his stomach was in knots as he sat beside his lawyer, waiting on the judge to enter the courtroom. Thanks to his public defender, he got the prosecutor to reduce the charge from second degree murder to manslaughter. He kept glancing toward the back of the courtroom, hoping that Nekole would walk through the door and take a seat. After all they had been through together, showing up for his sentencing would be the least she could do. After all, if it weren't for him, she would be sitting there, too.

The old, heavyset bailiff stood up. "All rise. This court is now in session. The Honorable Judge Gary Sweatt presiding."

Everyone in the courtroom stood until they were asked to be seated. Sweatt put a pair of half-moon reading glasses onto his grumpy-looking face. His stony expression scared Sirron to death. He wished that God would work his magic and get him out of this. If he did, Nekole would have hers coming.

The judge kept a frown on his face the entire time he read Sirron's plea agreement. Every so often, he would glance up, giving him a frigid stare. Sirron looked to his lawyer to see if he had seen the look that Sweatt had given him. He had talked to Sweatt earlier that morning in his chambers. The lawyer patted him on his shoulder, reassuring him that everything was okay.

Sirron glanced around the courtroom one last time, still hoping she would walk through the double doors. His heart skipped a beat after he saw the doors open up. To his disappointment, Detective Thomas came strolling in, stealing a seat in the back row. Their eyes met briefly. Thomas nodded, but Sirron turned away.

Judge Sweatt took a sip of water before he began. "Mr. Rand, did you knowingly and willfully sign this plea agreement?"

Sirron cleared his throat. "Yes, sir."

"Before we continue, is there anything the defense would like to say?"

"Yes, your honor," Sirron's lawyer said, standing up. "We would like to request a bond hearing as soon as possible."

"Denied. I don't give bonds on murder cases held in my courtroom. Is that clear?"

"Yes, your honor." He took a seat.

Sweatt took another sip of water. "Mr. Rand, I'm going to accept the terms of your plea agreement that the prosecutor has prepared. Just so you'll have some idea of the amount of time you'll be receiving, I'm gonna tell you. More than likely, you'll be receiving a sentence of ten years the next time we meet. However—"

"Fuck that!" the victim's brother yelled from the front row. His sister grabbed his hand, trying to get him to sit back down. "Nah!" He snatched away from her. "If my brother can't see his kids again, he shouldn't either."

Sweatt banged his gavel violently. "Order in my courtroom," he demanded. "No more outbursts. Is that clear?" Their silence answered his question.

Out of the judge's view, Sirron threw up a Blood sign, on the sly, to the victim's brother. The man mouthed the words, "I'ma kill you," at him, before Sirron turned back around.

"Mr. Rand," Sweatt proceeded, "You should consider yourself very lucky. You still have a chance to get out and live a productive life. So I suggest that you take full advantage of the programs that the state has available for you. Who knows, maybe you could write a novel or something. That is all. Court is adjourned."

x   x   x

The minute Sirron got back to the county jail, he headed straight for the phone. He didn't know if she'd accept the call, but he tried his luck calling Angie's house, collect.

Her boyfriend, Mack, answered. "Hello."

The operator came on. "You have a collect call from ... Sirron. If you would like to accept, press five now."

Mack pushed five.

"Ay, man, don't trip," Sirron said. "I'm Nekole's boyfriend. I was just calling Angie because I haven't been able to catch up with Nekole. I just want to ask her a few questions. That's all."

"It's cool." Mack yelled, "Angie, pick up the damn phone!"

"Who is it?" she yelled back from the kitchen.

"Some nigga named Sirran or Sirron or some shit. Just pick up the phone."

Mack hung up after he heard her pick up the other phone.

"How you doing, Sirron?" Angie said innocently.

"Wha' sup, man?" Sirron's voice was hostile. "Where's Nekole? I've been calling her aunt's house, but she ain't never there. She didn't even show up for none of my hearings. How she just gonna run off on me like that?"

Angie felt sorry for him. She was responsible for some of his pain by persuading Nekole to run out on him. Sirron was really in love with Nekole, and she knew it. Instead of telling him the straight-out truth, she decided to pacify him with a good lie.

"Sirron, listen. That dude that you supposedly killed, his brother came around asking questions about Nekole. We got scared thinking that he was gonna kill her, so she left town for a while. After she gets back on her feet, she's gonna send you some money and everything."

"You got a number or address to where she's staying?"

"I don't have it, but I can get it. It'll take me a while, though."

"A while?" he repeated. "Listen Angie, I'ma call you back in a couple of weeks. If you ain't got the information that I need to get in touch with her, including the address, consider your ass in the sling right along with hers." He slammed the phone down. "I can't believe this bitch," he said on the way to his cell.

x x x

Sitting Indian-style on the floor beside her bed, Nekole counted all of the money she had been saving. She had been working for two months and only saved up three grand. It was good, considering her circumstances, but she needed more. She still needed a place to stay and a car to get around in. She was definitely gonna have to stop clubbing with Pasha so much.

So far, she liked Kansas City and had plans to stay for good. It was a nice place for a girl like her to make a fresh start. She only wished that Sirron was there with her, instead of lying up in the white man's cage. After being ditched by Pasha last night, because she had a date with Maurice, Nekole really started to miss him even more.

She could imagine him lying on his bunk, staring out into space, wondering why she had done him the way she did. The thought made her stomach knot up. As soon as she got where she wanted to be, she would write him and send him a bankroll. Maybe even fly out there to visit him.

Someone knocked on her door. Quickly, she gathered up the bills, stuffing them into her dresser drawer. "Just a minute," she said, stalling whoever it was. Glancing around the room, making sure nothing personal was lying about, she opened up the door. Geno was standing there, holding a Taco Bell bag.

"I bought you something to eat. I know you're hungry after being asleep all evening."

"Thank you." She took the sack from him. "That was sweet of you."

"Do I turn you on?" he blurted out.

Nekole smiled. "What?"

"Don't worry. Toni went out with her friends." He stepped closer to her. "You can be honest."

"Geno, have you been drinking?" She could smell alcohol on

his breath, now that he was in her space.

"Yep. I'm drunk off looking at you." He attempted to kiss her.

She put her hands on his chest, stopping him. "You need to go take a shower Geno, then lie down until the liquor wears off."

Geno licked his lips. "I may be a little drunk, but I'm aware of everything. I'm aware that when a woman walks around a man's house in panties while his girl is away, she's either trying to give him some, or she's a fuckin' cock tease." He reached for her breast. "Now come on, before Toni gets back."

Nekole could see a hump growing in his pants. She wanted to reach down and caress it, but she remained in control of herself. Messing around with Toni's man under the roof of her own house was bad karma. She needed some dick bad, but she didn't want to get it like that. She'd rather continue playing the tease game, wearing skimpy clothes around the house.

"Stop it, Geno!" she said with authority.

He frowned, backing away from her. "Aw'ight. If you change your mind, I'll be in the shower." He left her standing there.

Slowly, she closed the door. She set the bag down, then dropped down on the bed, holding the pillow up to her chest. Her eyes focused on the ceiling while she thought. If she gave Geno some pussy, how would it benefit her? He seemed to be making damn good money at the shop. Looking at her new wardrobe and the way Toni lived, he didn't mind sharing it. A good shot of pussy might be the key to his safe. It worked for Toni. Besides, did she really give a damn if he was Toni's man or not? That never stopped her before. It was settled. She would become Geno's live-in mistress until she got everything she needed to move on.

She got up off the bed. A quick peek out the window informed her that Toni had not yet returned. She took off her T-shirt and panties and slipped into her robe. She left the room with a wicked smirk on her face. Just knowing that a dick was about to run up in her made her legs tremble.

Her plan to start a new life in Kansas City was about to be ruined. No more playing "Miss Nice Girl." Nekole's usual conniving, sneaky self was about to come out. It was the only way that she would be able to get ahead quickly.

Steam filled the bathroom. Nekole entered, tiptoeing, ready to surprise him with her naked body. Her robe fell to the floor, then she slid open the shower door. Geno looked shocked at the sight of Nekole standing there, naked. His once limp organ stood and saluted.

Starting with her toes, he slowly ran his eyes up her caramel-colored body. She had small breasts, and her pussy was shaven. She eyed him lustfully, licking her lips while he eye-fucked her body.

"Want me to wash it for you?" she asked in a sexy voice. She took the lustful look in his eyes as a yes.

Stepping into the tub, she reached back, sliding the door shut. She took the washcloth off the rack and lathered it with soap. The hot water ran down her silky mane, which stretched to her back. Gently, she ran the warm, soapy washcloth over his large body. After she finished washing him, she pressed her body up against his, kissing him passionately on the lips. Her small hand made its way down between his legs and began to massage his dick. She sucked his lips and chest, biting down on his nipples hungrily. She pushed him back against the wall as she traveled downward. Her tongue stabbed his deep navel while she jacked him off.

He moaned while he impatiently waited on her to take him into her mouth. Dropping to her knees, she continued to stroke him while kissing his thighs and pelvis. His body began to squirm with pleasure. Her touch was soft and gentle. Her kisses came as close to his dick as they could, without touching it. She stopped suddenly, then stood up. "I don't suck dick for free," she said softly, then jammed her tongue into his ear.

Geno grabbed her ass, lifting her up. She reached down and grabbed his dick, then he slid her down on it while holding her up. "Shit!" she exclaimed, feeling her pussy stretch to the size of his dick. He hadn't been up in pussy that tight since Trina's in his last year of high school.

She wrapped her legs around his big body, locking her feet.

Holding onto the back of his head, she worked her hips back and forth and buried her face into his shoulder.

"AH! AH! AH! AHHH!" she hollered. "Yesss. Gimme that dick, daddy!" She switched to a circular motion. Her pussy was so wet it felt like she had turned on a faucet inside her.

"Mmmm ... shitttt ... I'm ... I'm ... cum ... ming!" She dug her nails deep into his back as she grinded deeper on him. With one good thrust, she felt her vaginal fluid release all over his dick.

Geno was turned on even more because he had never experienced a pussy that came that hard. His plans to turn her around and get his nut doggy style were thwarted. "Unt unh. I'm not finished with you yet," she said into his ear. They got out of the shower dripping wet. She instructed him to sit down on the toilet, then she straddled him.

"Umph. Shit!" Geno gasped. Her pussy began to feel like she had turned up the temperature. She popped her pussy on his shaft in a steady motion. She placed her feet flat on the floor, then started springing up and down on him like a frog. She leaned back, allowing Geno the full sight of her shaved pussy sliding up and down on his thick dick. While she worked on her second nut, Geno got a look at her weird facial expressions. Her mouth hung open and her eyes were wandering around inside her head. The sound of their skin slapping together could be heard over their loud moans.

Geno began to feel the need to release the nut he had reserved specially for her. He grabbed her by her tiny waist to support her, spread her pussy lips and began stroking her clitoris. Pumping into her with no reserve, he filled her pussy with his hot, thick liquid. Her legs began to shake, and her pussy began to spasm uncontrollably. She felt herself cumming again and sat all the way down, absorbing every inch and every drop of him. Breathing hard, she got up, scooped up her robe, then walked sheepishly to her bedroom. She hadn't been fucked that good in a long time. She collapsed on her bed, eyes closed, dripping with satisfaction.

She would wait until after Toni came home before she would

get back into the shower, so Toni would think that she'd been in her room sleeping while she was out. Not fucking her man.

Toni stuck her key into the lock, opening up the front door. She stumbled in, dropping her Gucci purse on the couch. She had one too many drinks, and a good fucking was all she needed to top off the night. Something smelled funny. From left to right she looked, sniffing the air. Did she smell sex? Or was she just drunk and paranoid?

Geno was asleep when Toni crept into the room. Rushing out of her dress and heels, she slid into the bed next to him. She ran her foot up and down his calf while kissing on his chest.

He unconsciously rolled away from her. His eyes fluttered open after he felt her warm saliva on his body. Damn! The last thing he needed was for Toni to come home horny. After what he had just gotten from Nekole, he really wasn't trying to fuck her. Her pussy was good, but she didn't know how to take control like Nekole did.

"Baaaby," Toni whined. "I wanna do it." She grabbed his limp dick. "Want me to get it up?"

"Stop, Toni." He removed her hand. "I'm tired. I been on my feet all day."

She sat up in the bed with her mouth agape. "You tired? Since when did you start being too tired to get your dick sucked?" She got out of the bed. Suspiciously, she glanced around their bedroom. She hoped that Nekole hadn't been in her bed.

Geno wished she would hurry up and get her drunk ass to sleep. Toni remembered the funny odor she smelled when she walked into the house.

"Y'all think I'ma fool," she said. "That funky cock bitch!" She stormed out of the room.

Nekole jumped out of the bed when Toni came barging in. Toni's eyes grew as big as saucers when she saw that Nekole was naked. "No you didn't fuck my man in my house, bitch."

At first Nekole was too shocked to respond. But hearing the word "bitch" brought her back to reality. She didn't want to get

Geno in trouble, so she backed down.

"Toni, what the hell are you talking about?" Nekole grabbed a big T-shirt out of her dresser and put it on.

"You know damn well what I'm talking about." Toni's eyes were both red and watery. "You've been fuckin' my man."

Nekole pursed her lips. "Bitch, don't nobody want your fat-ass man. He's cool, but he's not my type. Sorry!"

"Why you naked then, bitch?" Toni stepped closer to her.

Nekole defensively put her hand up. "Don't walk up on me, Toni," she warned. "While we're arguing, give me three feet."

"This is my house," Toni reminded her.

"And? You're still gonna respect me," Nekole demanded. "Now, like I was saying, I just got out of the shower, then I passed out on the bed. That's why I'm naked."

Toni's eyes sharpened as she contemplated stealing on Nekole. Drunk as she was, she'd probably end up getting knocked out. Still giving her a hard stare, Toni backed out of the room.

"That must've been that bitch's funk that I smelled," she said to herself on her way down the hall.

Nekole was disgusted with herself for not kicking that bitch's ass. She swore that after this was all over, she would go upside Toni's head. Couldn't no bitch get away with talking to her like that.

Chapter 13

He had her legs over his shoulders, hammering his dick into her tight pussy. Her eyes were open, appearing to be staring at him, but she wasn't. While he was pounding her, he felt a strong hand grab him by the ankle, pulling him out of her. "Whaa—" he yelled.

The woman came to and her eyes focused in on her husband, standing over her lover with a shotgun pointed at him.

"Baby, nooo!" she screamed, reaching out for him. Her husband pulled the trigger.

Maurice's eyes popped open. He woke up, panting and sweating all over his sheets. He looked to the left and saw Pasha sleeping soundly beside him. No husband, nor shotgun, was in sight. It had all been a dream.

He yawned as he got out of bed, stretching his long frame. Seeing the unopened package of Trojans on top of his dresser reminded him that he hadn't used one last night. He was drunk, but he remembered her saying something about not wanting to use a rubber. He shook his head, disgusted with how stupid he could be when he drank. Every player had his weakness, and his was Moët & Chandon.

Now that he was up and walking around, he felt a queasy feeling in his stomach. He went into the kitchen and fixed himself a glass of grapefruit juice. He drank slowly while he pondered what he was going to do on this sunny Saturday. He'd start by going to the barbershop for a fresh taper.

He woke Pasha, then went to take a hot shower. By the time he finished and dressed, she had taken care of her hygiene in the bathroom downstairs, put on her clothes and was sitting in the living room, reading the paper. She looked up at him through soft green eyes, smiling when he walked into the living room. "You look good," she complimented him. She puckered her lips for a kiss.

He gave her two quick kisses. "You hangin' out with me today?"

She nodded. "Yes." She put down the paper and stood up. "Hold on, before I forget." She took two crisp hundred-dollar bills out of her wallet and handed them to him. "Your monthly payment."

"Good lookin' out." He grabbed his keys, activated the alarm and led her out the door.

Some changes were being made around Big Geno's Barber & Beauty. Tish, the lead beautician, had lost her position to Nekole. Geno had made up some excuse about some money coming up short. Instead of her beef being with him, she was furious with Nekole. She had a bad feeling about Nekole ever since Geno first brought her into the shop. All of her flirting and being friendly with everybody was just an act. There was about to be a lot of drama around the shop. Tish would bet her life on it.

Nekole nonchalantly moved her things over to Tish's booth without saying one word to her. There were no apologies, no "I didn't knows" or anything like that. Tish gave her an evil glare while she plugged her hand-held dryers into the outlets.

Nekole caught the glare out of the corner of her eye. She faced Tish. "Is there a problem?"

"Sure is," Tish confirmed, setting down the hair dryer.

Geno heard the altercation and jumped between them before it went any further. "Hold up! Y'all not about to tear up my shop." He turned to Tish. "If you have a problem, take it up with me.

Not Nekole."

Tish backed off. "This ain't over, bitch."

"You ain't trying to see me, Tish." Nekole smirked. "And don't forget to take your daughter's ugly-ass picture off my mirror."

"That's it," Tish said. She tried to swing on Nekole, but Geno caught her arm with his huge hand. Nekole took advantage of the situation. She stepped forward while Geno had a hold on her and hit her in the face.

"Unt unh, Geno, let me go," Tish demanded, trying to pull away from him. A speckle of blood ran out of her right nostril. "This bitch done stole on me."

"I said, cut the shit!" he hollered. "I'm not gonna say it again, Nekole." He gave her a serious, hard stare. Accepting defeat, Nekole backed away. He asked Tish, "You alright?"

"I'm cool." She kept her eyes locked on Nekole. "You gon' let me go now?"

"I don't want no more bullshit out of y'all in my shop. I'm dead fuckin' serious." He released his grip.

"You gon' get yours, bitch," Tish warned.

"Whenever you're ready," Nekole replied evenly.

"Silly-ass bitches," Geno said on his way over to his chair.

Pasha walked through the door, followed by Maurice. She had a huge grin on her face as she led him over to meet Nekole. She was cleaning out her sink when Pasha tapped her on the shoulder. Nekole spun around, drawing her arm back, ready to swing. The sight of Pasha standing there made her catch herself.

"Girl, you almost got knocked the fuck out," Nekole said, letting down her guard. "I done already stole on one muthafucka today."

"What the hell are you talking about?" Pasha quizzed.

"Nevermind. Wha' sup?" Her hazels caught Maurice, standing behind Pasha, and immediately recognized him as the guy in the Corvette. Once again, they exchanged predatory looks.

That's the girl who was driving Geno's truck, he thought. *I know they ain't friends. Damn, I hate to have to break Pasha's heart.*

Because I gots to hit that.

Pasha looked from Nekole to Maurice. Their savage looks didn't go unnoticed.

"You two know each other?" she quizzed.

Maurice said, "No. I mean ... I think I've seen her around before. Haven't I?"

Nekole shook her head. "Not that I know of," she lied. She didn't want her friend to suspect that she wanted her man. "You must be mistaking me for someone else. Anyway, I'm Nekole." They shook hands.

"Maurice," he said, noticing how soft her hand was. He wondered what her legs would feel like wrapped around him.

"Nice to meet you." Nekole grinned as she turned around to finish what she was doing.

Maurice said to Pasha, "I'ma be over here gettin' my shit cut." He felt kind of silly after the way Nekole had played him.

"Alright baby." She kissed him on his cheek.

His big ego was shot. He was sure Nekole had remembered him from the stoplight. That wink she gave him had to have meant something. Something clicked in his mind. She was driving Geno's truck that day. *That's the reason why she pretended not to have ever seen me. She couldn't be all up in my face while Geno was around. He would kick her ass out of the shop,* he thought.

He sat in a chair beside Old Man Ed, who was playing a game of chess with another older man.

"What's up, Ed? Geno?" Maurice said. They both were too busy to speak, so they just grunted. He watched Ed mistakenly move his rook instead of getting his queen out of the way of the other man's bishop. "Bad move, Ed."

Ed cut his eyes at him. "What? Stay out of my business youngster. I didn't make no—"

His voice trailed off as he watched his opponent capture his queen.

"Check!" the man said with a triumphant smile on his face.

Ed smacked the table with the palm of his hand. "Damn!" He

turned, facing Maurice. "Why you wait ... until after I made the move ... before you said something?"

"Don't blame me for yo' fuck up, Ed," Maurice said.

"You shouldn't have said nothing in the first place. All you did was fuck up my concentration."

Geno cracked a smile, listening to Ed's bullshit. "Cut the shit, Ed! Y'all been arguing about that game all morning. Put the damn game up." Geno took the cape off of a customer. "Pay up at the counter."

Lucki walked in carrying her barber's bag over her shoulder. She was wearing a blue KC Royals cap and jersey with a pair of baggy blue shorts that hung to her knees. Nekole was the first person that she fixed her eyes on. Nekole saw her and quickly turned away. Lucki smirked. She knew how Nekole would act after her first bisexual experience. She'd seen it many times before.

She pimped her way over to Nekole. Nekole put her head down, pretending to be concentrating on mixing a relaxer.

"Wha' sup?" Lucki said. "You've been ignoring me lately."

"Look, Lucki," Nekole responded, in a hushed whisper. "What we did was a one time thing, and it will never happen again."

Lucki blushed. "Yeah, okay," she said angrily. She stormed over to her chair almost knocking down a little boy.

"Damn, Lucki. Watch where the hell you going," Geno said. She ignored him and began unpacking her equipment.

Maurice sat in the chair, thinking about how to come at Geno about Nekole. From where he was sitting, he hadn't seen one sign that they even knew each other. But that was how two people acted when they were creeping on the down low. Then Maurice remembered seeing her driving Geno's truck. *Ah, that's it. She must be his little cousin or something.*

"Ay, Geno?" Maurice said.

"Close your mouth so I can get up under your chin," Geno instructed him. Maurice remained still while Geno cut away the little hairs around his goatee. "You can talk now." Geno positioned the chair so that it was facing the mirror.

Maurice turned his head from left to right, checking out the haircut. "Take the top down a little more."

"Aw'ight." Geno changed the guard. "What was it you was about to say?"

"What's up with you and Nekole over there? Y'all fuckin' around or what?" Maurice quizzed.

Geno became suspicious. "Why you ask that? I ain't never mentioned her to you."

"I saw her driving the Excursion the other day. You gotta be doing something with her if she ain't family."

Geno smiled. "Yeah. That's one of my new broads," he said proudly. "Fine. Ain't she?"

"Mm hmm," Maurice agreed. "Where you get her from?"

"She's from Cali." He wanted to impress Maurice. "She's staying with me and Toni."

"With you and Toni!" Maurice exclaimed. "What kind of shit y'all got going on at home?"

Geno explained the whole situation to him, not forgetting to mention what happened in the shower. Maurice imagined the fuck faces that she made while Geno was up in her. Evidently, Geno had fucked her good because she wasn't paying Maurice any attention.

"She's more like a friend," Geno said. "You know what I'm saying? I'm just helping her get on her feet. As far as us fuckin', that's something that just happened."

"So, she's free game then?" Maurice inquired. "Since y'all are just friends and all."

Right then Geno realized the mistake he had made. He had opened the door for Maurice to try to move in on his territory. He wanted to kick himself for saying that they were just friends. It was too late to take it back. If he did, it would look like he was trying to handcuff the bitch.

Geno shrugged. "Yeah. If you can pull her, pull her. Shit, I got a bitch at the crib."

Maurice stood up, dusting the hair off of his neck. "I don't want her," he lied. "It just fucked me up when I saw her driving your truck. I mean, I know you're a trick and all, but—"

"Nigga, fuck you."

Maurice laughed as they shook hands. "Pasha," he called out. She ended her conversation with Nekole and came running. "Pay the man, baby."

Pasha opened up her Gucci wallet and took out twenty-five dollars. "Here, Geno." She handed the money to him. "You got my man lookin' all handsome and shit."

"Yo' man?" Geno chuckled. "Girl, how you fall in love so easily?"

Pasha playfully hit him on the shoulder. "Shut up."

Geno continued to laugh. "Girl, you know I'm just fuckin' with you."

"No he ain't," Talib, another barber, said without looking up from the head that he was cutting.

She put her arms around Maurice. "Forget them, baby. They just hatin' 'cause you my man."

Maurice was growing tired of hearing her say "my man" in public. It was cool when no one was around, but out in the open, he had an image to uphold. Plus, he didn't want her to ruin his chances with Nekole. He had fucked friends before, but if Nekole thought that Pasha was in love with him, she might play even harder to get. Although, the look in Nekole's eyes told him that she was all for self.

"I'ma holla at you later, G," Maurice said, following Pasha out.

While Maurice was going out, Joker was coming in. He walked straight to E's empty chair and took a seat. E put the cape around his neck.

"What can I do for you, playa?" E adjusted the glasses on his face. "You want a line and shave?"

Joker looked over at Nekole, who had seen him walk in. Then he looked at E. "Cut this shit off my head. Give me a nice fade."

Nekole smiled, shaking her head. *Now he's cutting his hair off,* she thought. *He must really have a thing for me. Too bad, I'm still gonna turn him down.* She winked at him, then went on about her business. As soon as he was through, she knew that he would come begging her for a date.

Forty minutes later, Geno handed Joker a mirror. Joker smirked his new tight-ass fade. The low cut brought out the brown in his eyes, too. It was a look he hadn't seen in quite a while. She couldn't possibly turn him down now.

He paid E, then casually strolled over to her station. Her eyes were locked on the head of an attractive young lady whose hair she was styling. She could feel him standing over her. He sucked his teeth, feenin' attention. She still didn't look up.

The fact that she was ignoring him frustrated Joker. "How long am I gonna have to stand here lookin' stupid before you acknowledge my presence?"

She looked up, appearing to be surprised. "Hi, Joker."

"Notice anything different about me?" He turned his head from side to side.

She shrugged. "No."

"Look again," he said. This time he rubbed the top of his head.

"Oh, you got a haircut," Nekole said, as if she had just noticed. "I know you didn't do all that for me?"

"Sho' did. I'm trying to show you how much going out with you means to me."

She put one hand on his shoulder. "Listen, I should've just been straight up with you in the first place." She paused. "I think you're cute and all ... but I don't want to go out with you."

He was crushed. She could've at least given him a sympathy date. Now he knew that it was all a game from the very beginning. She had succeeded in making a fool out of him.

"So, let me get this straight," he said. "First you have me change from braids to dreadlocks. Then you lead me to believe that I'd have a chance with you if I cut my hair. Now you saying that I never had a chance?"

The girl who was getting her hair styled looked at Joker. "You did all that for her? That is so sweet. I wish somebody would go through all that trouble for me."

He ignored her and said, "You thrive on playing with niggas' minds 'cause you think you like that. Bitch!"

"I'm a bitch?" Nekole pointed at herself.

"Nah, you a ho-ass bitch."

"If I'm a bitch, yo' mama's a bitch, you trick-ass pussy," she said hotly. "I could've took your broke ass for what little you've got but I spared yo' trick ass, because what you done was sweet. Nigga, if we was in Cali your bitch ass would be leakin' for talking to me like that." She stepped to him, pointing her finger in his face.

Geno heard the commotion and grabbed his .38. Gun down at his side, he marched over to them.

"You got to raise up outta here, homie," Geno said. "Don't nobody get loud up in here but me."

Seeing the gun in Geno's hand, Joker humbled himself. "Yeah, alright." He bit down on his bottom lip. He gave her an evil glare while he slowly backed toward the door.

Tish shook her head. The place was about to go to shit a lot sooner than she thought. Nekole was trouble, and Geno acted like he was too blind to see it. She saw the way Nekole looked at Maurice. She hoped that Pasha would have enough sense to keep him away from her.

x   x   x

Johnnie Taylor blasted out of the jukebox. Middle-aged women danced with their too-cool husbands and sugar daddies to the rhythm of the blues. Stale cigarettes and old fish grease reeked through the whole joint. On weekends, the jukebox was replaced with a live band that sang old blues songs all night long. This was the place where Reece hung out when he wanted to get away from the young crowd and unwind over a few games of pool and a few beers.

Pasha chalked her stick while she eyed the table for her next shot. Maurice sipped on a cold Corona, waiting for her to fuck up.

They were playing for twenty bucks a game, and this was their second. He had let her win the first, missing every ball he shot. He planned to beat her out of a hundred dollars before they left. Teach her a lesson about trying to go up against him.

"Three in the side," she said, calling her next shot. She sunk it. She set up for the next. "Two to the five, in the corner." This time she missed. "Damn! I almost had you again."

He sat his beer down. "Watch out, lil' one. Let me show you how it's done." He chalked his stick. "Twelve ball, up in the corner." He sunk it. Then he cleared the rest of the balls off the table without giving her a chance to shoot again.

At the end of their seventh game, she found herself down a hundred dollars. "You quit?" he asked.

"Mm hmm. I can't win." She sipped her Corona.

He laughed. "Pay up, then." He held out his hand while she handed over the money. "Always bait ya sucka," he said, smiling.

"So I'm a sucka now, right? We gon' see who the sucka gon' be tonight," she joked. "You gon' have a mouthful of this pussy."

He put his arms around her waist and kissed her on the lips. "I hope it taste as good as your kisses."

Staring up at him, she said, "Would you fuck my friend Nekole?" She had been wanting to ask the question ever since they left Geno's.

Maurice looked confused. "If you want me to."

"Maurice, I'm serious. Would you, if she let you?"

He thought about it. "Nope," he lied with a straight face. "She don't even turn me on." He kissed her again. "You do."

They danced to the blues for a while, in silence. Then, "How come you don't want a picture of me like you have of everybody else?"

"Who's everybody?"

She toyed with the chain on his neck. "*Everybody* is the girls that I saw in all those pictures in your bottom drawer. You've got one of everybody but me. How can I be down?"

He grabbed her soft-ass cheeks. "You have to pop that pussy

on me better than they did."

"Mmm," she moaned. "I love it when you talk to me like that." She grabbed his dick. "Let's get out of here." She took his hand and led him toward the exit.

"We're using a rubber tonight," he said, watching her ass bounce in front of him.

"You said that last night and look what happened."

"I was drunk."

"Well, I guess we're on our way to the liquor store then, 'cause I want to feel your meat up in me. Not no damn rubber."

Chapter 14

Freak pulled his Cadillac into the car wash. He parked at the
vacuums, and his chrome rims kept on spinning. He hopped out,
wearing sweats, a T-shirt and a pair of Adidas flip-flops. He ran his
hand over his wavy head while searching for the change machine.
It was mounted on a wall, between the bays. His cell phone vibrated on his hip.

"Yeah," he answered.

"Wha' sup wit' it, nigga?" Maurice said in a low voice.

Freak inserted some ones into the change machine. "What the
hell you whispering for?"

"I'm in the bathroom. I got this bitch in my bed and I don't
want her to hear me."

"Aw, yeah?" Freak smiled. "Anybody I know?"

"Naw, nigga. Fuck all that. I gotta tell you about this new
broad that I'm scoping on."

Freak put the change into his pocket on the way back to the
truck. "I'm listening."

Maurice told him about Nekole.

While he was listening, Toni's Mustang pulled into the car
wash. She parked next to him at the vacuums. Instantly he
remembered her from Geno's shop. She was looking good with her
blond hair braided to the back in four braids.

Freak said, "So you think Geno is tricking off with this broad?

Just be careful, dog. I don't want y'all to end up gettin' into it over her. I got a hundred saying that she don't give you no play."

"Bet. I'll holla at you later."

Freak put the phone back on his hip.

The Mustang door opened and Toni got out, stretching her long legs. Reaching to her thigh, she pulled down her tight short-shorts. The yellow wife-beater she was wearing exposed the tattoo of her name and Geno's name on her upper arm. Taking off her glasses, she squinted from the bright sun while looking for the change machine.

That gave Freak reason to approach her. "You lookin' for change?"

She looked at him. "Don't I know you from somewhere?"

He smiled, letting his diamonds reflect the sun. "Yeah. I saw you up at Geno's. Remember?"

"Yeah. He's my man," she said proudly.

"Yo' man?" he said, playing dumb. "I didn't know y'all was like that."

Toni pointed a freshly manicured nail at him. "Now I remember. You're the little dude who was laughing at my baby because I didn't bring his lunch."

He leaned up against his truck. "What was I laughing for?"

"You was laughing and calling him a trick 'cause I was late getting there," she reminded him. "Don't act like you don't know."

"I was probably laughing because I was jealous."

She looked confused. "Jealous of what?"

He licked his lips. "'Cause he had your fine ass bringing him lunch. If you was mine, I'd be the one bringing the lunch." He looked her up and down. "I could get full just looking at you."

Her eyebrows shot up when she smiled. "I am like that, ain't I?" she bragged. She stepped back on her left leg, placing one hand on her hip. "Wait a minute. I know you ain't tryin' to holla?"

Standing straight up, he said, "Would I be wrong if I was?"

"Knowing that I'm your friend's woman, yes, you would be."

Slowly, he began walking around her, making a circle. "What

if I told you … that your man, Geno …" he looked at her ass and imagined what it would feel like in his hands, "…was fuckin' that girl he got staying with y'all?" His eyes concentrated on the mound between her legs, and instantly he felt an erection swelling. "And … that she's in charge of the beauty shop? Would I be wrong for telling you that?" He stopped, stared into her eyes and waited for his words to sink in.

Her body twitched and tears began to roll down her cheeks. Quickly, she put her hands up to her face so he couldn't see her crying. Collapsing into the seat of her car, she began to weep.

"You didn't have to tell me that." She wiped her face with the back of her hand. "Don't you think I suspected it? I knew. I was just hoping that the bitch would leave soon so things could go back to normal."

Touching her chin, he turned her face toward his. She looked even better crying.

"I wouldn't waste my time crying over him." He was setting her up for the kill.

"What you think I should do?"

"Move on," he said in a serious voice. "You can't let him treat you like a fool because he got money." He wiped the rest of the water from under her eyes with his thumbs. "Find somebody that'll make you feel good inside. You walk around like you're stress free, but I can see that you're hurting."

Still sniffling, she looked up at him. "Why don't you take me out? You seem to have all the right answers."

He shook his head disapprovingly. "Geno's a friend of mine. Much as I want to, I can't—"

"I can tell that you want me," she said, interrupting him, "by the way you're looking at me." She sniffled, looking down at her legs. "I don't want to leave him. But I do want to get even."

Looking down at the top of her head, he said, "If we do, it'll have to be on the super down low. Can't nobody … I mean *nobody* know."

Her head slowly lifted. "That's exactly how I would want it."

Freak pulled out his wallet, took out his business card, then handed it to her. "Give me a call when you're ready."

She took it. "I will."

"I'd love to see you in a thong, running around on some exotic beach."

A smirk appeared on her face. "Be careful what you wish for. You just might get it," she said in a sexy tone. She was feeling better already.

Toni put her legs inside her car and closed the door. She no longer felt like washing it.

"Call me," Freak said as he backed away.

Smiling, she waved goodbye as she pulled off. Keeping her eyes on the road, she picked up her glasses and put them on. If Geno was gonna fuck around with another bitch, she could fuck around, too. Freak had gotten her spirits back up by telling her how she deserved to be treated. She looked at the business card that he had given her.

Two businessmen are better than one, she told herself. *I'll let him hit it a few times and see if it pays off. Geno will get suspicious of us and become jealous, then he'll be begging for me to stop. By that time, Freak will be sprung and then they'll be bidding on this.* She had to pat herself on the back for coming up with such a brilliant plan. She hopped into the right lane, then sped up. "I've got the Midas touch," she sang. "Everything I fuck turns to gold."

Chapter 15

The warm shower water rolled down his muscular back, soothing his aching muscles. Eyes closed, he stood with his hands on the tile, enjoying the sensation. Sirron quietly uttered a prayer, asking God to somehow help him out of the mess that he'd gotten himself into. When he signed his plea agreement, he made sure that he kept his appellate rights open.

For a brief moment, Nekole's face had flashed inside his mind. He was lonely without her. Almost every minute of the day was spent wondering what she was doing, and who she was with. He wanted an explanation for her leaving him the way she did.

He stepped out of the shower to dry himself off. It was almost count time, so he had to hurry. He had an important call to make. It had been two weeks since he talked to Angie. She should know something by now.

After he put on his orange jumpsuit and shower shoes, he hurried to the phone. Normally he wouldn't wear shower shoes to the phone, for fear that a fight might break out. But with count time being only ten minutes away, he took a gamble that nothing would jump off.

Using his sleeve, he wiped the germs off the receiver and dialed Angie's number. While he impatiently waited for an answer, a guy walked past him with headphones around his neck, blasting Usher's "*U Got It Bad.*" He smiled to himself, thinking that the song was appropriate for his current situation.

Angie had her home stereo system up loud, blasting R&B music while she cleaned her house. She thought that she heard the phone ringing, so she rushed to turn it down. On the coffee table she set down her Pledge and dust rag, then picked up the phone.

"Hello," she said, breathing hard. She waited until the operator finished announcing Sirron, then pushed five.

"You got that information for me?" he asked rudely. He didn't bother with the hellos and shit.

"Damn!" Angie exclaimed. "Can't you speak first? Sirron, I haven't done nothing to you."

"My fault," he said, apologizing. "How you doing, Angie?"

"Fine," she replied. "I found out that she's staying in Kansas City. She got a job doing hair at Mack's cousin's shop, and she's doing alright."

"Kansas City? How she end up way over there?"

"I told you, that dude's brother came around trippin' and shit," she lied. "She had to disappear." She didn't want him to know that she was the real reason why Nekole left.

"You lying, Angie," he said angrily. "You said that she works for Mack's cousin, Geno. She didn't just happen to meet him. Somebody told her about him and I think that somebody was you." He glanced around to see if anyone was listening to his conversation. A fat white man, who was waiting on the phone, was staring directly at his mouth. "Find yo' fat ass another place to stand," Sirron snapped on him.

"I ain't trying to lose my place," the fat man said.

"I don't give a fuck. It's almost count time anyway. So go to your cell." He watched the scared man mope away. "Back to what I was saying, Angie." His voice was calm but serious. "If by some miracle I get out soon, I'ma holla at yo' ass just as soon as I take care of her."

"Alright, Sirron. Damn!" Angie gave up. "She's staying with Geno and his girl. She's gonna write you as soon as she gets on her feet. That's what she said and that's all I know."

"Gimme the number," he demanded.

Angie sighed. She deeply regretted letting herself get caught up in the middle of this bullshit. "Let me call and see if you can have it, 'cause I don't want Geno to trip—"

"Gimme the fuckin' number, Angie," he demanded.

She took a deep breath, sick of his temper. "Hold on." She picked up her cell phone and scrolled through her contacts for Geno's number. "It's area code eight one six—" she finished giving him the number, all the while hoping she wouldn't regret it.

He repeated the number, making sure that he got it right. After she confirmed it, he hung up the phone and ran to his cell to write it down. Immediately after count was over, he ran back to the phone.

The fat white man had come back, too. "Hey, I was next," he complained.

Sirron gave the man an evil stare. The man threw his hands in the air in defeat, then walked away. He had taken a beating over the TV the night before and didn't think he could take another one.

x   x   x

Geno stood in his driveway talking to his neighbor when his cordless phone rang.

"Hello." Unbeknownst to him, Toni had picked up the phone also.

The operator came on the line, announcing Sirron. Geno pushed five. "Who dis?"

"Sirron. Can I speak to Nekole?"

"Sirron who?"

"I'm Nekole's boyfriend."

Geno stepped away from his neighbor so he couldn't be heard. "Look here, man. I don't know how you got this number, but you can't call here no more. You ain't got no girl here."

"Stop playing games, man," Sirron pleaded. "I just want to talk to her."

"You don't understand," Geno said. "That's my girl now. So

whatever y'all had is over with." He hung up.

Toni hung up as well. She shook her head. "Trick-ass nigga," she said slowly. "I don't know why I even—" She began to cry. She knew everything, but actually hearing it out of his mouth was a blow to her heart.

She put her face in her hands. After a few minutes of crying, she remembered that Freak's card was in her purse. She found her purse and took the card out of her wallet. "I'ma show his ass how to play games since he thinks I'm some damn fool."

She quickly put the card back into her purse after she heard Geno come into the house. He walked into the bedroom. Toni was standing in front of the dresser, pretending to fix her hair.

"Toni," he said, "run down to the phone company and get the number changed."

No he didn't, she thought. *He likes this bitch so much, he's about to change the phone number so her real man can't call.* She was so enraged that she wanted to throw something at him. But she kept her cool.

"Why not just call the phone company?" she said evenly.

"Because if you go down there, they'll get right on it."

She knew he was getting rid of her so he could question Nekole about Sirron.

"Ride with me," she said, fucking with him. "We don't spend no time together."

"I can't. I gotta finish washing my truck." He pulled a couple of hundred-dollar bills out of his wallet and handed them to her. "It shouldn't cost too much."

Toni snatched her purse off the dresser. Her insides were on fire. *I'm gonna have the last laugh,* she thought as she walked away. *He's gonna pay for this shit.*

Geno walked outside with her and gave her an obligatory peck on the lips. He then picked up the soapy rag out of the bucket and started washing the wheels. He could see her Mustang pulling away out of the corner of his eye. After waiting a few minutes to make sure she was gone, he dropped the rag, then went into the house.

Nekole was lying across her bed in a pair of Scooby-Doo pajamas, reading *Let That Be the Reason*, when Geno barged into her room.

She sat up. "Don't you know how to knock?"

"I don't knock on doors inside my own house," he said smartly. He forced her legs out of his way, then sat on the bed next to her.

She could easily tell that he was disturbed by something. He had never used that tone with her before.

"What's up, baby?" She put her hand on his leg.

He pushed her away. "Who the fuck is Sirron? And how come I don't know about him? But best of all, why is he callin' my house?"

Nekole was confused. *How in the hell did Sirron get his number?* she thought.

"You still want that dude or what?" he quizzed.

She took his hand, rubbing it gently. "Baby, Sirron was my boyfriend when I stayed in LA. I have no idea how he got your number, but I'm gonna find out."

Geno thought back to something that Nekole said to Joker when they were arguing at the shop. He remembered her saying, "If we was in Cali, yo' trick ass would be leaking for talking to me like that." And for the first time he wondered what she was doing in Kansas City in the first place.

Geno said, "What made you leave LA? And what happened between you and ole boy?"

She sighed, pushing her hair back out of her face. She told him that Sirron killed a man that tried to rape her. The only reason she left was because she feared retaliation from the man's family. The only truthful thing that she told Geno was that she cut ties with Sirron to get on with her life.

Nekole massaged his neck. "I was gonna get in contact with him after I got back on my feet," she admitted. "But then I met you." She pulled his face toward hers, jamming her tongue into

112

his mouth. He was upset, and she wanted to give him something to soothe him.

Because of him, her stash was up to ten grand and he was gonna give her the cash to buy a new car. She got up, walked over to the window and closed the shades. Teasingly, she removed her shirt, showing him her hard nipples.

"Do we have time for a quickie before wifey gets back?" she asked seductively. She dropped her pajama bottoms and panties to the floor, then got into bed.

She grabbed her ankles and held up her legs, giving him a peek at what she had waiting for him. With no time for foreplay, Geno quickly pulled down his pants and positioned himself between her legs. He hit her with fast, deep strokes, wanting to punish her because of Sirron. Loudly she moaned, not only to boost his ego and clear his mind of Sirron, but also because his deep stroke was hitting her just right.

The phone rang.

Nekole's warm crevice was too good for him to pull out, but it might've been Toni, so he had to answer it. Reaching over, he picked the phone up off the small table that stood next to her bed.

"Hello," he said between breaths. Nekole continued to move her hips in a circular motion, watching the funny faces he was making. He couldn't help but smile when he heard the operator announce Sirron. Geno pushed five, then said, "Hold on right quick." He sat the phone down on the pillow next to Nekole's face.

"Ooh! Ooh, ooh, OHH, shiiit!" Nekole cried out after Geno began hammering her again. She knew that someone was on the phone, she just thought he was showing off for one of his friends. So she went ahead and put on a show. "Yes, daddy!" she hollered. "Ah, it's so big!"

Geno stopped suddenly on the down stroke. Picking up the phone, he said, "I told you nigga, that's my bitch!" Then he hung up.

Nekole peeped game right away. She pushed him off of her.

"Who was that on the phone?"

He avoided eye contact. "What you talkin' about?" Geno played dumb, but the guilty look on his face told her everything she needed to know.

Getting out of the bed, she threw her panties into the hamper, then slipped into her robe. After she finished, she looked up at him. "Please don't tell me that was Sirron."

He looked stone-faced.

She put her hand up to her forehead. "I can't believe you, Geno!" she yelled. "What kind of player are you? You didn't have to do him like that. Damn!"

"No, *you* didn't have to do him like that," he said defensively. "You're the one who left him after he went to jail behind yo' ass."

She frowned. "Get the fuck outta my room, Geno!" She pointed at the door.

"Aw'ight." He pulled up his pants.

Through all the commotion, they didn't hear Toni walk into the house. When Geno opened up Nekole's room door, he saw Toni coming down the hallway. Seeing him coming out of Nekole's room caught her off guard and she froze for a brief moment. When reality kicked back in, she stormed toward the room. Her mouth dropped open as he backed up. Nekole was standing next to her bed with an angry look on her face when Toni barged in.

Suspiciously, Toni looked back and forth at the two guilty faces. "What's going on?" she said evenly.

"Tell her, Geno," Nekole said, about to give him a taste of his own medicine.

"Yeah," Toni said, "tell me, Geno."

"I don't know what the hell she's talking about," he said unconvincingly. Toni knew too much of his business and could get him into serious trouble with the law if she chose to.

Nekole said, "Your man came in here trying to get some pussy."

Geno and Toni were both shocked at what she had just said.

Toni was confused. She thought they had already fucked. Now Nekole stood here saying that he was only "trying" to get some pussy.

Toni closed her eyes and asked, "Geno, what's going on?" She would have been furious if she hadn't just had a juicy conversation with Freak on her way home.

"She's lying," Geno argued. "I just came in here to see if she had seen the remote to the TV." His brain didn't work fast enough to come up with a good lie.

"The remote to the TV?" Toni grunted. With her arms folded across her chest, she glanced at Nekole. "I need to talk to you in our room, Geno."

Geno quietly walked past her to their room down the hall. "I remember when I first met you," she said to Nekole. "You told me that I didn't have to worry, because you didn't want my man."

"And I still don't," Nekole replied hotly.

Toni's arms fell down to her sides. "Hurry up and get your shit together 'cause I want you out of my house, tonight."

"Fine with me, bitch," Nekole said harshly. "I don't want to stay here no way." She picked up the phone and called Pasha.

"Hello," Pasha answered in a groggy voice.

"Come pick me up," Nekole demanded. "I'm at Geno's. Hurry up because they're over here trippin'."

"I'm on my way," Pasha said. "Do I need to bring my .22?"

"Nah," Nekole said, eyeing Toni, who was standing in the doorway, watching her. "If this bitch gets out of line, I'ma drag her ass out in the street and beat the shit out of her." Nekole hung up the phone, then immediately began packing her stuff. Toni was still standing in the doorway watching her. "You ain't got to watch me. I been ready to get the fuck out of here."

Toni rolled her eyes as she turned to walk away. "Don't let the door hit you in the ass on the way out!" she yelled over her shoulder.

Nekole went into the closet and grabbed her small Sentry safe where she kept the ten grand she had saved up. She stuffed her clothes into the suitcases that Geno bought her and carried them to the front door. She heard Pasha pull up outside, blowing her horn. Nekole went back to her room to make sure that she hadn't left anything. Then she left.

✗　✗　✗

At Pasha's apartment, Nekole made a nice, comfortable pallet on the living room floor. Pasha's place was small but clean and nicely furnished. Curling irons, combs and cosmetics were scattered about inside the bathroom. It was a typical place for a young woman who lived alone.

After Nekole washed Geno's smell off of her, Pasha showed her around so she could find the kitchen in the dark if she got hungry in the middle of the night. Nekole noticed something during the short tour – a picture of Maurice was in every room of the apartment, except for the closets. That was gonna be hard for her to get used to, especially since he looked so much like Sirron.

Still sleepy, Pasha went back to bed, leaving Nekole by herself. She picked up Maurice's picture off the TV, then curled up on the floor, examining it. She wondered if he was anything like Sirron. Was he tough and willing to do anything for his woman? Speaking of Sirron, he was probably ready to kill her. How could she blame him? Especially after that stunt Geno pulled. That had to have done more than just break his heart. It must have cut it in two. Somehow she was gonna find a way to set things straight with him.

She got up, setting the picture back on the TV. If she would have fallen asleep with it and gotten caught by Pasha, she wouldn't have anywhere to go. After a while, her eyes closed and she drifted off into a deep sleep, putting the horrible day behind her.

✗　✗　✗

After Geno hung up in his face, Sirron stormed back to his cell. His cellmate was sitting on his bunk reading the newspaper when he came in cussing and yelling.

"Trifling-ass bitch!" he yelled angrily. Breathing hard, he stared at his reflection in the mirror. His face was beet red and his eyes were narrow slits.

The power of a woman. His face balled up as he punched the mirror with his fist. Blood ran from his knuckles while he stood over the face bowl, looking down at them. His breathing began to slow as his temper cooled. Over and over, his ears played back Nekole's heart-stabbing moans of passionate lovemaking. The exact same sound that he'd heard many times in their bedroom. Now she was performing the same song for another man.

"I'm a goddamn fool," he said slowly.

His cellmate was an older man, around fifty, who practiced Islam. Day after day he went to the law library, trying desperately to get back the forty-five year sentence that he had received. He was a big, bald man with a long salt-and-pepper colored beard. He removed his glasses and wiped his eyes with the sleeve of his shirt.

"What's wrong, son?" he asked. Sirron had a look on his face that he knew was caused by a woman.

He had done two bids before this one and had seen it all. He knew that there were only two things that could drive a man to hurting himself inside the joint like he had seen Sirron do with the mirror. One was a death in the family, and the other was the lost love of a woman.

Sirron respected no one, but for some reason he felt close to his celly, Mustafa. During a time of loneliness and abandonment, he thought how one unconsciously became close to another sharing the same troubles.

"Ain't nothin' wrong," Sirron answered. He turned the faucet on and stuck his bloody hand under it. Then he wrapped it up with a towel and climbed up on his bunk. For a moment he said nothing. Then, he finally spoke up. "Man, this bitch," he said sadly.

Mustafa said, "I keep on telling you brother, you've got to rid your mind of that problem. Here it is, you done caught a case for her and haven't heard from her since you've been here." He shook his head, disgusted by Sirron's hard-headedness. "Let her go, young bro. She's only gonna bring you down."

Sirron put his face into the palms of his hands. Getting out of there was on his mind. He decided that the best and only thing for him to do was get in the law library and hope for a miracle. He hoped that there were some discrepancies in his case that his public defender may have overlooked.

"What time does the library open tomorrow?" he inquired.

By then, Mustafa was back into his newspaper. He closed it and put it down on the bed. He stood up and faced Sirron on the top bunk. "Noon. Why?"

"I think I'm gonna take your advice," Sirron said. "I'ma start putting all of my energy into trying to get out of here. Fuck lying around, stressin' all the time."

Mustafa smiled. "That's what I'm talking about, young brother. Tomorrow we'll go down there together."

Chapter 16

Tick. Tick. Tick.

The second hand on Maurice's clock turned slowly while he sat staring at it. He was waiting for the clock to hurry up and strike six. It had been a long day and he was ready to go home, call Kim and call it a night.

He checked the calendar on his desk to make sure that it was Kim's turn to be with him tonight. Yep, Kim was the lucky girl. He hadn't been with her in a while and figured that she was overdue for a good tune-up. Kim was a good source of income, but he knew his constant neglecting her would soon run her off. The best thing for him to do was to dedicate the whole week to her, put her portrait up in the living room and put a few of her belongings inside of his drawers. Then she would start feeling special again. A smile appeared on his face while he thought about how she liked to be choked during sex. Then he imagined her sitting in front of him with a short haircut with more waves than he had. He loved that big smile she wore, no matter what was going on in her life. She was smart, too. He was sure that someday she would make some lucky man a fine wife.

Derrick barged into his office, interrupting his thoughts. "Wha' sup," he said, taking a seat.

"Shit. What's up with you?"

"Finally finished doing the paperwork on them new Rams

that came in last week." He picked a piece of lint off his slacks. "You pull that ho yet?"

Maurice regarded him curiously. "Who?"

"The bitch that was driving Geno's truck. You know damn well who I was talking about."

Maurice waved a hand at him. "No, but you can go ahead and add her to my stable. Trust me, she's as good as got," he said confidently. He got an idea in his head. "As a matter of fact, we oughta go out tonight." The very mention of Nekole made him forget about Kim completely.

"I'm cool wit' that."

"Good. Because I'ma ride with you."

Maurice picked up the phone, calling Geno at the barbershop.

"Big Geno's Barber and Beauty," he answered professionally.

"What's up with you, big dog?"

"Finishing up on my last customer's head."

Maurice leaned back in his chair. "We thinkin' about stepping out tonight. I was calling to see if you wanted to meet up with us at the club."

Geno stepped away from the man whose hair he was cutting. He was checking his hairline to see if it was straight. "Yeah, I guess. I ain't doing nothin' else. What time y'all going?"

Maurice looked up at the clock. "'Round ten."

"Count me in." Geno hung up.

Maurice hung up the phone with a devious look on his face. He called Geno to come along, only because he knew that Geno would bring Nekole, trying to show her off. That's when he'd make his move on her. After all, Geno said that she was just a friend. He couldn't hate on Maurice for wanting a piece, too.

After he finished talking to Geno, he called Kim, telling her that he would see her after the club. Derrick and Maurice both got up and left the office. It was time to go home. On their way out of the front door, they saw Roger coming out of his office. He had a fine-ass black girl in tow.

"Reece, Derrick, what's up, yo?" Roger said cheerfully, walking past them. "That shit you told me really works."

To both of their surprise, the attractive girl paid them no mind at first. A few feet away, the attractive girl said, "Don't hate, don't hate," over her shoulder.

"Damn!" Derrick said. "What did you tell 'em?"

"Man, he bought that bitch. Why you think she didn't drool after she saw us? He's a John." Maurice chuckled.

"You just hating 'cause you haven't pulled Nekole's fine ass yet." Derrick walked off.

"I promise I'ma make you eat them words."

x x x

Maurice stepped out of the shower and dried himself with a green Polo towel. He slapped on some cologne, then applied some Dax wave grease to his head. He then opened up his closet, unveiling a row of expensive suits of all colors and styles. He selected a tan pinstriped Sean Jean suit, a cream-colored shirt and tie and a pair of cream-colored Mauris. To add a little pizzazz, he put on his diamond-studded white gold watch, a white gold diamond pinky ring and a pair of personalized cuff links.

Adjusting his tie, he eyed himself in the full-length mirror that hung on the outside of the closet door. *God knows he created a work of art when he made me,* he thought. He snapped his fingers remembering to put Kim's portrait up and scatter some of her belongings about. He'd wait until after he left the club before he called her. *Who knows,* he thought, *I might end up leaving with Nekole.*

He had just finished hanging Kim's portrait when he heard Derrick's car pull into his driveway. Checking the mirror one last time, he realized that he'd forgotten his earrings. He ran to his bedroom, got the earrings, secured his house and walked out the door.

Derrick blew his horn impatiently as he sat in his Silver Chrysler 300M on chrome twenties. He let off the horn when he saw Maurice walking toward the car.

"Hurry yo' ass up!" Derrick yelled. "Don't forget your VIP

card."

Maurice stopped suddenly. "Damn!" He ran back inside the house. From his kitchen drawer, he took out the gun that he had gotten from Freak. He stuck it in his waist. Derrick was fuming by the time he got back to the car.

"You's a slow muh-fucka," Derrick said. "Takin' all night and shit."

"Fuck you!" Maurice said, getting in. "I forgot my strap." He took it out and put it inside the glove box.

Derrick frowned. "What you need that for?"

Maurice let the seat back, making himself comfortable. "Shut up and drive, simp." The gun was making him feel powerful already.

Derrick sighed and put the car into reverse, backing out the driveway.

× × ×

Earlier that day, after Geno closed down the barbershop, he flew out to 82nd and Troost to Pasha's apartment, looking for Nekole. He parked his truck next to Pasha's, then ran up to her door. Pasha answered wearing a pair of gray sweats and a white T-shirt. She had a disgusted look on her face after she saw that it was Geno.

"We took the day off," she said smartly.

"Man, where Nekole at?" Pasha's large breasts, bulging through her shirt, did not go unnoticed by Geno.

She saw him staring at them and folded her arms across her chest. "She ain't here," she lied.

"Cut the bullshit, Pasha."

"I said she ai—"

"Who is it, Pasha?" Nekole interrupted as she appeared behind Pasha. She frowned after her eyes fixed on Geno.

He said, "Can I talk to you for a minute?"

"For what? To tell you the truth, I'm not feeling you right now, Geno."

He looked at Pasha, who was staring down his throat. "Can

you leave us alone? Please!" he said smartly. "Ain't Maurice callin'?"

Pasha rolled her eyes as she turned to leave. "Whatever," she said over her shoulder. She wanted to cuss his ass out, but she kept in mind that she worked in his shop. She couldn't afford to get fired.

Nekole stepped out on the porch, closing the door behind her. "What do you want? I hope that you're here to apologize; otherwise, you can leave now."

"I'm sorry," he pleaded.

She shook her head. "Unt unh, nigga. That ain't gonna work. You've got to say it like you mean it."

He sighed. "Aw'ight, damn. I'm sorry, Nekole. Is that better?" He looked around, then whispered, "Girl, you tryin' to make a playa like me look bad. I hope ain't nobody watchin'."

She pointed her finger at him. "See, that's your problem. You like to front too much."

He stepped closer to her, his face almost touching hers. "Gimme kiss."

Gently, she pushed him away from her. "Kiss Toni. She's the one you're in love with."

"Come on, man. Don't even go there. Slowly, but sho'ly, you're stealing my heart. Why you think I'm here?"

"Prove it."

"What I'm doing ain't proof enough?"

She shook her head.

"How can I prove it?" he inquired.

Nekole placed her hand on his chest, running it up to his head, pulling his face toward hers. She kissed him on the lips passionately. He grabbed her ass and pulled her against his body. When she felt his swollen manhood against her pelvis, she moved away.

"I'm gonna miss your sweet kisses," she said.

"What? I thought we was all good now," he said, confused.

She stared at him for a moment. The silence kept him in suspense. "It will be," she finally spoke, "if you do a little somethin'

somethin' for me. If you like me like you say, it shouldn't be a problem for you to take care of your mistress' needs."

He liked that. Saying that she was his mistress made him feel like she had accepted her place as being second in his life.

"What you need me to do?" he asked curiously.

"I need some money to get a car," she said. "What good does it do me to be second in your life if I can't get nothing out of it? I mean, shit, if I'm gonna be your mistress, you're gonna treat me like one."

Geno thought about it for a moment. Was she worth all of the money he had been giving her lately? He thought about all the times they had snuck around the house to fuck while Toni was asleep. She used to cover his mouth with her panties so Toni couldn't hear him moaning while she rode him on the laundry room floor. Yeah, she was worth it.

Three young dudes in a candy-apple red Impala on gold Daytons rode past, staring at Nekole. She sneakily glanced at the driver, who winked at her. He was sitting low, with his ball cap cocked to the left and one hand on the steering wheel. Geno saw her looking around him, so he turned around to see what had her attention. They threw up Blood signs at him, hoping he would bite. He didn't.

"I'll tell you what," he said, turning around. Nekole gave him her attention once again. She only looked at the dude in the Impala to make Geno jealous. "Let's go out tonight and I'll let you know tomorrow."

With a wave of her hand, she said, "Ain't no thinking about it. Either you gonna do it or you're not. I can always find me someone who will." She shrugged. "That's alright. Maurice said that he would hook me up if I came to see him. So, I'm cool."

He stroked his chin. "Maurice, huh?" Geno shook his head. He knew the game she was playing, but he couldn't help but admire her style. If he would've known that Cali broads were like that, he would've moved out there a long time ago.

"Aw'ight," he agreed. "I'll give you enough for a down payment. Is that cool with you?"

She smiled triumphantly, revealing a set of white teeth. When she was happy, her eyes became narrow slits that went halfway to her ear. "That'll do. Now, where we going tonight?"

"We goin' up to Spanky's."

"Who is *we*?"

"Me and a couple of my boys. Bring Pasha with you."

"Alright. We'll be there."

"Cool." He leaned toward her, trying to get a kiss.

She stopped him. "Don't push it. You're still in the dog house."

He backed up, throwing his hands in the air in mock surrender. "I'll just see you later, then."

On the way back to his truck, he heard her say, "I love you!" Then she went back inside. Even a thousand miles away from home, she could still work her magic.

Chapter 17

Spanky's parking lot was packed with expensive SUVs and cars of all types. It was a classy place, so you rarely saw girls prancing around with their asses hanging out, flagging down expensive cars. Royals, Chiefs and boss players graced the place with their presence when they wanted to have a good time within the city limits.

The line to get into the club stretched all the way around the building. Maurice and Derrick got a good look at all the fine honeys while they made their way to the front of the line with their VIP cards.

When they walked in, the dance floor was crowded with people doing the Cha Cha Slide. They grooved to the beat of the music on their way over to the VIP section. Derrick caught sight of a tall, chocolate, thick-in-the-hip girl with a long weave, staring a hole through him. He winked at her, acknowledging her presence, but kept on walking.

They took a seat at a table that overlooked the dance floor. Maurice motioned for the waitress to bring a bottle of his usual.

"It's some hoes up in here," Derrick said, looking around. Women were at the bar, playing pool and sitting on laps. It was like a convention. "You might have to find you another ride home."

"You been talkin' real slick at the mouth lately," Maurice said.

"I've got the game and gone with it."

Maurice smiled at his protégé. "Play on, playa."

The DJ played 50 Cent's *"In da Club."* Maurice took off his jacket and gave it to the girl in the coat check room. He hoped she wouldn't hold it hostage just to get next to him. He was on a mission tonight and didn't have time to get side-tracked. He had a gut feeling that Nekole would be in the house tonight.

"I see two freaks on the floor waiting on us," Maurice said. "Let's get on 'em."

Derrick followed him onto the dance floor where they cut in on two redbones who were dancing with each other. Maurice slid up behind one of them, grinding on her butt like he knew her. Instead of stopping him, she went on with the flow. Derrick was slower to approach the other one, but soon they were all over each other.

Maurice was all up on her, whispering in her ear. She smiled and squirmed from his breath tickling her neck. Suddenly, he felt a strong hand grab his shoulder. "Get off my woman!" he heard someone say.

The man spun him around. He was relieved to see that it was only Geno. Laughing at Maurice's expression, Geno said, "Man, let's go sit down and have a drink. You'll have plenty of time to fool around with these tramps later." Maurice noticed that Geno was sporting the biggest rock that he had ever seen on his huge finger. And the well-cut, tailored Armani suit he had on had to cost about two grand.

The two girls were shocked by Geno's unnecessary foul language. They were even more shocked after they saw Derrick and Maurice walk away. Anissa, the one Maurice was dancing with, smiled embarrassingly, then walked away. Her friend happily went on to the next man.

An open bottle of Moët chilled in a bucket of ice on the table next to two champagne glasses. The three of them sat down. Geno motioned for the waitress to bring another glass for him. When she returned, they poured drinks and sipped on the bubbly to loosen them up.

Maurice jumped up when he heard Chingy's "*Right Thurr*" come on. All the ladies in the house set down their drinks and rushed the dance floor.

Geno left Derrick and danced his way over to the DJ booth. He whispered into DJ Inferno's ear, then reached into his pocket and took out a hundred dollar bill. He rolled it up and slid it to him.

✖   ✖   ✖

There wasn't a parking spot left by the time Pasha and Nekole pulled up outside. Pasha drove until she found a spot up on the sidewalk. Both of them went into their purses, pulling out compact makeup kits. Satisfied with their looks, they got out the car, strutting across the street to the entrance. They both wore dresses with their lower backs out and three-inch heels.

As soon as they entered the club, they heard 2Pac's "*California Love*" blasting through the speakers. Nekole looked toward the DJ booth and saw Geno pointing at her. Impressed, she motioned for him to come over. He rushed over to her, greeting her with a big hug.

"Ass kisser," she said jokingly. "But that was sweet."

"You liked that, huh?"

"Yeah. That was cool." She grabbed his hand, leading him to the dance floor. "Let's do this."

Maurice unburied his face from Anissa's chest. He had bought her a few drinks to apologize for walking off on her earlier. If he had come up for air a second sooner, he would have seen Nekole and Geno walk past him.

Anissa tried to keep Maurice close to her by holding him tight. She fell in love with his groove and wanted to continue dancing with him. Her mind was already set on leaving the club with him.

"I need a drink, baby," he said, pushing himself away from her.

She grabbed hold of his arm. "Tell me what you're drinking, and I'll get it for you," she insisted.

He snatched away from her death grip. "I'm cool," he said, checking to make sure he hadn't lost a cuff link. "I'ma catch up with you later."

"Don't forget," she yelled at his back while she watched his tight little ass as he walked away.

Maurice was only two feet away from the bar when Pasha appeared out of nowhere. Her green eyes sparkled in the dimly lit place. She stood there smiling at him, looking better than he'd ever seen her.

"Can I dance with you, playa?" she asked, eyeing him up and down coolly. "You know you're the finest nigga in here, right?"

Ignoring her, he glanced around the club. He knew if Pasha was there, then so was Nekole. Geno had done exactly what he'd expected. What he didn't expect was for Pasha to be there. He liked Pasha, but Nekole just happened to have his full attention at the moment.

Giving up his eye search for Nekole, he focused on Pasha. "Baby, when did you get here?" He reached out and gave her a hug. The sweet fragrance of his cologne filled her nostrils, making her not want to let him go.

"A little while ago," she said. "I'm with Nekole."

"Nekole, Nekole," he said softly, acting like he couldn't remember who she was.

"You remember her. The cute girl with the chinky eyes and the doll face," she said, describing her for him. "Don't stand there acting like you don't know who I'm talking about."

"Aw, yeah, yeah. Now I remember. The girl with the long hair, right?"

"Mm hm. Come on, let's go take some pictures." She took his hand. "You are looking too good in that suit."

He pulled her back. "Let's get a drink first. I'll follow you."

Maurice lagged behind, getting a good look at her butt cheeks trying to bust out of her dress. She glanced back over her shoulder, catching him staring at her. That made her start switching her butt even harder.

Man, it's gonna break her heart after I fuck her friend, Maurice thought. *It's a damn shame I've got to be such a scandalous-ass nigga. Maybe in time, they'll learn to accept me fucking around with them both.*

Pasha gazed at the rows of alcohol behind the bar. Out of the corner of her eye, she could see Maurice staring her up and down. She was glad that his eyes were on her, because there was plenty of competition up in there. As good as Maurice looked in his suit, he could've had any broad there.

A medium-sized, athletically built brown-skinned dude, wearing a suit and a Kansas City Royals baseball cap, told the bartender to get everybody at the bar a round, on him. The bartender went from person to person, with a rag draped over his shoulder, fixing people's drinks.

"Can I get you something, sweetie?" the bartender asked Pasha flirtatiously. He fixed his eyes on her partly-exposed breasts. "Don't worry, it's on the big time Royals player standing at the end of the bar."

"Just a minute," she said to him, then turned to Maurice. "Let's see. I bet you want some Moët, right?"

"You know how I like it."

She smiled, turning back to the bartender. "Get us two glasses of Mo, please."

"Make it the bottle," Maurice said. "I can pay for my own drinks." The bartender shrugged and did as he was told.

Geno was on the dance floor, two stepping with Nekole. He stepped back away from her as he spun her around. While doing so, she caught a glimpse of Maurice standing at the bar, playing in Pasha's hair. The overcrowded dance floor was getting hot, causing sweat droplets to appear on Nekole's forehead. She quit dancing.

"It's a little hot in here," she said fanning herself. "Come on, you can buy me a drink." She pulled him over to the bar where Pasha and Maurice were conversing.

Geno saw Maurice and threw his arm around Nekole's shoulders. A mischievous grin appeared on his face. He stopped at the bar, pretending that he didn't see Maurice standing there.

Maurice's back was turned to them when Nekole stepped up to the bar, accidentally bumping into him. Quickly, he cut his conversation short with Pasha and turned around to the beautiful sight that stood between him and Geno.

"Excuse me," she said in a sexy, low voice. "I didn't mess up your suit, did I?"

He had temporarily gone into a daze again. For some strange reason, the very sight of her always left him speechless.

He collected himself. "It's cool." He could see Geno standing over her grinning from ear to ear. "I see you're in here with the finest woman in the house tonight."

Nekole blushed. "Thank you, Maur—"

"What you mean, she the finest woman in the house?" Pasha snapped. "What about me?"

He turned to Pasha. "I'm just doing a little light-weight flirting, that's all, baby." He kissed her on the forehead. "Just be cool and finish your drink."

She put her hand on her hip, looking up at him. "Don't talk to me like I'm a goddamn child, Maurice," she said hotly. She guzzled down the rest of her drink, then set the glass on the bar. "I have to go to the ... ladies room," she said drunkenly. "Nekole, you comin'?"

Nekole took her eyes off Maurice and focused in on Pasha. "Naw, I think I'ma hang out here with the boys."

Pasha spun on her heels, marching toward the restroom. "Fuckin' whore!" she said to herself.

Geno tried to use Pasha to get rid of Maurice. "You'd better go make up with your girl," he said, nodding in her direction.

Maurice brushed her off. "She'll be alright." He looked Nekole dead in her face. "You know how women get when another beautiful woman is in their presence."

She took that as a compliment and ran with it. "I'm glad I don't have that problem."

"I bet you don't." He picked up the bottle of Moët off the bar.

"Let me pour you a drink." He poured the champagne into Pasha's empty glass, then handed it to Nekole.

"Thanks. You're a real gentleman," she complimented him.

"Ain't he?" Geno said sarcastically. "It's too bad he don't know how to be a gentleman with his own girl."

Nekole suppressed a smile. The thought of two friends falling out over her created moisture between her legs. A little competition was just what Geno needed to loosen his pockets a little more. She could already feel the down-payment money for her new car in the palm of her hand. Though she already had more than enough to get one herself, she would never pass up the chance to spend someone else's money.

Nearly drunk, Maurice sipped on his drink while staring at Geno through red eyes. "You know a playa like me ain't got to be a gentleman all the time, Geno. Only when I'm on a mission."

Nekole couldn't help but ask, "What kind of a mission are you on now?"

He swallowed the remainder of his drink. "Taking somebody's woman." He smacked his lips.

Geno smiled nastily. If he responded to that comment, he would look like a hater in front of Nekole. If he didn't respond to it, he would feel like a straight up chump. He was in a no win situation, so fuck it. Why not get in his ass?

Geno stepped his huge frame around Nekole, getting up in Maurice's face. "What kinda shit you on tonight?" he said angrily.

Maurice sat the bottle of Moët on top of the bar. "You said she was free game, nigga," he reminded Geno. "Don't start hating now 'cause I'm trying to make a move."

Geno tried to calm down. "I don't even know why I'm trippin'. Ain't like you can take a bitch from me no way."

A frown appeared on Maurice's face. He didn't really think he could whoop Geno, but the Moët was kicking in like courage juice. Plus, he had his strap out in the car.

"Why don't you let the lady choose, fat boy," Maurice suggested.

That was it. Geno grabbed Maurice by the neck with one hand and picked up the bottle of Moët with the other. He was about to smack Maurice upside the head with it until Derrick appeared out of nowhere.

"Geno, what's up, man?" Derrick asked.

"Ain't nothin' up with that nigga and me no more," Geno replied.

"I don't give a fuck!" Maurice said. "You ain't shit but a hater anyway." Geno ignored him and started walking away with Nekole in tow. "Nigga, from now on you better keep every bitch you got away from me," he yelled, walking after him. He told the bartender to send the bill to his table. He paid no attention to the staring crowd as he walked back to VIP.

Derrick walked quickly, trying to keep up. "What the fuck was that shit all about?"

Maurice ignored him until he got to the table. He sat down and poured himself another drink. He swallowed it, poured another glass, then did the same.

Derrick waited on him to finish before he said, "You gon' tell me what all that was about? I leave you alone for a few minutes and you almost get your ass kicked."

"That was a fake out," Maurice said. "A tactic that I had to use in order to get wit' that ho. You know what I'm saying?"

"No!"

"It's simple. She won't fuck with me if she thinks that we're cool. With us being into it, it gives her a chance to work both sides to her advantage. After I fuck her, I'll apologize to him."

"What about Pasha?" Derrick quizzed. "Ain't they best friends?"

"I'm about to handle that right now." He could see Pasha looking around the club for him. She had been inside the restroom the whole time, and didn't have a clue what was going on.

Maurice leaned toward Derrick. "I need you to call Neosha. Tell her that you want her to come up here and kick it with us."

Derrick smiled, finally realizing what Maurice's plan was. "Aw,

I see what you up to. Now you about to fall out with Pasha, too?"

"Don't try to figure me out. Just make the call."

"Why are you so obsessed with that bitch, man?"

Maurice said, "To be honest, that bitch is poison. I know she is." He rubbed his hand across his face in bewilderment. "But I got to have her." He couldn't believe that those words escaped from his lips.

Derrick pulled out his cell phone and dialed Neosha's number. Maurice snatched the phone out of his hand.

"Don't do it here. Go in the restroom. I'm about to call Pasha over here. I want to be in the VIP tricking with her when Neosha walks in the door.

"Ain't you worried about gettin' into it with Neosha? You can't risk your whole stable over one ho."

Maurice brushed him off. "Just do what I told you to do. Then take a seat at the bar and watch a playa work."

Derrick stood up. "Aw'ight, playa." He started to walk off, then turned back around. "I hope this bitch is worth it. That ho better be worth ten hoes."

"Man, just go." He waited until Derrick left before he stood up, getting Pasha's attention, then called her over.

Once they got outside, Nekole began to pull away with Geno. She had almost forgotten about Pasha. There was no way she was gonna up and leave without letting her know first.

"Wait, Geno!" she exclaimed. "I gotta go back in there and tell Pasha that I'm leaving."

He looked down at her with his nose wrinkled up. "Fuck Pasha! She'll figure it out."

"Unt unh. I'm not gon' just leave her like that," she said. "Just because you and yo' boy are into it don't mean we are."

She tried to go back inside but he grabbed her. "Find Pasha, tell her what you got to say and come the fuck outta there," he commanded. "Don't say one word to that sucka. I'm through fuckin' with him."

"Damn, Geno, he was just messing with you," she said, trying to cheer him up.

"Just do what I told you to do."

"Okay, baby," she said humbly. "Be right back." She jogged lightly in her heels back into the club.

Pasha was giggling from the wet tongue that Maurice stuck in her ear. She had gotten a little tipsy and was ready to fuck. He stopped briefly to wet his lips with champagne then continued to tongue fuck her ear. Slowly, he eased his hand in between their bodies and began to play with her breasts.

She closed her eyes, feeling a tingling sensation between her legs. She reached the point where she didn't care who was around or watching.

"I want to fuck you," he whispered into her ear. His warm breath tickled the sensitive hairs inside her ear, causing her to squirm in her seat. "Would you fuck me right here if I asked you to?"

"Yesss."

"Ump umm," Nekole grunted, interrupting them.

They both looked up in a hurry and saw Nekole standing over them. "I don't mean to interrupt you two freaks, but I didn't want to leave without telling you first, Pasha."

Pasha had a frustrated look on her face. She had reached the point where she didn't want Nekole around while she was with Maurice. He had already told her that Nekole had left with Geno.

She forced a smile. "Okay. I'ma stay and kick it with him for a while. You have your key?"

Nekole was busy looking at Maurice. For a moment, she thought she was looking at Sirron, sitting there all hugged up with another girl. Somehow, she was gonna find a reason to be alone with him. She wanted to find out what he was like mentally and sexually.

"Nekole!" Pasha yelled, getting her attention.

She snapped out of it. "Huh?"

"I asked you did you have your key."

"Yeah, I got it. I'll see you when you get home." She glanced at Maurice one last time. "I'll see you later."

Verbally, he didn't respond, he just raised his glass at her. She didn't say it, but he could tell that he had an open invitation to get at her. He gave her a knowing wink before she turned to leave.

Geno looked into his mirror after he heard music coming from the car that pulled up behind his truck. A familiar-looking face hopped out of a green Nissan Pathfinder. She was petite and wore micro braids pinned up at the back. He searched his memory bank as he watched her strut toward the club. She was looking sexy in a pair of suede boots that came up to her knees and a loose fitting skirt.

He snapped his fingers, finally remembering who she was. "That's where I know her from," he said to himself. "That's Maurice's little broad, Neosha."

While Neosha was entering the club, Nekole was exiting. Neosha got a good look at the gorgeous woman as they passed each other. She would have bet her last dollar that Maurice had her number in his phone or had bought her plenty of drinks trying to get it. Knowing him, she was probably old news. With all of his cheating and neglect, Neosha often wondered why she still loved him.

"Hi," Neosha said, speaking to Nekole, who almost bumped into her. Nekole, being snotty, ignored her and kept on walking. On a normal night, Neosha would have copped an attitude and tried to fight her. But at the moment, all she wanted to do was sit across from Maurice and have a few drinks.

Entering the club, she heard Jagged Edge's "*Where the Party At*" bumping through the speakers. Derrick eased up behind her.

"Buy you a drink?"

Her frown turned into a smile when she turned around and saw Derrick's yellow face.

"Hey, boy. I thought you was one of these fools." She gave him a hug. "Where my man at?"

He nodded toward Maurice's table. The frown returned after she saw Maurice freaking the shit out of Pasha in the VIP. She bit down on her bottom lip.

"That's why I called you over here tonight," Derrick said. "You see that shit right there? I'd kick his ass if I was you."

She handed Derrick her purse and stormed across the room to his table. Maurice dipped Pasha's fingers into his glass and was sucking the champagne off them. The loud sounds of Neosha's boots hitting the hard floor made him turn to look. But it was too late. Neosha punched him in the eye.

"Shoot!" he hollered, grabbing his face. It took a minute for him to figure out what was going on.

He felt the cut under his eye. Before he could get up, Neosha grabbed the empty Moët bottle, drew back and busted him upside his head with it. Pasha watched in horror. Derrick saw what was happening and took off in their direction.

The bottle didn't break. Pasha tried to escape, but not before Neosha struck her across her back with the fat end of the bottle. She fell to the ground, holding her back, screaming out in pain.

Derrick finally made it over to where they were. Neosha raised the bottle again, but before she could swing, she felt Derrick's hand wrap around her neck. He took the bottle away from her. She kicked and clawed until he pushed her down. Soon the bouncer stepped in and assisted him.

Maurice was on the floor, holding his head in a daze. He wasn't sure where he was or what had happened. The crowd was hyped and circled the area, screaming for the bouncers to let Neosha go. Cuffing her hands behind her back, they immediately escorted her out of the club.

Derrick helped his friend up off the floor. By then the police and paramedics had come running into the club, clearing away the crowd.

Maurice saw them putting Pasha on the stretcher. "What the fuck happened?" he said groggily.

"Shit got out of hand, playa," Derrick said, shaking his head.

Chapter 18

The next morning, Maurice sat in his office popping pain pills and drinking coffee. He wouldn't have shown up for work, but he had used up all of his sick days and couldn't afford to lose his job right now. His commission, plus the scam he had going, brought in about ten grand a month, easily. The only other way he could've made that kind of money was by selling dope. That or luck up on a corporate job, which he knew wasn't happening.

Subconsciously he fiddled with the bandage that was wrapped around his head. Before he left the hospital last night, he stopped and made sure that Pasha was gonna be alright. The doctors informed him that she would be fine. Neosha didn't swing the bottle hard enough to break any bones, but her back and shoulders were bruised badly.

"Neosha, Neosha, Neosha," he repeated to himself.

He always thought of her as his ghetto girl, and last night she proved it. He still couldn't believe that she hit him over the head with that fucking bottle. *Doesn't that bitch know that she could've killed me?* he thought to himself. Did she even care? As much as he didn't want to, he had to cut her off completely. Any girl who had the guts to do that to him, he didn't need. If he ever saw her again, she had an ass whooping coming.

Maurice sat back in his chair, looking out of his huge window. An attractive white lady and a teenaged boy were looking at a

Dodge Stratus. He saw the owner conversing with two stuck-up-looking white guys in cheap suits. He closed his eyes, trying to forget about the pain in his head.

"Knock, knock," a female voice said.

His eyes opened slowly. Nekole was standing in the doorway looking fine as a muthafucka.

He sat up in his chair, wondering what it was that brought her there. For a minute he was speechless, like he always was at the sight of her. He didn't know why, but this girl brought butterflies to his stomach.

She stepped into his office. "You do remember me?" she asked.

He smiled. "I'd have to lose all the brain cells in my head to forget something as fine as you," he said coolly, trying to collect himself. "Have a seat."

Nekole sat in one of the two leather chairs and crossed her legs. "I was out car shopping, so I decided to stop in and see how you were doing."

"How'd you find out where I worked?" he quizzed.

With a shrug, she said, "You know all car dealers put their names on the back of every car they sell. I got yours off of Pasha's."

"She know you're here?"

She shook her head. "You know better than that." Her eyes remained on him. "So, how ya feeling?"

He touched his bandage lightly. "I'm cool. How's Pasha?"

"Banged the fuck up," she said, then set her purse on his desk.

They stared at each other lustfully. Neither said a word.

Maurice cleared his throat. "Why don't we get down to what you really came for," he said, hoping that she was gonna come on to him.

She knew what he wanted her to say, and she wanted to say it, but she also wanted to make him sweat a little.

Uncrossing her legs, she said, "Okay. I really came to … check out that Dodge Ram Quad Cab out there." She smiled for a minute. "You think my credit is good enough?"

Evidently, she knew about the loan program that he had

going.

Resting his elbows on the armrests, he interlocked his fingers and said, "If it's credit that you're looking for, you've come to the right place."

Standing up, she placed a finger on his desk and slowly walked around it to where he was sitting. He turned toward her. "Why don't you run a check on me right now?" she said seductively.

The only button that was fastened on her pink button-down shirt was the middle one. Part of her breasts, as well as her navel ring, were exposed.

"First we ha—" She bent over and kissed him on the mouth, ceasing all conversation.

Slowly, she kissed him with her eyes closed.

"Mmm," he moaned, tasting her sweet saliva. She took her tongue out of his mouth and guided his face into her chest. He had forgotten about the pain in his head altogether.

"Be gentle, baby," she murmured, feeling his teeth biting down on her left nipple. "Yeeesss."

Suddenly, she backed away from him, stopping everything. He sat there with his chest heaving, staring up at her. Buttoning her shirt, she walked back to the other side of his desk.

"We through?"

"For now," she said evenly. "I came here to buy a car. Not to fuck."

He rubbed his hand over his face, laughing to himself. "That's cold."

"Ain't it?" She reached into her purse and pulled out a bundle of money, tossing it on his desk. "That's ten grand. I've been pre-approved for an eighteen-thousand-dollar loan from Beneficiary Loan Company, co-signed by Geno Armstrong." She gave him a wicked little smile. "So, I won't be needing a loan from you."

Once again, he was left speechless. This girl had a lot of game.

"What's the matter?" she asked. "Cat got your tongue?"

He looked down at her crotch. A wide V-shape bulged out the front of her pants. "Not yet," he replied.

She caught the remark after she saw what his eyes were focused on. "This kitty cat ain't no stray. So I should warn you that it's very high maintenance." She sat down and crossed her legs so he wouldn't be distracted. "Now, could we start the paperwork on my new truck, please?"

"Aw'ight," he said, opening his desk drawer. "But one of these days, we're gonna finish what we started."

"You definitely got that coming. But, you can't kiss and tell."

"I'm a playa, baby. Not a hater."

"We'll see."

x   x   x

"So you coming or what?" Freak asked. "I don't have time for games. I think you fakin'."

"I told you that I was coming," Toni whispered into the phone. She was in the bathroom, pretending to be peeing while Geno was in the bedroom, getting dressed to go out. "As soon as he leaves, I'll be on my way."

Freak was sitting on the edge of his bed, oiling up his muscular frame. "Aw'ight. I'll be waiting."

"I hope you got some protection, 'cause I ain't trying to get—" Geno walked through the door. "Okay, girl. I'll see you Monday," she said, pretending to be talking to one of her girlfriends. "Bye." She hung up.

"What the hell is Keydra talkin' 'bout now?" he asked.

"How do you know that I was talking to her?" She wiped herself, pulled up her shorts and flushed the toilet.

Geno grunted. "That's the only friend you got besides me. Yo' attitude is too bad."

That's what you think, she thought to herself. *That was your boy on the phone, begging me to come over. And I'm gonna fuck him tonight.* She held back a smile while she stood beside him, washing her hands in the sink. *If he only knew what I was thinking, he would slap my ass through the wall.*

Geno left the house about an hour later. Toni could tell that he was going to meet Nekole by how anxious he was. She gave a fuck, but then again, she didn't. She was going to lay up with a hard body tonight, and that was all she could think about at the moment. At first she was out for revenge, but after the three wonderful dates that she and Freak had been on, she started to develop feelings for him.

After a quick shower with her favorite shower gel, she slipped into a colorful sundress and a pair of sandals. No underwear would be needed for what she was going to do. She was trying to get fucked tonight. She made Freak wait long enough. She looked in the mirror one last time, blew herself a kiss, then grabbed her keys and headed out the door.

A warm breeze was coming in from the South. Taking advantage of the wonderful weather, Toni hit the button that dropped the top of her Mustang. She popped in Beyoncé's CD, *"Dangerously in Love,"* then took off down the road.

Toni cut her lights out before she pulled into Freak's driveway. He lived in an all white neighborhood in Prairie Village, Kansas. He warned her before she got there that his nosey white neighbors be tripping about him having company pull up at all hours of the night.

Raising the top to her car, she checked her face in the mirror and walked up to the front door. Freak answered the door wearing house shoes, red pajama bottoms and a tank top. Without a word, she put her arms around him and began kissing his lips and face. He backed up so he could close the door. Toni continued to kiss him savagely, pushing him back against the wall. He relaxed, letting her take control. Roughly she licked and bit his chest, then dropped to her knees, tonguing his navel while pulling down his pajamas. He put his hand on top of her head, pushing it down to his dick. Most of it fit into her mouth on the first try. She took it out, swallowed, then forced it down her throat, sucking it and wiggling her tongue around inside her mouth.

Freak closed his eyes while she did her thing. He felt kind of bad for what he was doing behind Geno's back, but he did nothing to stop it.

× × ×

Geno and Nekole were riding in her new Dodge Ram on the way to the show. She sat on the passenger side, twisting up a blunt, while he sipped on a glass of Remy Martin V.S.O.P. He felt his cell phone vibrating on his hip.

"Hello," he answered.

"Big G, this is Beno, man. I'm trying to get three of them thangs, like right now."

"Damn! Me and my lady friend are on our way to the show. You can't wait?"

"Not really, man. It's kinda poppin' down my way and I wanna get it while the gettin' is good," Beno explained.

Geno thought for a moment. He had never revealed to Nekole that his real income came from slanging bricks of cocaine. If he made the move with her in the truck, she would probably put two and two together. He didn't need that. It was bad enough that Toni knew all of his business. That's why he was scared to exchange her for Nekole.

If he didn't drop everything and go meet Beno, he was gonna miss out on fifty-seven grand, and that, he wasn't about to do. He would just be as discreet as he could while he handled his business.

"Aw'ight," Geno finally said. "Meet me at my house on 68th in about …" he glanced at his watch, "fifteen minutes."

"Don't be bullshittin', Geno, man. I know how you is."

"Fifteen minutes." He hung up.

Geno made a left, passed the median, then made another left, heading back north on Ward Parkway. A confused look appeared on Nekole's face when she noticed that they were going in the opposite direction.

"Where we goin'?" she inquired.

"I gotta make a quick run."

She frowned. "But the show starts in twenty minutes!" she exclaimed.

"We gonna make it, baby. Just calm down."

She became suspicious. The closer she got to Geno, the more

143

she noticed that he made sudden moves, like a nigga who had the sack. But she never saw any physical proof that he fucked around, except for the ten grand cash that he gave her to put down on her new truck.

Beno was parked outside the house on 68ᵗʰ in his blue Suburban. He waited impatiently for Geno to show up. All of a sudden, a red Dodge Ram came flying over the hill and whipped into the driveway. Beno didn't move until he saw Geno's big head after the interior light came on.

"Be right back," Geno said on his way out the truck.

This was the first time that Nekole had heard about Geno having another house. She could've moved in there a long time ago and never had to deal with Toni's shit. She reminded herself to talk to Geno about that after he finished taking care of his business.

Beno stepped out of the Suburban, wearing sweat pants and a tank top. He held a black gym bag in his hand.

"Wha' sup, baby?" Beno said, giving Geno a handshake.

"Shit. Let's hurry up and do this." Geno unlocked the door and they both went inside.

Inside the house, Beno was told to wait in the living room while Geno ran upstairs to the attic. Tucked away in a corner was a large trunk with an old Master Lock securing it. Opening it up, he took out three kilos, then locked it back up.

Beno was bent over, looking at a big goldfish trying to get away from two killer piranhas inside the fish tank. He glanced up after he heard Geno coming down the steps.

"Everything straight?"

"Yep." Geno set the dope on the dining room table. "Come on back here."

"Who in the car wit' you?" Beno asked as he set his bag down on the table.

Geno smiled proudly. "I got a bad one in the car," he bragged. "Stop and take a look at her on your way to your truck."

"Man, I ... I ... ain ... ain't fittna be ... doing all that." Beno

144

stuttered when he became excited.

"Hatin'a get you nowhere." Geno grabbed the gym bag. "Is this my money?"

Beno looked up from checking out the dope. "Um ... ye ... yeah. But ... buut, I'ma need my bag back."

Geno emptied the stacks of money onto the table, then tossed him the bag. It wasn't until after Beno was gone that he put up the money.

x   x   x

Leaning back in the seat, smoking on the blunt that she had rolled earlier, Nekole waited impatiently for Geno to return. She saw Beno come out of the house, moving quickly, with the black bag in his hand. He even looked like he was doing something illegal. She made a mental note to remember where the house was. The episode was enough for her to want to start investigating Geno's background. If he was fucking with dope, he was gonna have to start kicking in more than he was.

When it was halfway gone, she put the blunt out so Geno could get his buzz on, too. A few minutes later, he climbed his big body into the truck.

"You ready, baby?" He took a sip of his now watery drink. "Where the blunt at?"

She took it out of the ashtray and handed it to him. Her eyes watched him closely as he inhaled the smoke into his lungs. He saw her watching him, but he avoided all eye contact.

"Geno?"

"Huh?"

"What did you just do? If you don't mind me asking."

He hesitated for a moment, searching for a good lie to tell her. A suitable one didn't come to mind quickly. What else could he have been doing, meeting Beno at a secret place, taking time out of their date, if he weren't dealing drugs? Then Beno came and went, carrying a black gym bag. A seven-year-old could've figured out what they were up to.

His silence confirmed her suspicions. Even though she knew

that he was in the right by keeping his business secret, she was still a little hurt. She thought she had his nose open wide enough that he would keep no secrets from her.

"You sellin' dope, Geno," she blurted out. "I wondered how you gave me that ten grand so easily." She wanted him to go ahead and confess.

Blowing smoke out of his nostrils, he threw the rest of the blunt out of the window. "I don't know if you forgot or not, but I am a business owner."

She smirked. "Not gonna confess, huh?"

He lifted his shoulders. "Ain't nothin' to confess."

Her attention went to a white kid who was standing up in the back seat of the car next to them. If that's how he wanted to play it, she would leave it at that for the time being.

x x x

Mustafa and Sirron had their heads buried deep inside two old, thick and confusing law books. Weeks had gone by and they still hadn't found anything useful. Several times, Sirron become frustrated and wanted to give up, but Mustafa wasn't trying to hear it. He didn't want Sirron to spend his young life locked up. If he could help set him free, he would feel better about his chances of winning his own appeal.

"Hand me your case, Sirron," Mustafa said, closing the law book. "I'ma take it back to the cell and go through it again."

Sirron eagerly tossed him the small stack of papers. "Good luck, man." He lowered his head down onto the table.

Getting up out of his chair, Mustafa stretched his old bones, then walked over to the door and beat on it. "CO," he called out. "I'm ready to go back to my cell." He looked down at Sirron. "Keep ya head up, young bro. Everything is gonna be alright. Insha'Allah."

Sirron didn't respond, nor did he lift his head. He wasn't gonna go home for ten years. All of this law library shit was a waste of time, he thought. What he should've been doing was writing some of his old hoes so he could start getting visits. His mother kept his books straight, so he was cool with money. Female companionship was what he needed.

That night he stayed up late, writing letters to every heavyset girl he knew out in the world. It wasn't no use trying to get in touch with the fine ones. A nigga in jail was of no use to them. There were too many ballers out there who kept them on lock. Big girls paid like they weighed.

Mustafa had his shirt off, exposing his hairy, graying back, reading Sirron's case. *Young people these days are so stupid,* he thought. He couldn't believe that Sirron would rather sit on his bunk, writing letters, than work on his own case. Unknown to Sirron, Mustafa wasn't working for free. If he did happen to luck up and beat his case, Sirron would owe him dearly.

Mustafa left a daughter behind who needed financial help out in the free world. If everything worked out, Sirron would be the one who would help her.

Hours went by. Sirron had fallen asleep a long time ago, but Mustafa was still at work. Yawning, he took off his glasses, then set them down on the bed.

"Shit!" he said to himself. He had gone over every single page, coming up with nothing.

He was just about to give up for the night when a thought entered his mind. He didn't remember seeing Sirron's signature on his Miranda form. Just to be sure, he looked over the document once more. Just like he thought, Sirron's signature was nowhere on the form.

Instantly, he jumped up off the bed. "Sirron, get up!" he yelled, shaking him awake.

"Whaat?" Sirron mumbled, smacking his dry lips. "Man, I just went to sleep. You need to take yo' ass to bed." He rolled over, facing the wall. "Put that shit up."

"Do you remember signing a Miranda form before you made your statement?"

Knowing that Mustafa wasn't gonna let it go, he sat up, wiping the sleep from his eyes. "What?"

Mustafa spoke slowly. "Do you remember signing away your Miranda rights?"

"Miranda? Nah, I didn't sign nothing. They just pulled out a tape recorder and I started talking. All I was trying to do was make sure that Nekole didn't go down with me."

A triumphant smile appeared on Mustafa's face. "I think we have a chance to get you out of here, young bro. At least out on an appeal bond."

"The judge said he didn't give bonds on murder cases."

"He didn't because of the statement you made during your interrogation. I read it in your report. Without your signature on this form," he held it up at him, "it's like you never confessed."

"You bullshitin'?"

"No, I'm not. Insha'Allah." He snatched the covers off of Sirron. "Get up! We've got a motion to prepare."

Chapter 19

"*Love Jones*" was showing on the big screen television inside the living room of Nekole's new home. She had finally sucked Geno's dick and told him that she wanted to be his wifey. Of course, she was only bullshitting. As a result, he bought her a small house in Raytown, far away from his home with Toni.

Geno had driven his RV out to California for the week, no doubt going to get some more drugs. Pasha was still in a lot of pain and didn't want to hang out. That left Nekole lonely when she wasn't running the shop.

She sat on her couch in front of the TV with her arms and legs crossed, shaking her foot nervously. "I'm not gonna sit here by myself tonight," she said to herself.

Digging into her purse, she searched until she found Maurice's business card. She picked up the phone and called his home number. Now she too had butterflies in her stomach while she waited for him to pick up.

Maurice stood over his stove, frying chicken. He had the phone up to his ear, talking to Tamisha, when he heard the line click.

Tamisha asked, "So what time is dinner gonna be ready?"

"Hold on right quick. My line is clicking." He clicked over. "Hello."

"You on the phone?" Nekole asked in a sexy voice.

Smiling, he said, "Yep, but it ain't nobody special."

Nekole picked up the remote, turning the volume down on the TV. "Hang her up, then."

"Hold on a minute." He clicked back over. "Tamisha, let me call you back in a little while, okay, baby?"

She sighed. "Aw, man!" she pouted. "Why come I can't never get no quality time? Here we are planning a dinner date, and then you get a call. Now, all of a sudden, you gonna call me back. Fuck that shit man!"

"Tamisha, don't—" he stopped in mid-sentence after he heard Nekole hang up on the other end.

Tamisha heard it as well. "The bitch hung up."

"What are you talking about? What bitch?"

The line clicked again. "Hold on." He clicked over. "Hello."

"You left me on hold," Nekole reminded him.

He turned the stove off. "I didn't mean to," he explained. "I had a little problem on the other line."

With her feet propped up on the glass coffee table, Nekole fiddled with her belly ring. "It's cool. Now you gotta leave her on hold like you done me."

"So, to what do I owe the pleasure?" He drained the chicken grease into its proper container.

"I've been thinking about you."

"Good or bad?"

"Mmm, a little of both." She slid her hand down under her pajamas and began rubbing her bald pussy. The sound of his soothing voice turned her on. "What you got on, baby?"

Tamisha finally hung up. He looked down at his legs. "Right now, I have on a pair of Polo briefs and some house shoes. And you?"

"I got on some Nekole's secret."

He grabbed his dick. "How can I find out what the secret is?"

"Grab a six pack of Coronas and something to smoke on, then head this way."

"I heard he bought you a house."

"And?"

"And, you're inviting me over there?"

"Like you said, he bought *me* a house, and I'm inviting *you* to come over and kick it with me."

He shook his head. "Girl, you playin' a dirty game."

"That's because I'm a dirty girl. He's out of town anyway. Now bring your scary ass over here and fuc—see me, boy."

He laughed after he heard what she almost let slip. After he wrote down her address, they hung up. The chicken went into the trashcan instead of his stomach. He now had a yen for some cat. It was dick that she had called for in the first place. He didn't know what took her so long to ask for it.

The first thing he did was hop into the shower. One thing that turned a woman on was a man who smelled good. When he finished, he lotioned his body, making sure that his feet and knees were just as smooth as his face. The Dax wave grease made his hair wave like an ocean current. He put on a fresh T-shirt, jogging shorts and a pair of Nike flip-flops. He didn't want to dress up just to go over there and get undressed.

Before he left, he took his gun out of the top drawer, putting it inside his pocket. Going to see a woman over to her man's house could be dangerous. Whether Geno bought it for her or not, it was still his in a sense. So he wasn't gonna go alone.

In the bathroom, he checked his face in the mirror one last time. *Damn*, he thought as he looked at his reflection. *That knot Neosha put on my head is still there.* He cut out the light and shut the door.

The phone rang as he was walking by. He looked at it, wondering if he should answer it or let the machine pick up. It rang again. This time he answered it, just in case it was Nekole calling back.

"Hello," he answered. There was silence. "Hello."

"Hi," a familiar female voice said. "'Member me?"

"Yes. How you doing, Pasha?" He closed his eyes. He didn't have time to patch things up with her right now, or ever.

"I'm fine." She sounded so sweet and innocent. "I'm barely walking, but I should be alright in a few weeks." She paused. "Look, Maurice, we've got some things that we need to discuss."

"I don't mean to be rude, but I'm in kind of a hurry."

Don't mean to be rude? thought Pasha. *I can't believe what this nigga just said. I get my ass kicked because of him and don't get so much as an apology. But he don't mean to be rude. I don't know why I bothered. I should've took his absence as a hint.*

"Okay," Pasha said sheepishly. "I'll just call you some other time."

"Cool. Talk to you later."

Pasha slammed the phone down. She got up off the couch, limping to her bedroom. Her body collapsed onto her bed. She squeezed her pillow tight and started to cry.

After Nekole hung up the phone with Maurice, she hopped into the shower as well. She was excited about seeing him and couldn't wait to feel his body next to hers. Deep down, she wanted him just as bad as he wanted her, but she was gonna take her time with him. If he turned out to be the nigga she thought he was, Sirron might not ever see her again.

She lotioned her body with her favorite scent – cucumber melon. She loved how good it smelled and hoped that he would, too. She was ready by the time she heard Maurice's Corvette pull into her driveway. Her toenails were polished, her nails were done and her hair was pulled back into a wavy ponytail, making her eyes even more slanted than they were already.

He rang the doorbell.

She hurried toward the door, then stopped about three feet away from it to calm herself down.

"Hi," she said, after she opened the door.

The first thing he noticed was her pretty bare feet. His eyes wandered up her long, smooth legs to the oversized Scooby-Doo T-shirt that hung down to her thighs.

"You look good," he complimented her. He handed over the six-pack of Coronas. "Can I come in, or is that all you wanted?"

"I'm sorry." She had a few nasty thoughts of her own, looking down at the crotch of his shorts. "Come in."

Not only was the outside of the house nice, but Geno had furnished the whole interior with expensive furniture and appliances. Maurice wondered how in the hell he afforded it all.

He made himself comfortable on the sofa while she took the beer to the kitchen. To his surprise, she had the old movie "*The Mack*" playing on the screen.

"You're a Goldie fan, huh?" he yelled toward the kitchen.

She came back into the living room carrying two open bottles of Corona. "Yep. If I would've been the same age that I am now, back in the seventies, I would've been his main whore."

He laughed. "Damn." He took a beer from her. "Not his main ho."

"I stay down for my man and whatever he does," she stated firmly. "Did you bring the greens?"

"Aw, yeah." He pulled out a quarter ounce of light green. "I forgot to get the blunts."

"That's okay. I got some in the back."

His eyes were fixed on her booty as she walked down the hallway. Man, he couldn't wait to hit that. Geno was probably hitting it good, but his stomach was too big for him to really get up in it. She looked pretty flexible herself. He grinned, unable to hold back his excitement. As big of a player as he was, he couldn't believe how he was reacting over one broad.

When she returned, he noticed that she had changed clothes. Now she was wearing a tank top and a pair of silk shorts. Her nipples damn near pierced her top. He loved those small, perky titties.

She took a seat in a chair next to the sofa where he was sitting, then emptied the greens onto the table. She broke it down, sprinkled some into a zigzag, then twisted it up.

"You don't mind smoking papers, do you?" she asked. She left the blunts on her dresser because they would have made her too high, and she wanted to remain in control of herself.

"Paper's cool." He couldn't help but stare at her. It wasn't just her beauty and booty, her style attracted him as well.

"So, have you talked to Pasha?" She put the joint between her lips, then set fire to it. "That's your girl, ain't it?"

He smiled shyly. "There you go."

"What you mean ..." she coughed, "there I go?" She passed the joint to him.

Accepting it, he smoked on it for a minute or two. "You bringing up someone that I'm trying to forget." He sipped his beer. "I'm trying to get next to you."

Picking up her beer, she got up, walked over to the love seat, then dropped down next to him. She made sure that her leg touched his. Sitting back on the sofa, she faced him while he coolly puffed on the joint. The sight of his juicy lips, sucking, made her wet. She wanted to get on top of him and ride him forever.

He could see her hazels gazing at him out of the corner of his eye. That's why he made sure that he looked extra cool, blowing the smoke out of his nostrils.

"You are so fine. You know that?" She gently touched the knot on his head. "That crazy-ass girl don't play about you." She chuckled. "You must have some fire-ass head."

He passed what was left of the joint to her. "You think that's funny?"

"Naw, boy. I was just teasing."

For half the night they sat, drank, smoked and talked about everything from sex to the goals they were trying to reach. Maurice admitted that he was a player who manipulated women every time he got the chance. She told him that even though she was a female, she was down for her crown and would do anything for the scrilla.

Then Sirron's name came up. She admitted that most of her feelings for Maurice were because they looked so much alike. Maurice's face had attracted her at first sight. Then, just to score some points, he told her that he staged the fight with Geno and the one between Neosha and Pasha just to get next to her.

Nekole thought he was just as devious as she was. She sat Indian-style on the couch while he lay back on the armrest with his foot in her hand. Her soft hands massaged it while he shared his plans for their future. She wanted to be with him, but she was not about to jeopardize the good thing she already had going with Geno. At least not anytime soon.

Their conversation ran out. There was nothing left to discuss at four in the morning. By his calculations, he should have been in her panties two hours ago. She hadn't even hinted around that she wanted to have sex with him. If she didn't make a move within the next thirty minutes, he surely would.

All of a sudden, she got up and disappeared into the back room. He sat up on the couch preparing for whatever was about to happen next. His eyes were on the TV, but he wasn't watching it.

R. Kelly's "*Sex Me*" could be heard coming from her bedroom. "You gonna sit there all night or are you gonna come back here and keep me company?" she asked seductively.

Turning to face her, he saw that she had changed again. Nia Long could have walked into the room and wouldn't have diverted his attention away from her. With her hands up, touching both sides of the doorway, she stood there in a black lace and satin chemise with a matching thong.

He licked his lips as he got up to follow her into the bedroom. It was just as plush as the rest of the house. The whole bedroom set was mahogany and thick, walnut-colored carpet covered the entire floor. Her bed stood about three feet high with a small, two-step mahogany staircase next to it.

"Why don't you relax on the bed and make yourself comfortable?" she suggested. "I'll be back in a minute." She disappeared again.

Maurice hurried out of his clothes, then neatly placed them on the seat of a mahogany rocking chair that sat in a corner of the room. Getting down on the floor, he did fifty push-ups to harden the muscles in his chest and arms.

The sheets felt cold and crisp, like she had just changed them before he showed up. He lay in the huge bed, pulling the comforter up to his waist, then waited for her to return.

Nekole snuck off to the kitchen. Out of the cabinets, she got a jar of honey and a small bowl. Emptying a third of the honey into the bowl, she let a little water from the faucet run into it to make it less sticky, then stirred it until it became creamy. She took off her chemise and thong. After scooping some of the concoction, she rubbed it all over her neck, titties, stomach, in between her thighs and even her feet. She slipped back into her chemise and headed back toward her bedroom. She wanted her body to taste naturally sweet when he kissed her.

Maurice was sitting up in the bed with one hand behind his head, flexing his six-pack when she returned. *Damn, he's fine,* she thought as she swayed over to him. He pulled back the covers so she could slide right in.

Their lips locked and they held each other tightly. He rolled over on his back, pulling her on top, letting his hand travel down to her ass. He massaged her cheeks while she kissed his neck, face and chest wildly. He moaned while she grunted, both sounding like animals.

She seized his arms and put them up toward the headboard. His body went into submission, letting her take control. She ran her tongue from his forehead all the way down to his hairy pelvis. She held his dick with her tiny, warm hand, stroking it while she kissed the surrounding area. Lifting his balls, she planted a kiss between them and his asshole.

R. Kelly sang, "I feel soooo ... freaky tonight. And I need someone ... to make me feel alright." Then the beat came on.

Suddenly, she stopped and came up for air. She sat up on top of him, then took off the chemise. Her titties bounced slightly as she threw it toward the rocking chair. He could feel her pussy's nectar oozing through her thong. Grabbing hold of her hand-sized titties, she massaged them.

"Have you ever had some Caliii pusssyyy?" she sang, moving

her hips in a circular motion.

He flipped her over on her back and repeated the same process she performed. He slid two fingers inside of her while he kissed her inner thighs. She tried to guide his face to her pussy. He tricked her like he was about to do it, then he kissed her on the crack, just below it. Frustration had her constantly trying to find his juicy lips with her pussy, but he kept ducking and dodging her attempts. Two could play that game.

One thing he noticed while he kissed her was that her skin had its own, yet familiar, taste to it. Tired of the foreplay, he pulled off her thong and spread her legs. Just as he was about to enter her, she placed both of her hands on his stomach, stopping him.

"What's wrong?" he asked.

"We can't do it on the first night," she said, panting.

"What?" he hollered, then caught himself. "What you mean?" he said, a little softer this time.

She pulled him down on top of her. "I just wanna be held by you, baby," she said softly. "Just hold me. We ain't gotta be in a rush." Her titties pressed up against his chest as she squeezed him tightly.

A smile appeared on her face after she felt him squeeze her back. She liked him a lot, but she wasn't gonna change the way that she did things for nobody. Her magic had worked on everybody else. Why wouldn't it work on him, too? She wanted to see how much of a player he really was. If she could hook him like she did with every other guy who crossed her path, then she was gonna use him like Goldie. One thing she was sure of, no nigga on this earth would ever make a fool out of Nekole Mitchell. At one time Sirron may have owned her heart, but she always got what was coming to her out of him.

Maurice could see the game that she was playing. She was a lady and she wanted to be treated like one. He could respect her for that. He'd chill out and play the gentleman role, for now. But she would pay later.

Chapter 20

For the entire week that Geno was in California, Nekole and Maurice kicked it together. They went out to clubs, amusement parks, swimming and horseback riding and dined in exotic restaurants. And just like that first time they kicked it together, the nights ended with serious foreplay without going all the way.

He paid for every outing. He even let her talk him into putting a set of spinners on his car. She said it would make him look even sexier when he prowled the streets.

Derrick, Freak and his mama noticed how distant Maurice had been all week. He wouldn't return any of Derrick's phone calls and hadn't stopped by to see his mother. He started showing up for work late and would leave early, before Derrick could get a chance to talk to him.

Freak had seen Maurice and Nekole out in traffic, but didn't disturb the two lovebirds while they were spending their quality time together. Since Toni was out of town with Geno, Freak started spending more time at his office. He was falling for Toni as well; that's why he didn't blame Maurice for spending so much time with Nekole. There's always that one special girl who can touch a man's heart, no matter how much of a player he claimed to be.

Even Pasha had gotten the 411 on her friend and ex-lover. It didn't come as a shock; she saw it coming long ago. From the first time that she introduced them, she knew they were attracted to each other. The bad thing about it was that she was still deeply in love with Maurice. Plus, they were about to share a bond that could not be broken until death, but she could never catch up with him to discuss it.

Derrick became frustrated with all of his friends. Maurice didn't kick it with him. Geno didn't kick it with Maurice. He saw Freak and Toni creeping one night, so Freak avoided Geno whenever possible. Everything was going to shit. The very same thing that had motivated them to be the players that they were was coming between them.

x   x   x

Maurice returned home from a very profitable day at work. He took a cold shower, then fixed himself something to eat. Before he sat down, he pushed play on his answering machine so he could hear his messages.

Neosha had called for the fiftieth time, apologizing for the way she acted at the club that night. Michelle had called for the sixtieth time, wanting to know where he had been and why she hadn't heard from him. Kim called to see how he was doing. Some unknown person kept calling and hanging up. He figured that someone to be Tamisha, still mad at him. Then Kim called again saying that she had graduated from nursing school, and she was officially a Registered Nurse.

There were no more messages. Nekole hadn't called since Geno had gotten back from California, and he still hadn't fucked her.

He flipped through the channels until he found BET. It just so happened that "*The Mack*" was on. Right away he began to think about the first night he and Nekole spent together. He thought he had her figured out. She was playing the role of The Mack, and he was Chico, the girl who got mad at Goldie inside the restaurant because he was spending her money on that white girl. Nekole may not have spent her money, but he knew that she was spending her time with Geno. He had to laugh at the jealous thought.

He heard a car pull up in front of his house, then a door slam. Setting his fork down on his plate, he got up to look out the front door. Peeking out, he saw a face he recognized.

He snatched open the door. "What?" he said harshly. It was Neosha.

"Can I come in?" She noticed the knot on his head but fought back the urge to look at it.

"Look, bitch," he snapped. "Stay the fuck away from me. If you come around this muthafucka again, I swear I'ma beat the shit out of you."

Her face balled up. "Do it now, pussy," she said, rushing him.

He backed up so he could come in out of the neighbors' view. She swung her small fists wildly. He grabbed her arms, slinging her over the couch. She flipped and hit her head up against the table. Before she knew it, he had one hand around her throat was smacking her hard across the face with the other.

Smack! "You stupid-ass bitch!" he yelled. *Smack! Smack!*

"Okay, Maur ... ice," she cried. Her lip and nose were both bleeding.

"No, it ain't okay." Snatching her up, he pushed her into the kitchen. Bent over the counter, she coughed and gasped for air. Maurice took a knife out of the dish rack. Twisting her hair in his hand, he pulled her back to him, exposing her throat, then put the knife up to it.

"Bitch, you bet not breathe," he said, barely moving his lips.

She was shaking, crying and trying hard not to swallow. "Mau—"

"Shut up! You ain't so tough now, are you bitch?"

"Pl ... ease, don't—"

"Bitch, I said shut the fuck up. I'ma teach yo' ass a lesson." He dragged her through the house, all the way to the bathroom. He tossed the knife into the face bowl, but kept his grip on her hair.

She screamed loudly in pain and agony. "Please stop! I promise I'll leave you alone," she pleaded. He pulled on her hair.

"Ahhhhh!"

Bending over the bathtub, he turned on the hot water. Forcefully, he put the top part of her head under the running faucet.

"Ahhh—" Some of the very warm water ran into her nose and mouth. She could feel the water on her scalp getting hotter by the second.

"Maurice, pleease. Stop, please!" she begged.

He shut the water off before it got burning hot. As soon as he released his grip, she jumped up, screaming. She slipped on the wet floor but quickly regained her balance on her way to, and out of, the front door.

"Good riddance!" Maurice yelled.

"That pussy tried to kill me," she said hoarsely to no one in particular. Climbing into the driver's seat of her Pathfinder, she put it in drive and sped away.

Maurice sat back down and began to finish his now cold dinner.

x   x   x

Later that night, Maurice pulled out of the club parking lot. He had gone to happy hour and had a few drinks to help clear his head about what he had done earlier. To validate his actions, he kept telling himself that the bitch had it coming.

After leaving the club, he turned off of Blue Ridge and hopped on 71, going north. The powerful V8 engine was accelerating fast as he eased his foot down on the pedal.

Nekole had his head fucked up. The bitch was playing him like he did other bitches. When did shit like that start happening to him? It never did, until Nekole. Eventually, he would get over the fact that he'd played the fool, but she was contagious, and he couldn't pull himself away. His thoughts were interrupted by his cell phone vibrating. "Hello," he said somberly.

"Hi, stranger," Nekole said in her usual sexy voice.

"Stranger, huh?" He tried to hide the frustration in his voice. "Ain't you one to talk?"

She chuckled. "You mad at me, baby?"

"Nah, I ain't mad. Why should I be mad?" He got into the left lane, then slowed down to the speed limit.

"Because I haven't called." In truth, Nekole not calling didn't have anything to do with Geno being back in town. After they had spent that week together, she wanted him to crave her. Just to make sure that he was feenin' for only her touch, she would park in front of his house late at night to see if he would call another one of his women over after he didn't hear from her. If he did, they never showed. She knew right then that she had a new fish caught on her hook.

He heard a police siren going off behind him. Glancing in his rearview mirror, he saw a blue police car all up on his bumper.

"Damn!"

"What's wrong, baby?" she said with concern in her voice.

"I'm being pulled over." He got off on the Longview exit, then pulled over in a McDonald's parking lot.

"What did you do?" she asked curiously.

"Ain't no telling about these cocksuckers out here. I'm on Longview Road."

"I'll call back and check on you in a few. Don't call my phone."

"Aw'ight." Through the mirror, he saw two policemen coming his way.

"Shut off the engine," the shorter of the two ordered.

He did as he was told.

The taller one asked him to step out of the car and produce some identification. He gave them his driver's license. Leaning back against the door of his car, he waited patiently while they ran his name through the computer.

The short officer found it amusing that his wheels were spinning while his car was in park.

"Cool," the officer said. "I wish I could afford a pair of those for my car." He studied Maurice carefully. "You a crack dealer?"

"No. I'm a car *salesman*," he replied, emphasizing salesman.

He thanked God that he left his gun at home and prayed that they wouldn't smell the alcohol on his breath.

The tall officer removed a pair of handcuffs from his belt, walking toward Maurice. "Turn around and put your hands behind your back, please."

"What I—"

"Now!" he yelled. The short officer stepped up, just in case the prisoner tried to resist.

Maurice cooperated. They cuffed him and put him in the back seat of their police car.

"What are y'all gonna do with my car?"

"I would think that you would want us to tow it."

"Yeah," the tall officer said. "Those wheels are way too expensive for us to leave unattended. *Car salesman.*"

x x x

Toni was out bowling with some friends. At least that's what she told Geno. She was really somewhere laid up with Freak. So Geno picked up a bag of Indo and a bottle of Remy, then headed over to Nekole's. He was sitting on her couch, playing football on the Xbox, when the telephone rang.

"I'll get it," she yelled from the kitchen.

"Naw, I got it," Geno said, reaching for the cordless phone. "I'm waiting on a call."

Nekole picked up the phone right before he said, "Hello." She remained silent while she listened in on his conversation.

"Wha' sup, Big G? This Chuck, nigga."

"I know who it is," Geno said smartly. "Wha' sup, Chuck?"

"I need a whole one."

"Shid, you know it's kinda dry out there right now," he said in a low voice. He set the controller down. "So I'ma need twenty-three for it. That cool?"

"I guess so. You want me to meet you on 68th?"

"No. I got a couple of 'em out in my truck. I'm in Raytown, at Nekole's. Out there where you seen my truck parked at that time."

Triple Crown Publications presents . . . **Contagious**

"I know where you're at."

"Call me when you get close by. I'll meet you outside. She don't need to know my business."

"Bet that." All three of them hung up.

Nekole walked into the living room and took a seat beside him. His cell phone began vibrating on the coffee table.

"Hello," he said, answering it.

"Geno, this Maurice. I'm in jail, man." He sounded desperate. He called all of his females and didn't receive an answer from any of them. Freak's voicemail kept coming on, and Derrick was in Joplin, Missouri. He didn't want to call his mother from jail unless he had to. Geno was his only option.

"What you doing in jail?"

Nekole said, "Who is that?"

"Maurice," Geno said. "He's in jail."

Maurice spoke. "I got into a fight with Neosha earlier today and that funky bitch called the police on me." He sighed. "I got plenty of bread at home man. I just need you to post my bond so I can get out."

"How much is it?"

"Two thousand. But it's only four hundred through a bondsman."

Geno sucked his teeth and said, "I ain't got it, player." He hung up the phone.

Nekole's eyebrows shot up. "Damn. How much was it?"

He shrugged. "A couple grand. Now the nigga wanna be my friend because he needs something. If he's so much of a player, why he ain't got one of them hoes running up there to get him?"

"Who knows," Nekole said as she got up to go to her bedroom.

She pulled her small safe out from under her bed. Out of her stash, she took two grand and stuffed it into her pocket. The phone rang as Nekole came walking back into the living room. Geno picked it up and looked at the caller ID. It was Chuck.

"I'm about to go over to Pasha's, baby," she said, picking her

164

keys up off the table. "I'll be back in a little while."

"Aw'ight," he said, then continued talking to Chuck who was four blocks away. Geno was glad she was leaving. He hoped she would be gone before Chuck pulled up.

She got into her truck and took off in a hurry. What would be more perfect than her making his bond and being out front waiting when they released him? She would feel better about the way she had been treating him.

Taking out her cell phone, she dialed Pasha's number.

"What?" Pasha answered.

"Don't what me, girl. What's wrong with you?"

"Don't even trip. What do you want?"

"I have a question. What jail would they take you to if you were arrested on Longview Road?" Nekole listened while Pasha gave her all the information that she needed. She also told her not to call a bondsman, because one was probably already there.

"Thank you, Pasha."

"If you see Maurice any time soon, would you please tell him to call me? It's very important."

"What makes you think that I'm gonna see him?"

"Girl, please. Bye."

x   x   x

The guard opened the door to the cell. "Maurice Jones."

"Yeah," Maurice said, standing up.

"Step out please," the guard instructed him.

"What's going on?"

"Bond has been posted," he said nonchalantly.

"By who?"

"Enough with the questions. Let's go."

When he got to the front desk, he saw Nekole standing over by the pay phones, talking to the bondsman. He smiled, happy to see her.

He signed his release papers and received his belongings in a brown paper bag. The bondsman told him not to forget to show up for court and to call if he couldn't make it. They shook hands, and that was it. By then, Nekole had gone back to her truck to wait for him.

She was on the phone, talking to Geno, when Maurice climbed into the passenger seat.

"Alright, baby," she was saying. "I'll see you in a little while. Bye." She hung up. Without looking over, she felt Maurice staring at her. "What?"

"You're something else. You know that, don't you?"

She put her index finger up to her lips. "Shhh. Let me take you to your house and give you a bath first. Then we can talk about it. Okay?"

Chapter 21

"I've got to hurry up and get back home," Toni said, putting her clothes back on. "I wanna be there before he gets back. Plus, I need to wash this sex smell off of me."

Freak continued to lie there, wallowing on the spacious hotel bed. "You better hope that he don't come in ready to fuck," he said, smiling.

She sat down in a chair and began putting on her socks. "I hope not. I've already cum too many times tonight to even dream about going again. My pussy sore as a muthafucka." She put on her shoes. "Besides, I'm sure that Nekole gave him enough pussy to last him for a while. Whore."

Freak laughed. "You ain't got room to talk. You supposed to be at the bowling alley with your friends. Instead you ended up on your back in my hotel room."

She looked at him confusingly. Her eyes remained on him while she stood up, walked over to the bed, then lay down beside him.

Rubbing his hard abs, she said, "Thought you said you loved me?"

"I do." He kissed her cheek. "But that doesn't change the fact that you got a man."

She rolled over on top of him, then licked his nose. "What if me and Geno broke up?"

He frowned. "Look, baby. Just because we're doing our thing don't mean I want to come between you and Geno. He's still a friend of mine." He got out the bed and started putting on his clothes. "Please don't create no bullshit between me and him."

Toni sneered at him. "But you love me." She grunted. "Yeah, right." She got up off the bed, picked up her purse, then stormed out the door.

Her cell phone rang as she was pulling out of the parking lot. Freak's number showed up in the caller ID.

"What you want, Geno's friend," she said, answering the phone.

"Baby, why are you acting like that?"

A black Ford Escort ran a stop sign, almost striking the side of Toni's car. "Fuckin' bitch!" she yelled. "God, these people can't drive." She shook her head. "Now what were you saying?"

"All I was trying to say, before you stormed off, was that it would be different if y'all just happened to break up for a different reason. Like if he went to jail or got killed. Don't leave him because of me. You understand what I'm saying?"

"I do, but ... I don't know, man. I'm a little confused right now. Look, I'ma call you tomorrow. Okay?"

"You mad?"

"I'm fine. I just need to take the time out to figure out what I want to do." Nelly's "*Dilemma*" came on the radio. She turned up the volume a little. "You never know, me and him might work things out."

"Aw'ight. Call me."

"Bye." She hung up.

With Geno, Toni knew that he could, and would, give her everything she wanted. With Freak, things *could* be the same. The question was, *would* they? Was he really in love with her or just in lust? If she gambled on love, and lost, she would lose everything. If she won, it would be all good. She chose her third option, which was staying with Geno, kicking it with Freak on the side and putting the rest into God's hands. *Damn*, she thought, *life is a bitch.*

x   x   x

Freak sat in his Escalade, watching a blue TV screen on one of his six TVs. Instead of pulling off, he sat back in his seat to think for a minute. Things were getting out of hand. He should have never told her that he loved her. That wasn't nothing but his dick talking.

On the down low was how they were supposed to keep their relationship. Now she was talking like she was ready to leave Geno for him, and that wasn't cool. Nobody, not even Maurice, knew that Freak made most of his income by washing Geno's drug money through his loan company. He couldn't take the chance of blowing that for some pussy. So he made up his mind. He was gonna have to let her go.

x   x   x

Maurice stepped out of the tub after Nekole finished washing him up. She handed him a towel and told him that she would be out back on the deck when he was ready to talk. After he finished, he put on a pair of boxers and slipped on his flip-flops.

Nekole was leaning up against the wooden rail, looking up at the stars, when he stepped out onto the deck. She had taken her clothes off and put on his robe.

She turned around when she heard his footsteps. That arrogant walk and look that he had vanished. Now he had the look of a man who had been hurt. She could see that he was ailing and could feel his body yearning for hers.

He stopped a few feet away from her.

"Come closer," she said, motioning with her finger. "I got something for you." He took his time approaching her. Impatiently, she grabbed his arm, pulling him toward her. "I missed you, baby." Pulling his head down to hers, she kissed his lips.

Maurice untied the robe, then picked her up and set her on the rail. She removed the robe so he could get a good look at what he was finally about to get.

"You plan on teasing me again tonight?" he asked, admiring

the view.

She shook her head slowly. "Go 'head and hit it, that's what it's made for."

Using her feet, she pulled his boxers down to his knees. Her legs spread, and he stepped between them. He picked her up and slid her down on his hard shaft.

"Umph," she grunted, feeling him deep inside of her. She wrapped her arms around his neck. "Fuck me, baby."

He hit her with slow and hard thrusts while she popped her hips back and forth. Taking his time, he carried her over to the patio table, set her down and continued to dig up in her. She lay back on the table, holding her ankles in the air.

"Mmm ... oh ... ahh," she moaned loudly. He put his fingers into her mouth for her to suck on.

He didn't race for a nut like he did with most of his women. Instead, he took his time and relished the tight, warm feeling around his dick.

They couldn't hear it, but Nekole's cell phone was ringing and would ring for the next two hours. But she would be too occupied to answer the call.

In a rage, Geno threw the cordless phone against the wall. He was mad because she wasn't answering her damn phone. About an hour before, he had called Pasha and learned that Nekole had never come by her apartment. In fact, she had called trying to get some information on bonding somebody out of jail. Geno knew that somebody had to have been Maurice.

He couldn't understand it. A house, car and money, what else could he have done? Some women were ungrateful. He felt like the biggest fool. It was his own fault that he thought with the little head instead of the big one. She was in love with him. Wasn't she? Or was she in love with what he could do for her?

Like the police did in a dope house, he searched her room, looking for nothing in particular. He wanted to see what kind of secrets that she might have been hiding. Nothing incriminating was in the closet, the drawers or behind the TV. The only place left to look was under the bed.

"Un huh," he said, pulling the safe out from under her bed.

It was locked, but he knew how to get into it. He took a butter knife, jammed it between the opening of the safe, then slid it sideways until the latch popped open. He whistled at its contents. There had to be over ten grand inside. He cleaned it out, then pushed the safe back under the bed.

"Bitch owes me this much," he said.

He jumped in his Excursion and headed to Maurice's house. He was halfway there when he changed his mind. He made an illegal U-turn, going the other direction. It was bad enough that he had tricked all that money off with her. He would really feel like a fool if he drove around looking for her. But he had to be sure. So he turned back around and headed to Maurice's house, once again.

From the corner he could see Nekole's Dodge Ram parked in his driveway. Pulling over down the street, he cut out his lights. Out of the console he took a chrome, snub-nose .357.

"Both of them got me fucked up," he said. He ignored the burning feeling inside his big stomach.

He had just grabbed the door handle when he saw a police car cruising slowly up the block. He let the handle go and started the engine back up. They flashed the spotlight on him but kept on going.

Geno silently thanked God. If they would've arrived a minute later, they would have seen him get out with the gun in his hand. How would he have explained that?

After he put his gun back up, he pulled away and headed to his own home. He had a woman at the crib who loved him. Instead of being at home, he was out riding around, chasing a whore. A whore that he was in love with. He made up his mind to try to forget about her and make things right with Toni.

As he headed down Food Lane, he wondered what he would have done if the police hadn't shown up.

His cell phone rang. "Hello," he answered.

"Hey, fat daddy," Toni said.

"Wha' sup, baby?" He tried to hide the anger in his voice.

"I just called to let you know that I was at home."

"Okay. I'll be there in a minute." He hung up.

Toni was already in the bed when he got home. A quick shit and a shower had him ready to call it a night. He climbed into the bed, snuggling up next to her. Gently, he began kissing on her back and neck. She squirmed, then her eyes fluttered open.

Not now, she thought. She could feel his hand traveling down her stomach to her pussy. Reaching under the covers, she found his hand and pushed it away.

"Stop, baby," she whined. "I got to be at the doctor's office early in the morning."

"Come on, babe," he pleaded. "We ain't did it in so long, I forgot what it feels like."

That's your fault, she thought.

He cupped her titty.

"Baby, I said I was tired. Damn," she said, irritated.

Geno remembered playing her the same way that night he first fucked Nekole. He also remembered why he was playing so sleepy, because he had already been fucked good.

Once Toni's breathing was deep and steady, Geno eased out of the bed and tiptoed over to the dresser where her purse was sitting. It was already open when he reached in and pulled out her wallet. He saw a Visa, MasterCard, driver's license and Freak's Savings & Loan business card. What was she doing with his card in her wallet?

He wouldn't have suspected anything, but it was tucked behind her driver's license like she was trying to hide it. Next he picked up her cell phone and went through her calls. Freak had called her three times and she had called him twice.

The burning feeling returned to his gut. Enraged, he snatched the covers off her. The breeze hit her half-naked body.

"Baby, w—"

"Get up, bitch!" he hollered, snatching her up by the arm.

She had a terrified look on her face. "What I do—" he slapped her across her face, letting her fall into the corner. "Oow!" she cried, holding the side of her face.

"You fuckin' my friend?" he quizzed.

"No, baby," she cried. "I wo—"

He snatched her up by her neck, pushed her against the wall and started choking her.

"Ple ... ease ... d ... on ... t," she said in a strained voice. He squeezed her neck until her face turned red, then let her go. She slid down the wall to the floor, holding her throat, coughing.

Standing over her he said, "I gave you a house, car, money and this is how you pay me back?" Breathing hard, he turned and walked off, shaking his head unbelievingly.

She rose to her feet, then went after him. Just as he was about to walk out the front door, she yelled, "Geno. Please don't leave me, baby! I only did it because you fucked that bitch in our house!"

He stopped. He believed her. She got her ass kicked because she had given him a taste of his own medicine. Now that very bitch that he let wreck his home was busy lying on her back in his friend's bed. His love life had gone from sugar to shit real fast. And it was all because of Nekole.

"Call Freak and end it," he said in a low voice. "Don't tell him that I know. Just end it." With that, he walked out the door.

Chapter 22

Geno's Barber & Beauty was packed with young women between the ages of sixteen and thirty, trying to get their wigs done for the concert. There was a crowd of guys waiting for cuts, but it was nothing compared to the women's side.

Nekole had been busting her feet all morning, curling, washing, relaxing and styling hair. Pasha had to be called in on her day off to help out. Nekole had been ignoring all the vicious stares and cold remarks Pasha had been making since she walked through the door. She didn't have time for Pasha's bullshit. More important things were on her mind.

It was noon and Geno still hadn't shown up for work. She had no idea that he'd seen her truck parked in Maurice's driveway last night. But she did know that he was probably angry because she had disappeared. That's not what she was tripping on. She wanted to know why her safe was empty when she came home that morning. He had no right to take her shit, and she was gonna check his ass about it.

Lucki was fading Joker's hair. Every once in a while, she'd cut her eyes in Nekole's direction.

"You got a problem with Nekole or something?" Joker inquired.

"That bitch is pissing me off, walking 'round this muthafucka like I ain't never got the pussy."

Not sure of what she meant by that, he changed the subject. "When are you gonna get some different shit? That last shit you had wasn't shit."

"Shit, nigga, you smoke too many sticks. Your tolerance level is up too damn high."

"Yeah. 'Cause when I get wet, I like to get wet. You dig what I'm saying?"

"Don't worry. I got some new shit coming this week."

The front door opened. In walked Neosha, wearing a dark pair of expensive shades. She looked at no one as she quietly made her way over to Tish's station.

Tish looked up from washing out her combs. "Hey, girl."

Neosha waved politely. She was about to take a seat over in the waiting area, but Tish motioned for her to come over.

"You're next since you had a appointment." She waited patiently for Neosha to sit down and get herself situated. "Ain't you gonna take them off?" Tish said, referring to the shades.

"No!"

Tish put her hands on her hips. "Neosha?" She sat there like she couldn't hear. "I don't have time for your ghetto-ass bullshit today."

Neosha looked back at her. "Girl, please. Just do my hair. Would ya? Thank you."

Tish sighed. "Whatever."

Pasha combed Kelly's hair and kept a mean stare on Nekole at the same time. She didn't recognize Neosha with her shades on, or without the micro braids in her hair. Neosha took them down the night before so Tish could give her a wrap.

Nekole caught Pasha muggin' her. "Ahh!" Nekole grunted, tired of being stared at. "Why you keep muggin' me?"

Pasha put down the comb. "Bitch, you know why," Pasha snapped. The entire shop got quiet. "Don't try to play stupid up in here."

Nekole shut off her hair dryer. She smiled devilishly. "So you mad at me 'cause your man's sniffin' up my ass crack?" She pointed to herself.

"Bitch, please! Maurice ain't doing nothing but playing yo' tramp ass just like he do all of his bitches. So you ain't nothin' special."

"Speak for yourself because I got him eating out of my panties. I made that so-called *player* sleep with me naked for a whole week. Then sent him home with his nuts just as full as they were before he got there."

Rolesha, another beautician who worked there, slapped five with Nekole. "I heard that. That nigga sho' be up in here acting like he's like that."

Old Man Ed shook his head. "I know you ain't did that to my partner. Not Maurice Jones."

"The hell if I didn't," Nekole said. "Then I disappeared on him. Had his ass sitting by the phone, praying that I called. That nigga was fucked up and love struck."

Neosha wasn't sure of what Maurice they were talking about until Ed said his last name. She leaned forward and took off her shades.

"Maurice *who*?" Neosha said to Ed.

"Yo' Maurice," Tish said, putting in her two cents. Until then, she had forgotten that Neosha fucked around with him, too.

Pasha looked over at Neosha. "I see we got another one of his fools up in here," she said, referring to the bruise under her eye.

When Neosha looked at Pasha, she immediately recognized her as the girl from the club. She was surprised that Pasha didn't seem to have a clue as to who she was. Five months had passed since Neosha had been there to get her hair done, that was why she had never seen Pasha or Nekole before that night at the club. And now that she thought about it, Nekole was the girl that she saw coming out of the club that night. She almost didn't recognize her without the makeup.

Neosha stood up. "Ain't you the bitch whose ass I kicked at the club a couple of weeks ago?"

Pasha regarded her curiously. She wasn't sure, but with braids in her hair, it could've been her. Regardless if she looked like her or not, the bitch had confessed and that was enough.

Pasha picked up her shears and charged Neosha with them. In a desperate attempt to get away, Neosha pedaled backward, tripping over Tish's chair. Tish jumped in front of Pasha with her arms stuck out.

"Put the scissors down," Tish demanded.

"Move, Tish," Pasha said, holding the shears in the air. "I'm about to stab the shit out of that bitch."

"Unt unh, Pasha. I can't ... I won't let 'you do that. Think about this, now."

Big E crept up behind Pasha, grabbed her wrist and shook the shears out of her hand. She bent down trying to retrieve them, but he kicked them away. He had to twist her arm to keep her from trying to fight him.

"Oouch! Ow!" she screamed. "Let me go, E."

"Not 'til you calm yo' ass down," he said, leading her down the hall.

"Let me go, goddamn it!" Pasha insisted.

Nekole laughed out loud. "It don't make no sense how girls get themselves caught up over a nigga that don't care about either of them. I flips the script. I bring the bitch up out a nigga."

She and Rolesha laughed.

Embarrassed, Neosha stormed toward the exit. "I'll see you later, Tish," she said over her shoulder. "I can't believe the shit I go through behind his bitch ass," she said to herself on her way out the door.

Geno parked his truck in his private parking spot. He was tired from being up all night thinking. Two hours of sleep was all he got before the hotel manager called letting him know that it was check out time. Toni called his phone all morning, but he didn't answer. He didn't want to hear her excuses, but he did want to hear Nekole's.

He grabbed his barber's bag out of the back seat before he got out. While he was stretching his long frame, he saw Neosha marching out the front door.

"Ay, girl," he hollered to get her attention.

She came to a halt. "What?"

He approached her. "You still messing around with that sucka Maurice?"

"Sucka? I thought ... look I ain't got time to chat, alright." She tried to step around him, but he grabbed her arm. "What the fuck is your problem? I'm trying to get outta here." She glanced back at the shop, making sure that Pasha wasn't coming. She sighed. "What do you want, Geno?"

Geno stood there and told her the whole story about Maurice and Nekole. Then he lied, like Maurice was the one who bought her a new truck and a house. To add insult to injury, he planted in her mind that Nekole could be pregnant. He also lied when he told her that Maurice bragged to him about beating her up.

"He bragged about beating me up?"

"Yeah," he said sincerely. "He's a dirty dude, for real. I told him, Neosha's a good girl, man. You don't fuck good people around like that."

"Hmph. I'm glad you told me that. Pussy gon' pay for fucking with this bitch like that." She took her keys out of her pocket. "I gotta go, Geno. Thanks for the info." She walked to her truck.

"Remember what I said."

x   x   x

Toni walked into Freak's Savings & Loan, strutting right past the receptionist without introducing herself. The short chocolate girl jumped up, trailing her to Freak's office.

"Wait a minute!" the girl yelled. "You can't just walk back there."

Ignoring her, Toni kept on walking. Freak was in a meeting with his secretary when she came barging in. He flinched, thinking that it was the Feds coming to get him. He relaxed after he saw Toni standing there.

"I told her she couldn't come back here," the receptionist explained.

Freak put his hand up, signaling her that it was alright. "She's a friend of mine," he said. He looked at his secretary. "Excuse me for a moment. We can take this up after lunch."

Toni stood there staring at him until the two women left the office. She was amazed at how professional he could be when he wanted to. Outside the office, he was a totally different person.

"I had it out with Geno last night," she said, taking a seat in one of the two chairs in front of his desk.

"About what?" he quizzed, afraid that they'd been found out.

Her eyes went to the floor, and her hands started to fidget. "He knows about us."

His mouth fell open. From that moment on, he knew that his life would never be the same. He wondered how he found out and what Geno was gonna do about it.

"You told him?"

"He went through my purse and my cell phone," she said in a low voice.

"Yo' cell phone?" he said, leaning forward. "You mean to tell me that you didn't have sense enough to erase your numbers?"

"I'm not a professional cheater, Franklin," she said, calling him by his real name.

"Maybe not, but I know you got common fuckin' sense." He stood up and ran his hand over the top of his head. He was in a fucked up position. "So what did he say?"

She wiped the tears from her eyes. "He told me to break it off, but I'm not supposed to tell you that he knows."

His eyebrows shot up. "Aw, yeah? I wonder why?"

She shrugged. "My guess is that he wants to make things right with me."

Freak grunted. "You've got your part figured out. What about me? How can I face him now?" He punched his file cabinet. "Damn!"

She stood up and walked over to him. "Don't be mad—"

He pushed her away. "Stay the fuck away from me."

She looked confused. "What are y—"

"Baby, please! I need to think." He put his hands up to his head, massaging his temples. "Do you have any idea what this could mean for me?"

She put her head down, shaking it slowly.

"I didn't think so." He marched over to the door, snatching it open. "Get out!" he said harshly.

She walked to the middle of the doorway and stopped. "I'ma make it up to you. I promise."

He said nothing.

Giving up, she continued on out the door. He slammed it behind her.

× × ×

Nekole went inside Geno's office to call Maurice for the third time that morning. Still no answer. She left a message for him to call her. Just as she was about to leave, Geno walked through the door. They both flinched after they laid eyes on each other.

She was the first to speak. "I'm glad you finally made it. I need to talk to your ass."

"You need to talk to me?" he asked. "I need to talk to you." He dropped his bag on the floor.

She knew what he was tripping about, but she wasn't trying to hear it.

"Fuck all that," she said, waving her hand. "Where's my damn money?"

"That's my money," he said seriously. "You think I'ma keep on taking care of you while you go out and fuck around? Bitch, you got me fucked up."

A confused look appeared on her face. "What are you talking about? I told you that I was going to Pasha's h—"

"Bitch, you wasn't over no goddamn Pasha's house!" he shouted. "So stop fuckin' lying before I slap the shit out yo' ass."

Geno's loud voice interrupted Old Man Ed's chess game. The barbers shut off their clippers and the beauticians stopped doing hair. They all wanted to hear what he was shouting about.

Geno walked to the office doorway. "If I call Pasha in here and she tells me that you weren't with her, I'ma go upside yo' mutha-fuckin' head, so tell the truth."

Nekole stood there quietly. It was obvious that he had already talked to Pasha, so there was no use in lying. She was so anxious to pick Maurice up last night that she forgot to tell Pasha to vouch for her. How things were between them right now, Pasha would-n't have covered for her anyway.

"You're right," Nekole said softly. "I wasn't with Pasha."

He slammed the door closed. "I know goddamn well you wasn't." He walked up on her. "Where were you last night while I was waiting at your house for you like a damn fool?"

Geno was so hot that she could feel the heat radiating from his body. And from past experience, she knew that she was not about to leave the room without getting into a physical altercation.

She swallowed. "I spent the night with ... Maurice," she said timidly.

"With Maurice, huh?" Geno bit down on his bottom lip as he drew back and smacked her viciously across her face.

"Ow!" she hollered as she fell back into his desk. Without hes-itation, she picked up a pen off the desk and rushed him with it.

He tried to block it, but ended up being stuck in the arm. If it hurt him, he didn't show it. Immediately, he grabbed her wrist and squeezed until it fell from her hand.

Ed, Lucki, Rolesha, Jamisha and a few of the barbers ran to the office. The sound of Nekole crashing into the desk had gotten their attention. When they opened the door, they saw Geno hold-ing her down with his knee and his hands around her throat.

"Geno!" Ed yelled, grabbing the big guy from behind. "Let her go, Geno."

"Oh my God!" Jamisha hollered. "Help her, Joker."

Joker jumped in, assisting Old Man Ed.

Toni pulled up outside. She had stopped by KFC to get Geno some spicy wings for lunch. She thought it would be good if she surprised him by not being late for once. Plus, she hadn't talked to him last night and wanted to see if he was feeling any better. Her jaw hurt and her neck was sore from the fight they had.

The employees' stations were empty when she walked in. The curious customers stood, looking down the hallway, trying to see what was going on. Setting the chicken down, she hurried down the hall, squeezing her way through the nosey crowd.

Joker and Ed had a hold on Geno while Rolesha and Jamisha made sure Nekole was okay.

"You gon' give me my money, too, pussy," Nekole said, wiping blood from her lip.

"I ain't givin' you shit," he stated. "Bought yo' punk ass a car, got you in a house and this is how you treat me?" He broke loose from their hold. "That's my muthafuckin' money."

Nekole managed a smile. "That's cool, Geno. I ain't even gon' trip. You'll be calling me in a week, begging to suck my pussy."

"Come on, Nekole," Rolesha said, grabbing her by the arm. "Joker, help me take her outside."

Breathing hard, Geno watched them escort her out the door. Toni stepped to the side to let them pass. That's when Geno saw her.

"Would everybody please return to their stations," Toni ordered. "The drama is over, now let's go."

While everybody cleared out, Toni stood there staring at Geno. She had come there hoping to make up. Now her plans were shattered. He was in love with Nekole and that was all there was to it. He didn't have to tell her because she could see it in his eyes. That's why he put his hands on her. Nekole hurt him just like she had done. She could deal with the fact that he fucked her, but what she couldn't deal with was him taking care of her, too.

Geno sat on the edge of the desk. Toni removed her hair from her face, then folded her arms across her chest.

"So you bought her that new truck she's been parading around town in. And ... you bought her a house." She shook her head. She couldn't believe it.

He said nothing.

"If you see a fool, bump his head," she said. "That's what my daddy used to say." She sighed. "I guess I can't get mad at her. Can I?"

He still said nothing.

She turned around and began to walk away.

"Where you goin'?" He finally spoke.

"I'll be at Freak's house." She paused to let her words sink in. "When you're ready to talk, call me. You know the number." She continued out the door.

"You do that and it's over for me and you, for good!" he yelled. "You hear me, bitch?"

She ignored him and all the stares that she received from the people inside the shop on her way out.

Geno slammed the door closed. He collapsed in his office chair and put his hands over his face. *Two days of bullshit,* he thought. *Could it get any worse?*

Chapter 23

Joker drove Nekole home in her truck. She didn't want him to, but he insisted, saying that she shouldn't be alone right now. She jumped in the tub to soak her aching body. Joker was sitting in front of the TV eating a sandwich when she called his name.

He put the plate down and rushed to her aid. Her breasts were exposed, but she had a washcloth covering up her pussy when he came in. He saw that and quickly turned away.

"Damn, nigga, you act like you ain't never seen a pair of titties before." She laughed. "Ain't like you about to get no pussy."

"Why you call me in here?"

"I want you to bring me the cordless phone." She took the washcloth off of her pussy, wrung it out, then put it over her face.

"Man, I'd like to smell that," he said on his way to get the phone. He was back within a minute. "Here."

She took it from him. "Thank you." He was about to walk away until he heard her say, "Joker."

"Huh?"

She handed him the washcloth. "Go sit in a corner and sniff that." She chuckled.

"You got jokes, huh? It wasn't funny when Geno was kickin' that ass, was it?" He laughed his way to the living room.

She smiled, causing her jaw to ache. Geno's huge palm felt like a fist going across her face. *Punk-ass nigga*, she thought. She couldn't remember the last time Sirron had hit her. If Geno didn't give her money back willingly, she was gonna take it. Evidently he had no idea who he was fucking with.

Nekole dialed Maurice's number. Again, no answer. So she left him a message, explaining what happened with Geno. She also said that she needed to be fucked real good and held by him. He didn't have to call; just come by, because she was waiting.

The next call she made was to the cab company so Joker could take his helpful ass home. She wanted to be alone. Maurice was coming over and she had to get prepared. Now that Geno was so-called through with her, she was gonna have to use Maurice. It was all his fault anyway. At least, that's what she'd tell him.

Joker turned off the TV and was looking through her CD case for something romantic when he heard a horn blowing outside. Glancing out the front window, he saw a yellow cab pulling into the driveway.

"What the fuck," he said to himself.

Nekole came walking into the room wearing a pair of shorts and a tank top. Out of her purse she took a fifty-dollar bill and handed it to Joker.

"That should cover the fare," she said. He had an embarrassed look on his face. "What did you think? We were gonna have a few drinks and end up fuckin' or somethin'?"

He smirked. "You know what? I don't know what I thought. It was good just being around you for a while."

"Thank you." She gave him a hug. "If you want, you can leave your number so I can call you."

The cab driver blew his horn again.

He jotted his number down on a tablet that was on the table. "Call me."

"I will."

x x x

Derrick was sitting on the edge of the bar stool, sipping on a beer, waiting for Maurice to sink the eight ball. He hadn't brought it up yet, but he wanted to know why Maurice let that girl knock him off his square.

Maurice shot the eight ball and missed.

"Damn it! My hand is shaky as a muthafucka." He drank some of his beer.

Derrick stood up. "Yo' game is fucked up in more ways than one." He sunk the ball with ease.

"I ain't gonna dispute that, Derrick." Maurice leaned up against the bar. He knew what he was getting at. "Man, that bitch is poison."

After he ordered another round, Derrick sat on the stool, waiting to hear an explanation for how he had been acting.

"That bitch had me tripping for a week. She freaked me to death for seven nights and didn't let me get the pussy." He shook his head. "Then the bitch cut me off for a few days. I ain't never in my life been treated like that."

"You let her do it."

"Fucked up thing about it is, I really dig the bitch," Maurice said seriously. He took a swig of his beer. "I never had a broad who took control of our relationship like she did. She's the first bitch I ever opened up to."

"About what?"

"About everything. She got me drunk, high, rubbed my feet and relaxed me to where I felt free to expose my inner self to her. She's a cold piece of work." He tilted his bottle.

"Sounds to me like you done fell in love, nigga."

"Unt unh," he grunted, still sucking on his beer. "I'm through with that ho, man. Any bitch that—" His phone vibrated on his hip. "Hello?"

"Did you get my messages?" Nekole asked. Levert was singing in the background.

He pointed at the phone, signaling Derrick that it was her. "Yeah, I got 'em. I've been busy. I had to go get my car from the impound."

"Too busy for your booby, huh?"

"Evidently," he said smartly.

She chuckled. "I'ma ignore that 'cause I probably deserve it. Anyway, I cooked you a nice dinner, got a hot bath waiting and a bottle of your favorite on ice. You coming?"

Damn, she knows how to hook a nigga, he thought. If he kept on fucking with her, he was gonna find himself proposing to her.

"Yeah, I'll be there," he said coolly.

"You want me naked or wearing lace?"

"Naked. Give me about an hour," he said, looking at Derrick, who was shaking his head.

"Bye." She hung up.

"Simp-ass nigga," Derrick said hotly. "Man, you used to be my mentor. Now you my simptor."

Maurice put his hand up. "Chill out, nigga. Your boy is back," he said convincingly. "I ain't even gonna show up."

Derrick smiled approvingly. "You playing her game now, huh?"

"Unt unh. I told you I was through with that bitch."

"So my boy is back?"

"I ain't never left. I just got side-tracked."

Tamisha walked through the door, looking around for Maurice. She spotted him racking up the balls on the pool table. Stopping at the bar first, she ordered a pitcher of Budweiser and had it sent over to their table.

Just as Maurice was about to shoot, he saw her walking toward him out of the corner of his eye. He set the stick aside and gave her a hug. The first thing Derrick noticed was how well she fit in her jeans. Her red thong was peeking out the top of them. The Tweety Bird tatted across her lower back made his mouth water.

She turned around in time to catch him staring at her behind.

"You see something you like, Derrick?" she asked.

"More like something I want," he said, flirting with her.

Maurice put his arm around her waist. "What do you think, baby? You want to give him a shot of that?"

She elbowed him in his stomach. "Boy, you better quit playing. Ain't nobody gettin' this nookie but you."

"Yeah, right," Derrick said doubtfully.

"You right," she admitted. "Hank gets a shot every now and then, too."

Maurice scowled. "Who the fuck is Hank?"

"He's long and thick. Some girls call him 'dildo.'"

They laughed.

"Re-rack 'em, Derrick. My boo wants to play with us."

While Derrick racked the balls, Maurice put his tongue down her throat.

"Mm," she moaned. "You think I can get some of that sweet dick?"

"I don't know. I'm still mad at you about the other night when I went to jail."

"I was sleep, baby," she explained. "You know damn well that if I knew I would've come and got you on the bus if I had to."

"You would've, wouldn't you?" he said, looking into her eyes. "I'ma take you to another world tonight, baby."

"Ooh, I can't wait. Let's get a bottle and go now," she begged. "My hormones are on fire."

"Not yet, baby. I gotta kick it with my man for a little while. We ain't kicked it in a minute."

"I'm cool with that."

"We'll leave in a few." He went and got her a stick so she could play, too.

✗ ✗ ✗

Two hours had passed and Maurice still hadn't shown up. Nekole called him several times with no answer. She wondered if he was in jail again. Had he run into Neosha? Did he run into Geno? All kinds of questions and worries ran through her head.

An hour later, she popped open the bottle of Moët and began drinking it by herself. The food and bath water had gotten cold, and so had she.

Hoping to come up with an answer to her questions, she got out the phone book and called every jail and hospital in the city. None of them had him. Slamming the phone down, she picked up the yellow pages and threw it up against the wall. It fell on the table, knocking the lamp over.

She saw lights and heard a car pulling into her driveway. With a big smile on her face, she rushed to open the front door. To her disappointment, it wasn't him. A purple minivan had used her driveway to turn around.

She sighed.

It was now three o'clock in the morning. Still not a word from Maurice. She swallowed the last of the Moët, then tossed the bottle into the trash. At a drunken pace, she stumbled to her room and crawled into bed. Sleep didn't come easily. For over an hour, she lay there watching the ceiling spin around and around.

Finally, she got it. Maurice hadn't shown because he was giving her a taste of her own medicine. He wasn't sprung after all. He had gotten the pussy and disappeared on her. She wondered if that was his plan from the very beginning, or if he was simply paying her back for what she had done to him. Whatever the answer, she still felt like a damn fool. She'd fucked up with Geno to fuck with Maurice. And now there was no Maurice. Ain't no pain like that from the opposite sex. And that went for everybody. Including her.

Chapter 24

Maurice rolled over in his bed, facing Tamisha, who was sleeping soundly. She was a beautiful person. He didn't know why he couldn't just settle down and be with one woman. After his experience with Nekole, he wasn't sure if he wanted to be a player anymore.

Gently he placed a finger on her neck, running it all the way down between her legs. Even while she was asleep, her pussy remained moist. She was probably having a wet dream, he thought. He touched her clitoris, moving his finger in a circular motion. She twitched. Then he saw her legs easing apart so he could dig into her crevice.

"Mmm …mmm …" she moaned, feeling his finger enter her. She began moving her hips up and down.

The ringing of the phone interrupted them.

"Noo!" she whined. A phone call could easily ruin a person's whole day. Man, how she loved morning dick. There was nothing like a good orgasm to start off the day.

"Hello," Maurice answered.

"Have you talked to your daddy?" his mama asked. He could hear the anxiety in her voice.

"Unt unh," he said. "When was the last time you talked to him?"

"Last night. He and Jesse went out and I haven't heard from

him since."

Maurice assumed right away that he had crept off with the young girl from the restaurant. He didn't appreciate the stress that his dad was causing his mother. She was too old to be going through that type of bullshit.

"You talk to Jesse?" he asked.

"Karen said Jesse came home last night. He said he hadn't seen Steve since last night."

Maurice sighed. "Well, I'll see if I can catch up with him." He looked over at Tamisha, who had begun sucking on her own titty nipple. His dick got hard instantly.

"Get your ass over here and fix my flat tire. I'ma go find his ass myself," his mama said.

"I'm on my way, mama."

Tamisha frowned.

"Why ain't you at work?" she inquired.

"We're closed for inventory."

"Inventory? Yeah right. You over there taking inventory on one of those tramps. Now get up and bring yo' ass over here." She hung up.

Tamisha sighed. "What's wrong with mama?"

Maurice sat up on the edge of the bed, scratching his head. "Steve's cheating," he said solemnly.

Her mouth fell open. "Get outta here."

"Saw him myself. He's got a young bad one, too."

She got up and put on his robe. "Well, gon' over there and tend to your mother. I'ma clean up your house and cook you a big breakfast."

x   x   x

Nekole threw up three times that morning before she started feeling better. After a shower and two bowls of Lucky Charms cereal, she was ready for the day ahead. She squeezed into a pair of shorts, a Nike T-shirt and put on a pair of all white New Balances. The shoes didn't go with the shirt, so she changed and put on some Air Force 1's.

Hopping into her truck, she burned rubber out of the driveway and sped off down the street. Her nosey, old white neighbor stood on the porch, holding her cat and shaking her head. "There goes the neighborhood," she said to herself.

Nekole's first stop was at the dealership where Maurice worked. The sign in the window said that they were closed for inventory. She got back into her truck and headed to her next destination.

Tamisha's gold Acura could be seen parked in front of Maurice's house from a distance. His Corvette wasn't in the driveway. She whipped into the driveway, parking in his spot. Grabbing the pocket knife out of her console, she exited her vehicle and marched up to the door.

Bam! Bam! Bam! She beat on the glass door. Impatiently, she continued to beat on the door until Tamisha showed up wearing his robe. Tamisha flinched because she knew that Nekole was trouble the minute she laid eyes on her.

"Who the fuck are you?" Nekole asked.

"Tamisha. And you are?"

"His muthafuckin' woman, bitch. Now, where is he?"

"He's not here." Tamisha was confused. She had never heard of Maurice having a woman until now. "I'll tell him that you came by." Tamisha tried to close the door.

Nekole grabbed the handle, stopping her.

"No, you won't. What you gon' do is get the fuck up outta here," she demanded.

Tamisha stood speechless. She didn't know how to act or what else to say. She had never been in a situation like this before. She was never a fighter, and she wasn't about to become one today.

"Let me call Maurice," Tamisha said, walking to the phone. She picked it up, but Nekole slammed it back down.

"What part of 'outta here' don't you understand?" Nekole gave her a hard stare.

Tamisha was on the verge of crying. "I'll just get my stuff then." She went to the bedroom.

"You do that." Nekole waited in the hallway with her arms folded across her chest while Tamisha got dressed. She wanted to laugh because she couldn't believe how much of a punk Tamisha was. Judging by Tamisha's looks, Pasha's looks and hers, she would say that Maurice had good taste when it came to women.

When Tamisha came out of the bedroom, her eyes were red and her face was wet. Sniffling, she picked up her keys and purse off the table. Without a word, she opened the front door and walked out.

"And don't come back!" Nekole yelled. Then she slammed the door.

When Maurice returned home, he was shocked to see Nekole's Ram instead of Tamisha's Acura parked at his house. He didn't know what to think and prayed that Nekole hadn't hurt Tamisha.

The TV was off, the curtains were closed and he smelled weed when he walked into his house. Nekole was sitting in the recliner, staring at a blank TV screen, puffing on a joint. She picked up the remote to the stereo and pushed play.

Shortly, Luther Ingram began singing, "If loving you is wrong ... I don't wanna be right." The volume was set just right.

"You stood me up last night," she said evenly.

He closed the door. "Where's Tamisha?"

She shrugged and continued to smoke her joint.

There was no sign of a struggle, so he figured that Tamisha had left peacefully.

"What you want?"

Putting the joint out, she stood up and walked toward him. "I came here to fuck you up for what you did last night." She stopped directly in front of him. "Then I realized that ... that I was in love with you."

"How'd you come to that conclusion?" he said nonchalantly.

"Because you had me stressin' last night," she admitted. Leaning forward, she kissed him. "And feenin'." She kissed him again. "And going damn near crazy."

"Really?"

Again, she pointed the remote at the stereo and pushed skip. She tossed the remote on the sofa. Grabbing the bottom of his shirt, she pulled it up over his head.

Now Marvin Gaye was singing *"Sexual Healing."*

"Get up, get up, get up, get up, let's make love tonight. Wake up, wake up, wake up, wake up, 'cause you do it right."

"What you doing?" he asked as she began to lick his nipple.

"I need sexual healin', baby," she said softly as she unbuttoned his pants.

Dropping down to her knees, she came face to dick with his huge, even though limp, organ. He closed his eyes and tilted his head back. "Mmm," she moaned as she took his dick into her mouth. Slowly, she swallowed as much of it as she could. Then she pulled it out of her mouth and stood up.

Maurice was breathing hard, and his facial expression was begging her to finish. She walked to the beginning of the hallway, then turned around. "There's a meeting in your bedroom," she said then continued down the hall.

× × ×

"Shit! Mmm. Hmm," Maurice moaned in his sleep. His eyes fluttered open, then he saw what had him feeling so good.

Nekole was facing the opposite direction, riding the shit out of him. Her back muscles flexed and her ass cheeks clapped as she bounced up and down on him in a steady motion.

"Ooh! Ooh!" he moaned as she sped up, trying to make him cum with her.

"Oh my God it's ... it ... Ah ... Ah ... Ahhhh, shit!" she screamed, feeling her vaginal slime ooze out of her onto his dick. Panting, she looked back at him. "Did you cum, too?"

"About a minute before you."

She smiled. "You minute man," she said, climbing off of him. She collapsed beside him and wrapped her body around his. "I don't know how I fell in love with you so fast."

"My game is strong," he said confidently. He hoped that he didn't have stinking-ass morning breath. If he did, he couldn't smell it.

"I know you're in love after all that good pussy and head I gave you all night. And this morning," she added, looking up at the ceiling. "That's the first time I ever swallowed."

"Last night was?"

"Umm hmm. I never swallowed Sirron's cum, so consider yourself special."

He smiled. "I have to admit. You're the only girl that has ever sucked my dick and balls at the same time."

She put her head on his chest. "This mouth is all yours now, baby. And so is my body. It's up to you how you want to use it."

Her last words caught his attention. What did she mean by, "It's up to you how you want to use it?" He thought back to something she had said that night they watched " *The Mack*" over at her house. She said, "I would've been his main whore." Meaning, his number one ho. Was she inviting him to pimp her? Or was it just talk in the heat of passion?

"What do you mean by that?" he quizzed.

She sat up in the bed, Indian-style, tucking the sheet between her legs. Her perky nipples pointed at him.

"There's a lot I haven't told you about me." She paused to let her words sink in.

"Good or bad?"

She shrugged. "It depends on how you look at it."

He sat up against the headboard, waiting to hear her story. "I'm listening."

She took a deep breath before she began. "When I was in Cali ... I used to scope out ballers, date 'em, then set them up for Sirron to rob them. All of the robberies didn't go as planned ... and a few of them ended up dead. Right before I came here, we hit this guy for a lot of money. Enough for us to stop hustling and open up our own business."

Maurice listened carefully, taking in every word of what he thought of as a confession. Why was she confessing? He wasn't sure, but if he had to guess, he'd say she wanted him to be her new

Sirron.

"The guy who we robbed tried to resist," she went on, "and so we had to kill him. That's why Sirron's in jail right now." She grabbed his hand and began cleaning out his fingernails with hers. "Anyway, the police kicked in his house and took all of the money. I figured that I had done too much to too many people to stay in LA, that's why I came here." She looked him in the eyes. "Then I met you."

Maurice cleared his throat. "You ever kill anybody yourself?" he asked, not really expecting the truth.

She gave him an incriminating look.

Nothing that she said to him that morning surprised him. She had just confirmed what he told Derrick about her the other night at the bar. She was poison. A tamed serpent ready to strike at her master's command, but who was also capable of striking without one.

In just a few short months, her poisonous venom had spread through his and Geno's veins, causing them to be at each other's throats. Long time friends had possibly turned into lifetime enemies. Over what? A piece of pussy. A pussy so poisonous and sweet that it lured more than a few young men to an early grave.

In a roundabout way, he and Geno had battled to become her new master, and Maurice had won. Now the question was, was he gonna accept the position and run the risk of ending up like Sirron? Or would he end it now and let her go on about her business?

"So are you through with all that?" he asked. He could sense that she was up to something.

She shrugged. "Maybe. That depends on you."

He could understand how her beauty could enable her to lure and trap the average man. What he couldn't understand was how something so beautiful on the outside could contain such a malicious, wicked person on the inside.

Not even she fully knew the lengths to which she was willing to go to be rich. She walked around every day carrying the second root of all evil between her thighs. She knew it, and she used it to her advantage, hoping to obtain the first as well. Money. Whether it be by hook or crook, she was gonna get her share.

"What did you have in mind?" he inquired.

She lay down beside him, putting his warm arm around her cold body. "Let's get some sleep. We can discuss it some other time."

Something told him to separate himself from her completely. Because if he didn't, he would regret it for the rest of his life.

x   x   x

Geno drove to the shop in the new BMW that he had bought that morning. It had been a good month for his drug business, and he celebrated by buying the new car. His supply was running out fast, and soon he'd be back on the highway to California for a re-up.

Since Toni left, he had turned back into a whore. He stayed out all night, kicking it with different bitches. At the club, he bought up the bar, splurging money and getting his name out in the streets where he didn't need it. He was no longer moving kilos undercover. Everybody was starting to know that Geno was the man with them thangs.

He called Freak on his cell phone.

"Hello," Toni answered.

"So that's where you been laying up at, huh?" Geno said jealously. "Put Freak on the phone, bitch."

Even though he was upset, he still couldn't afford to get into it with Freak. He needed Freak just as bad as Freak needed him. He couldn't take his money to just anybody to get it washed. That would be a stupid thing to do. He had already done enough stupid things to last him a lifetime.

"Hello," Freak said.

"What's up, friend?" Geno exited 71, then turned onto Prospect.

Freak caught the sarcasm, but ignored it. "Wha' sup?"

"Man, just because you went behind my back and fucked my

bitch don't mean that our business stops. Or does it?"

"She didn't have no place else to go, Geno," Freak explained.

"If you hadn't been fucking her behind my back in the first place, she wouldn't have needed a place to go. Would she?" He was getting hotter by the second.

Freak couldn't think of a good defense because he knew that he was in the wrong. He had dirty-macked Toni just to get some pussy. He didn't spit no hellified game at her to get in her drawers. He told on her man in order to get it. There was nothing playerish about doing what he had done, and he knew it.

"Anyway," Geno continued, "I got some cash that I need you to take to the laundromat. That's if we're still cool like that."

"Yeah man. I mean ... you know that I didn't intend for none of this shit to happen. You're like a brother to me."

"Right," Geno said. "Just like my brother Maurice. Having brothers like y'all helps me understand why Cain killed Abel."

Freak didn't know if he should take that as a threat or not. He wasn't a stranger to gunplay, so that wasn't what scared him. He knew that he wouldn't pull his gun on Geno unless he had to. But then it might be too late. Geno held the cards, so Freak had to wait and see how he was gonna play them.

"Like I said, Geno. It wasn't—" He stopped in mid-sentence because there was no use in trying to explain himself. He was wrong, and that was all there was to it. "I'll tell you what, man. Since I'm a bigger man than that, I'ma go ahead and call it off between me and her."

Toni looked at him, confused. If Freak left her alone, where would that leave her? Back at home with mama, that's where. Back to a house full of bad siblings. Back to budgeting her money. Back to square one.

"You do that, Freak," Geno encouraged him. "Then things between me and you will be back to normal. But Maurice, I'd shoot that nigga dead if he ever crossed the line again."

"I hear ya. Look, let me get up and get myself together. I'll give you a holla in a minute."

"I'll be at the shop." He hung up.

After Freak got off the phone, he got up and hurried to the bathroom to take a shower. He had felt Toni's cold eyes on him and didn't want to face her yet. To be truthful, he was the one who had gotten her into all this. But in order to save his friendship with a long time friend, he had to rid himself of her.

Toni was fully dressed and sitting up in his bed when he came out of the bathroom. She was staring out the window with tears rolling down her face. Freak stood there watching her.

"So it's over between us, too, huh?" she asked without looking at him.

"Shid, I guess so. I ... Geno and I go way back, Toni, and I can't let you come between that." He sat down next to her on the bed. "Besides, I don't have another choice. If we keep this shit up, somebody's gonna end up hurt and I don't want it to be me. So before that happens, I'd just rather end it altogether."

"So the only one who gets fucked is me, right?" she said, pointing to herself. "I let you fuck me and ended up fucking up everything I had. Fuck am I supposed to do now?"

"It ain't my problem," he said coldly. He knew that if he wasn't tough about it, he might start feeling sorry for her.

"It ain't your problem," she repeated to herself. "Then I guess I'll be going." She got up and gathered her things. "You seen my purse?"

"It's on the kitchen table," he reminded her.

She walked to the door, then stopped and turned around. "Ain't nothing I can do to change your mind?"

Her face was so pretty, serious and sincere. He turned his head so he wouldn't have to look at her. "I don't think so."

Slowly, she turned back around and began to walk away. She picked up her purse and got another bag out of the closet. When she opened up the front door, she hesitated, hoping that he would come running to stop her. He never came.

He heard the front door close. In the last month, he had, in fact, grown to love Toni. He couldn't understand why Geno had

put her on the back burner for some stranger. If their situation had been different, she would've been his main girl. He was sure of that.

Chapter 25

Once again, Nekole and Maurice found themselves spending all of their spare time together. Shopping sprees and family barbecues. They even spent a weekend in Vegas. It seemed like he had forgotten everything that she had told him that night. But he hadn't. He hoped that he could change her into a normal, one-man woman, just like she was changing him into a one-woman man.

Geno had come and taken all of the furniture out of Nekole's house, and he still refused to give back her money. She was jobless now that she no longer worked at the shop.

Toni and Freak were no longer fucking around. But he did help her get into a nice apartment. His feelings for her wouldn't go away overnight. If she needed some money to pay a bill or something, she could always come to him. But they could never be a couple. Not as long as Geno was running the streets.

Since Freak wasn't fucking her anymore, Geno started kicking it with him again. They went out to clubs and out of town to Atlanta and Texas, but things weren't the same without their third amigo there. Secretly, Geno missed the shit out of Maurice, though he wouldn't say that out in the open. As far as anyone knew, he would rather see Maurice dead than to speak to him again. People couldn't understand how he could feel that way about his friend, and all because of a woman.

Michelle, Yvonne, Kim and Tamisha had all started to drift

away from Maurice. He no longer returned their calls or took them out anywhere. Pasha had been trying to hunt him down because she had something very important to discuss with him. Just like everybody else, he was dodging her, too.

Maurice was sitting at his desk looking up travel agencies on the Internet. His door opened and Derrick walked in, carrying two boxes of chicken. He hurried up and hit escape on the keyboard, taking him back to the main menu, so Derrick wouldn't see what he was doing.

Derrick set one of the boxes down in front of Maurice. "Two legs and a breast," he said. "And a pepper."

"You finally got it right," Maurice said, opening up the box.

Derrick sat watching Maurice while he ate his chicken. Maurice could feel his eyes on him, but he didn't say anything. He knew what was on Derrick's mind, and he wasn't in the mood to answer questions about his love life. Nekole was somebody he could relate to, and he didn't want to be a player any more. Derrick was gonna have to accept it.

Fed up with Maurice avoiding eye contract, Derrick went ahead and spoke up.

"You's a trick ass nigga," Derrick said angrily. "You preach all that bullshit about game and players and you don't practice it your damn self."

"Nigga, fuck you!" Maurice said. He dropped the chicken and stood up.

"Aw, you wanna fight now." Derrick smirked. "You act like a bitch when it comes to her, but you want to get tough with me." Derrick got up. "*Yo' boy is back. I'm through with that bitch. She poison,*" he said, mocking Maurice. "That wasn't nothing but a bunch of bullshit."

"Nigga, I'll beat yo' bitch ass," Maurice said, storming around his desk. He couldn't bring himself to hit Derrick, so he pushed him into the water cooler.

Derrick bounced off and came at him. Maurice sidestepped, grabbed him, then put him into a headlock.

"Why you wrestling?" Derrick murmured, barely able to breathe.

"Nigga, you'd better be glad I'm wrestling." They both fell to the floor, knocking over one of the chairs. Derrick squirmed, but couldn't get loose. "Give up, D, man."

"Fuck you," he murmured.

Nekole parked next to Derrick's 300M. She grabbed her purse and her Subway sandwich bag and got out of her truck. Something was on her mind that she wanted to discuss with Maurice over lunch. She had been holding off for over a month now, waiting on the perfect time to bring it to him.

From outside his office door, she could hear them rumbling. Opening it, she saw them on the floor tussling. Chicken and fries were scattered all over the floor. Both of them were breathing hard and out of gas. Hurriedly she closed the door before anybody could look in and see them fighting, and set her stuff down.

"Break it up, y'all," she said, rushing over to them. She grabbed Maurice's arm, trying to break the hold. "Let him go, Maurice." Gritting his teeth, he squeezed even harder. "I said stop it before your boss comes in here."

Finally he released his grip from around Derrick's neck. Derrick tried to swing, but Nekole jumped between them.

"Derrick, please. Stop this shit," she pleaded, not wanting them to get caught. Maurice needed his job, and for the moment, she needed Maurice.

They stood on each side of her, breathing hard, eyes red and chests swelled up.

"Now y'all need to shake hands and apologize to each other," she said, hoping it was over.

"I ain't shakin' shit with that nigga," Derrick said. He walked away, bumping into her on his way out. She ignored it so things wouldn't escalate any further.

Ten minutes later, everything was back to normal. While Maurice was in the restroom cleaning himself up, she had straightened his office and put everything back into place.

Now she was sitting at his desk, eating her Subway sandwich while he sat behind his desk, drinking water and replaying in his mind the things that had just taken place. It seemed that since he met her, he was losing everybody around him.

She looked at him. "You okay, baby?"

"I'm cool."

She left him alone for a few minutes so he could gather his thoughts. What she came to ask him was gonna take a lot of thought, and she wanted him to have a clear head while he contemplated it. She was in a bind and had found a sure fire way to get out of it.

A block away from the dealership, Pasha waited impatiently at a red light. She was irritated, mad, anxious and in love, all at the same time. All she did lately was go to work and come back home. Her life was about to change, so she was trying to get mentally prepared for it.

The light turned green and she pulled off. When she made a left into the dealership, she didn't see Nekole's big Dodge Ram parked beside Derrick's car. It wasn't until she was walking toward the front door that she spotted it.

Slowly, she began to back away. After so many failed attempts to reach him, she was now giving up. Evidently, they were not meant to be. Maurice was with Nekole, where he was happy. Why should she burden him with her problems?

Tears streamed down her face as she bolted out into traffic, almost running into an old Chevy Caprice.

Nekole was cleaning up the mess from her sandwich while Maurice went to talk to his boss. The phone rang. She didn't know if she should answer it or not. It rang again. Her attention remained on what she was doing. Then it rang a third time.

She picked it up. "Midwestern Chrysler and Dodge. This is the office of Maurice Jones," she said in a professional voice.

"Who is this?" Neosha asked, knowing that he didn't have a secretary.

"This is Nekole."

"Nekole?" she said hotly. "Damn, bitch. What you got on Maurice that he's so in love with you that you get to answer his office phone? Yo' pussy ain't gold."

"It's obvious that yours ain't even copper 'cause I'm here and you're not. Bye."

She hung up in her ear.

At no time after Maurice got back was the phone call from Neosha mentioned. He sat down behind his desk doing some paperwork while Nekole stood behind him massaging his shoulders.

"So, boy," she began. "Have you thought about what we talked about a month ago?"

"What you mean?" he said without looking up.

Stopping the massage, she sat on the edge of his desk facing him. "Remember when I told you that my body was yours and it was up to you how you chose to use it?"

"Mm hm." He leaned back in his chair.

"Well ... I think it's time that you used it."

"What you got in mind?"

"It's like this, Maurice." Her voice took on a serious tone. "I need some money, and a whole lot of it. I've got some things that I want to do, and I only know one way to get it done."

"You want to set somebody up?" he asked, already knowing the answer.

"Not want. I'm gonna do it ... with or without you. But I'd prefer that we do it together." She stood up and started pacing the floor. "I don't know if you know, but Geno don't rely on the shop alone to pay his bills." She stopped pacing and faced him. "He's slangin' more bricks than he's cuttin' heads."

"How you know?" he quizzed.

"You don't fuck somebody for months and not get to know 'em. Now, I can't say for sure where the money is, but I definitely know where he keeps the dope stashed."

"So you want to break in?"

She shook her head. "No. I want to snatch his ass and make

him cough up the money. Ain't nothin' I can do with a bunch of dope."

"You're crazy."

"And you owe me," she said, pointing a finger at him. "I had everything. I risked it and lost it all when I came and got your ass out of jail that night."

He didn't respond.

"And for your information, I'm not crazy," she said seriously. "I'm just out to get mine, by any means necessary."

"What's that supposed to mean?"

"By hook or crook, nigga. If I gotta go out and hook for it or if I have to get into some gangsta shit, I'ma get it. Now is you down?"

He stared into her cold hazel eyes, knowing that if he did go along with it, they would have to go as far as killing Geno. Because there was no way he was gonna let them rob him and let it go. If Geno had it like she said, he would surely kill him, her and everybody around him before he'd let it get taken.

Maurice sighed. "I ... I can't do it, Nekole," he said in a low voice. "You're asking me to do something that I don't do, and ain't ever gonna do. Especially not to somebody I know."

A look of disappointment appeared on her face. "So, you don't love me?"

"Yes, I do," he said, standing up. He walked around the desk to where she stood. "I can't chance ruining my life like that. I got my own thing going here and I'm not about to jeopardize that for nobody. Not even you."

She looked down at the floor, appearing to be hurt. Then she looked at him.

"Well, I guess that's it then." He looked at her but said nothing. "I mean, you're right, you do have your own thing going on here. Now I gotta do my own thing." She walked to the door.

"You ain't gotta do it."

"Are you gonna take care of me, Maurice?" she asked, raising her voice. "You gonna buy me all the nice things I want? You plan on marrying me and buying me a big house out in Belton? Is yours mine?"

He remained quiet.

"I didn't think so." She opened up the door. "I'm sorry that I wasted your time. I thought there was a G buried somewhere inside of you." She looked him up and down. "But I guess it ain't." She closed the door and left.

A second later, the door opened again. "I forgot my purse," she said, picking it up off his desk. Then she was gone again.

He wanted to run after her, but thought it was best that he didn't. Hell or jail was the path that she was on, and he wasn't about to follow her.

Neosha pulled into the parking lot across from police head-quarters. She grabbed her purse, locked her Pathfinder, then walked across the street to the building. Sitting at the front desk was a short, shriveled old man doing a crossword puzzle, pretend-ing to be busy.

She stood at the counter, waiting on him to acknowledge her presence.

"Hellooo," she said.

He looked at her like she was disturbing him, and his job was-n't to serve her.

"Wha'do ya want?"

"I'd like to talk to someone who handles fraud and embezzle-ment, please."

×   ×   ×

"Can I speak to Joker?" Nekole asked.

"Who dis?" Joker questioned, hoping it was who he thought it was.

"Aw, you done forgot about me already?"

"Hell, nah. I was just playin' it cool, that's all. Wha' sup wit' ya, playgirl."

"I need you to come over here and keep me company," she said seductively. "I want to ask you something."

"Twenty minutes too long?"

"Make it fifteen, baby. I can't wait."

"I'm already gone."

Joker could hear Prince singing "*Adore*" through her front door. Impatiently he rang the doorbell until she showed up.

She wore a big smile. "Come on in," she said. "Give me five minutes, then come on back to my room."

Excitement was in his glassy eyes. He had been getting fucked up all evening and this was just what he needed to end his day. He couldn't think of a better place that he could've been at the moment.

He fixed himself a glass of Remy and was just about to sit on the couch when he heard her call his name. On his way to her room, he smiled and hummed to the tune of Prince's song.

Lying on her back across the bed, naked and spread eagle, Nekole stared at him lustfully. When she saw the hungry look in his eyes, she knew she had him on the hook. He stood in the doorway.

"What would you do to get this pussy?" she asked.

He smiled. "Probably anything," he answered truthfully.

Sliding her hand down between her legs, she started fiddling with her pearl tongue. "Would you kill for it?" He nodded his head, yes. "Would you steal for it?" Same answer. "Would you rob for it, daddy?" She rubbed it harder.

"Mm hm," he said, getting aroused.

"You promise, baby?" He nodded. "Then come over here and get it, daddy."

In one swallow, he downed the drink then rushed out of his clothes. He was anxious to do the one thing that he'd been wanting to do for a long time—fuck the shit out of her.

x x x

Sirron came back from court with a big grin on his face. His first stop was at the phone to call Angie. He wanted to tell her the good news so she could tell Nekole. Maybe then she'd come back to him.

Angie picked up on the first ring, then pressed five. "Hello."

"How you doing, Angie?" he said cheerfully.

"Sirron?"

"Yeah, girl. Why you say my name like that?"

"Because you don't sound like a lunatic today."

He laughed. "Girl, you crazy. Have you talked to my boo?"

"Nope. I haven't heard from her. Didn't you call her?"

"Yeah. But I didn't get a chance to talk to her." His voice went from happy to sad.

"Aw, yeah? What's up? Why you so uppity today?"

"Because," he said. The excitement had returned to his voice, "I went to an appeal bond hearing today and was granted one."

"That's good. Ain't it?"

"Hell yeah. Only problem is, my bond is a hundred thousand. But it's only ten grand through the courts. I was hoping you could catch up with Nekole so you can see if she can help me."

"I'll try to get in touch with her for you. Last time I called, Geno's number had been changed. So I might have to call over to ... no wait, I've got Toni's cell phone number."

"Write down my address so you can give it to her."

"Hold on, let me get a pen."

When she returned, he gave her the address and told her that he would not be calling back. If Nekole wanted to get in touch with him, here was her chance. If she didn't, she'd better hope that he never came up with the money on his own.

✗ ✗ ✗

Joker put on a pot of coffee, fried some eggs and sausage, then served Nekole breakfast in bed. The covers slid down and exposed her breasts when she sat up to take the plate. He sat beside her.

"So, how was it?" he asked, referring to the dick that he gave her last night.

She waited until she finished chewing her food before she spoke. "I didn't know you had it like that. You got a big-ass dick," she said, stroking his ego. "It's gonna take a while for my pussy to stretch open that wide."

He blushed. "So, where are we going with this?"

After setting the plate next to the bed, she rolled over on top of him and started kissing his chest. "That depends on you."

"Wait a minute. What's up with you and Maurice?"

"He wasn't the G that I thought he was." She continued to kiss him.

"How so?" he asked curiously.

"I need a man who's down for *my* crown, just as well as he is for his," she replied. "Ya know what I'm saying?"

"I hear ya." He rubbed her back. "Let me guess. You want me to do whatever it is that he wouldn't do? Because it's obvious that you want me to do something."

She sat up on top of him. "I can't tell you unless you're gonna help me. I need a man with his boots laced up, ready to do whatever it takes to live better. You feel me?"

"Well, you've come to the right man this time. 'Cause I need to come up, bad."

Reaching down, she inserted his dick inside of her. "Ummm," she moaned. She began to ride him. "That gangsta shit turns me on."

Chapter 26

Joker pulled up to the pay phone at James' Liquor Store. He put two quarters in the slot, then dialed Geno's cell number.

"Yeah," Geno answered.

"Wha' sup, nigga. This Joker."

"Hey, Joke. Wha' sup?"

"Man, I'm trying to get a half of one of them thangs."

Geno became suspicious. *How in the hell does Joker know my business?* he thought. "Joker, how did you get my number?" Geno asked curiously.

"My nigga Beno gave it to me," Joker explained. "Man, I'm all good."

That eased his suspicions a little. "That's cool, but I only sell whole ones and I'm down to my last two."

"I can come up with enough money to get a whole one."

"How long you gon' be?"

"Really, I've got it on me. Just let me know where you want me to come."

Geno gave him the address to his house on 68th Street. His instructions were for Joker to park in front of the house and wait for him to get there.

Joker checked the chamber of his snub-nose .357, then put it in his pants. The next call that he made was to Nekole, telling her that everything was ready to go.

Geno closed up the shop in a hurry. Joker had called while he was cleaning up, so he would have to come back early in the morning before the shop opened. Nekole was leaning up against his truck when he came outside. He was happy to see her, but didn't show it.

"How you been, big G?" She flashed a smile.

"I've been cool, stranger," he said sarcastically.

"You're the one who left me. Remember?"

He opened up the passenger door and threw his bag onto the floor. "I've got a run to make," he said, glancing at his watch. "I ain't got time to sit here and chat."

"Well, I guess I'll see you around." She started walking away, knowing that he would stop her.

"Don't give up so fast," he said. She stopped and turned around slowly. "Why don't you ride with me while I make this run?"

She pretended to think about it. "We ain't going nowhere bad is we? I mean, you might be holding a grudge and planning to kill me or something."

"What if I let you hold my gun?"

"Well," she paused and looked at Geno. The look in his eyes pleaded for her to go with him. "I think I can do that." She got into the passenger seat.

Geno took his gun out of the console and handed it to her. "You happy?"

"You trust me?"

"Even though you snaked me once, yeah, I trust you." He started the truck, then put it in drive. "My life is in your hands. Where is your truck?"

"I parked it behind the shop." She put her head on his shoulder. "I fucked up with you once, but that don't mean that I wasn't down for you. I just want you to know that."

"You still down for me?"

"I can show you better than I can tell you." She tucked the gun in her waist.

Joker was smoking on his third stick of wet while he sat parked in front of Geno's spot on 68th Street. He checked the chamber of his gun one more time. It wouldn't be his first time committing a robbery, but he was sure that this would be his biggest lick yet.

He put the stick out in the ashtray after he saw Geno's Excursion coming over the hill. He put on a pair of gloves.

"Here we go," he said to himself.

Nekole sat up, looking out the windshield. "Is that Joker's car?"

"Yep," Geno confirmed, turning into the driveway. "That's who I'm meeting."

She faced him. "So you into drugs and shit?"

"If you say so." He put the truck in park.

"I'm comin' in with you," she insisted. "I'ma hold onto the gun while you handle your business. If he even blinks, I'ma blow his head off."

"Naw, you ain't gotta do all that. Just wait for me here. "

"I told you I'm still down for you. Let me prove it. That's the least I can do."

"You ain't scared?"

"Nigga, please. I'm from killa Cali." She opened up the door. "Let's do this."

Joker got out of the car, carrying an empty black gym bag over his shoulder. He shook Geno's hand. Nekole stood on the side of Geno with her hands on her hips like she was his bodyguard or something.

"Sorry about what happened at the shop, man. You too, Nekole," Joker said.

"It's all good."

They both followed Geno inside where he instructed Joker to wait in the living room until he returned. Just like Beno, Joker was staring at the fish when Geno came down from the attic.

"Come back here, Joker," Geno said. He set the kilo on top of the dining room table. Nekole was standing behind him.

Joker set the bag on the table and put his hand on his hip,

close by his gun. Geno took the bag and opened it up. A jolt of fear shot through his body when he saw that the bag was empty.

"Where the money at?"

Nekole winked at Joker, signaling him that Geno was unarmed.

"I was hoping you'd tell *me*," Joker said with a cold look on his face.

Geno caught the cold stare and reacted immediately. He turned to Nekole.

"Gimme my gun."

She took a step back, pulled the .40 caliber out and aimed it at his chest. "Do what he says, Geno. We didn't come to kill you, but we will if we have to. So I'd advise you not to try me."

For the first time in a long time, Geno was scared to death. His heart rate sped up and his palms started sweating. He didn't want to die tonight. Not over paper money. He'd do whatever he had to do to make it out of there alive. But if he ever saw them again, there would be hell to pay.

"The money is downstairs," he said nervously.

Joker pulled the .357 out of his pants. "Lead the way."

Down in the basement, he led them to an old washing machine that sat against the wall. Geno twisted the knob to cold/rinse, then to final spin. After he pushed start, the top popped open. Reaching inside, he began taking out stacks of money, putting them into Joker's gym bag.

When he finished, he closed the bag and handed it over to Joker.

"What the fuck is that?" Nekole said, seeing the small amount of money.

"Sixty thousand. That's all I—" Nekole cocked the gun, stopping him in mid-sentence.

"I told you not to try me, Geno," she said. "I don't know if I told you this, but I killed a nigga before in this same situation. Now show us where the real money is before I deaden yo' ass right here in this basement."

"Fuck all that," Joker said. "We got enough money. Let's get the fuck outta here."

She shook her head. "Naw. We ain't going nowhere with that chump change. This nigga gon' show us where the real money is. Ain't you, Geno?"

Geno went from scared to angry. Not only had the bitch betrayed him again, but she wanted to send him to the poor house as well.

"It ain't here," he explained.

"Well take us to it," she demanded. "Now move yo' fat ass up them steps."

They all got into Geno's truck and drove to a 24-hour storage unit. After he punched in the code at the gate, they drove to Unit 26 and parked.

Geno unlocked the padlock and raised the door. Inside was a bunch of brand new washers and dryers for the laundromat that he was about to open up. He opened the doors to two of the dryers.

Joker damn near fainted when he saw that they were loaded with cash. He had never seen so much money at one time in his life. He reached into one of them and pulled out a stack.

"You've been a busy boy, Geno," Joker said, laughing loudly. "I would've robbed yo' ass sooner if I knew you had it like this."

He looked at Nekole. "Let's load this shit up."

Voluntarily, Geno showed them where a package of laundry bags and a money counter were. They filled the bags and Joker carried them to the truck.

"Y'all got the money," Geno said. "Y'all can just leave me here."

"Why, so you can hunt us down and kill us?" Nekole said. "I don't think so. I hate to do it, but you gotta die tonight, Geno."

"Huh?" Geno said in a cracked voice. "Nekole, please don't do me like that. I promise I won't do nothing to you or him."

Nekole lowered the door until it shut. "Shoot 'em, Joker," she ordered. He raised the gun up to Geno's chest, then hesitated.

"Either you kill him now or worry about him killing us later."

"Joker, don't kill me man, please," Geno cried.

"I've been knowing him too long to do this, Nekole," Joker explained to her as he began to lower his gun. "Let's just let 'em go."

Coward muthafucka, Nekole thought. She closed her eyes and fired three times, knocking Geno to the floor. "Let's go."

After they locked the unit back up, they hopped in Geno's truck. Joker didn't waste any time bolting out of the gate, headed anywhere.

"Where we headed?" he asked, just driving.

She didn't answer right away. Her hands were shaking. She didn't want to kill Geno, but she had to. It would take a while, but she would eventually get over it. Just like she'd done the last time. Ridding herself of coward-ass Joker was the next thing on her agenda.

"Gimme your gun so I can get rid of it," she said.

Without thinking, he took the gun out and handed it to her. "Where to?"

"Go back to Geno's so we can get yo' car. The last thing we want is for the police to find it over there."

"Hell naw."

Cautiously, he turned onto the block, creeping toward the house. His old Chevy Camaro was still parked in front of the house, untouched.

"I'ma follow you," he said, opening the door.

"First we gotta go in there and get that dope off the table. Ain't no use in leaving it."

"I'll get it." He casually walked up to the house.

After she put Joker's gun under the seat, she checked the clip from the .40 caliber. Satisfied with the five rounds that it held, she went up in the house behind him. Joker picked the dope up off the table, looked at Nekole, then turned and ran toward the door. He never heard the blast as the first bullet ripped through his face, lodging in his skull. The second shot hit him in the throat and exited out the back of his neck. His body fell to the floor, twitching violently.

After she wiped off the gun, she bent down, placing it in his hand. They wouldn't know who shot him, but the police would at least think that he shot Geno. That way, if she got caught, she would only have one murder to answer to. Nekole wiped down everything that she thought she touched then left, closing the door behind her.

The owner of the 24-hour storage unit woke up after he thought he heard gunshots. He hurried into his clothes, grabbed his .38 and hit the door. His golf cart moved at a slow pace as he made his rounds around his property.

All looked well until he approached Unit 26 and heard someone screaming for help. Quickly, he jumped from the cart, running to the door.

"Somebody, please help!" Geno cried as he lay on the ground, bleeding.

It took a minute for the man to find the right key. By the time he got it open, Geno had passed out. Right away, the man turned around and ran for help.

Chapter 27

Nekole hid out all week at an expensive hotel in Overland Park, Kansas. It didn't take long, using the money counter, to find out that she was $965,000 richer. But as usual, things hadn't gone as planned. While watching the news, she learned that the owner of the 24-hour storage unit had found Geno alive.

He hadn't told the police who shot him, nor did they mention anything about a robbery. This led her to the conclusion that he planned to come after her himself. Even though she still had Joker's .357, she didn't feel safe. She had to come up with a plan to rid herself of him, for good this time.

Nekole stood on the balcony smoking on a blunt when she heard her cell phone ring. After taking one last puff, she threw it over the side, then ran to get her phone.

"Hello."

"Hey, girl," Angie said cheerfully.

"Angie?" A big smile appeared on Nekole's face. "Girl, it's good to hear from you. How you been?"

"I'm cool," she replied. "So how is everything going in KC?"

Nekole flopped down on the bed. "Great, I guess I could say. It's starting to get cold, so I'ma have to get used to the change in climate."

"You don't sound like things are great."

She sighed. "Enough about me. What's up with you, girl?

When you coming to kick it with me?"

"Bitch, please. I ain't got no money right now to be taking no trips and shit." Angie took a cigarette out of her pack and fired it up. "Mack done lost his job, and I'm the only one working around here."

"No, shit? Well listen, I want you to get off your fat ass and be at Western Union first thing in the morning 'cause I'm wiring you five grand."

"You ain't got to—"

"Yes, I do," Nekole insisted. "I love you, and you're the reason why I got it like I do. So stop acting like that."

"Aw, yeah, girl. Speaking of money, Sirron called and wanted me to tell you that they granted him an appeal bond. It's a hundred thousand, but if you go through the courts, you'll only have to pay ten."

That almost brought tears to her eyes. "Are you serious?" she said excitedly.

"Mm hmm."

Nekole fell back on the bed, kicking her feet. "Yes! My prayers have been answered. In that case, I'ma wire you twenty grand in the morning. Five is for you, five is for my aunt, if you'll take it over there. I tried to call, but I think her phone is off. And the other ten, I want you to get Sirron out with," she said quickly. She took the time to catch her breath. "Now, after you post his bond, I want you to put him on a plane to KC. Then call me with the details so I can pick him up at the airport."

"I will. But when this is all over and I get some free time, we gotta talk."

"I promise I'ma take you on a cruise to Jamaica and tell you everything."

"Aw'ight, now. I'ma hold you to that."

"You do that. Just make sure that you go get my man tomorrow."

"I'ma handle everything, bitch. Don't worry. Bye." She hung up.

Nekole walked back out on the balcony. She looked up at the clear blue sky and inhaled the cold, fresh air into her lungs. With Sirron out, Geno was no longer a problem for her. He would protect her no matter what kind of trouble she was in.

She knew he would be furious about that thing with Geno, and about her abandoning him. But the nine hundred and something thousand that she took from Geno should be enough to heal his wounds. She couldn't wait for him to see how much of a good girl she'd been.

× × ×

The next day, Geno was released from the hospital. His whole upper body was still in pain but he was alive. Luckily for Geno, Nekole had her eyes closed when she squeezed the trigger. The first shot hit him in the hip and went straight through. The big gun jerked in her small hands, causing the second bullet to hit him in the shoulder, and the third shot missed him completely.

Toni sat with him through surgery and stayed every night that he was there. Secretly, she had been hoping he wouldn't make it so she could be with Freak. But as luck would have it, he survived the tragedy.

There were two reasons why Geno didn't tell on Nekole. One, because he planned on killing her. And two, she had robbed him of almost a million in illegal drug money. Reporting something like that would only arouse the Feds' suspicions.

Toni pulled her car around to the front entrance, waiting for Geno to come out. Two nurse's aides helped him, on crutches, out to the car. She hurried around to the passenger side and helped them get him in.

They were headed up 71 on their way out to Geno's house before Toni finally said something.

"You gonna tell me what happened?"

"Not yet. I gotta figure out what I'm gonna do."

"What you mean by that?"

He looked at her for the first time. "I need to go to LA as soon as possible. I got to hit my plugs and get shit back up and running." She glanced over at him but didn't say anything. "Muthafuckas took me for half my worth. That was the money that I copped with."

"Who did it?" she inquired, really wanting to know what went on.

"If I tell you, I can't kill 'em," he said seriously. "I'ma lay back and get my grind on for a minute. At least until I get my bread back right. Then I'ma find both of them suckas and fuck 'em real good."

"If I make that move with you, Geno, you gon' have to pay me twenty thousand up front." She hit her signal, then jumped on the exit. "Since we ain't together no more, I can't risk going out there and getting caught up with you for free."

"I gotta talk to my banker, but I should be able to get it to you by tomorrow. I'ma gas the RV up, so be ready tomorrow night."

This nigga hasn't once thought about thanking me for staying at the hospital with him all week, Toni thought to herself. *He got just what the fuck he deserved. His bitch Nekole hasn't sent so much as a card or called to check on him, but I bet she's on his mind. The storage owner should've left his fat ass to die in that unit.*

Sirron stood in line at mail call, waiting for his now weekly letter from Mustafa's daughter. For the past few weeks they had been writing back and forth to one another. In her letters she talked about wanting a real man in her life and how much she was looking forward to meeting him.

Promise after promise he made to her, saying that if she did this time with him, he would marry her after he got out. She knew he was bullshitting, because he had never seen what she looked like. Mustafa didn't even have a picture of her. But it didn't matter to her, because it just felt good to hear.

"Sirron Rand," the CO said, reading his name off of a letter.

Sirron put his hand up. "Pass it," he hollered out.

Mustafa was standing over the sink shaving his head when Sirron came in waving the letter.

"Got another one from my ba-by," he bragged.

Mustafa stopped shaving and faced him. "Christy wrote you and didn't write me?"

"I didn't hear your name at mail call," he said smartly. He hopped up on the bunk to read it.

The next hour was gonna be a good one, only Sirron didn't know it yet. He was sitting at the table eating and watching TV when the CO walked into the pod.

"Sirron Rand," the CO called out.

He looked up. "Yeah?"

"Pack your shit. You've just made bail. I'll be back in a minute. Be ready."

The spoon fell from his hand as a rush of excitement went through his body. With a big grin on his face, he ran to his cell.

"Mustafa!" he yelled. "Get yo' old ass out the bed. I'm about to go home!"

Mustafa's eyes popped open and he sat up in the bed. "What?"

"Somebody made my appeal bond." He snatched the covers off his bunk, then stuffed them into his laundry bag. "You can keep all my commissary."

After he finished packing his stuff, he gave Mustafa a hug. Mustafa was glad and sad at the same time. They'd grown close to one another in the past months, and he hated to see him go. That was one of the reasons that he never made friends in the joint. Sometimes he'd get attached to them and start believing they were family. And in a way they were.

"Look out for my daughter as soon as you get yourself together," Mustafa said, breaking the hug. "Go see her as soon as you get some money. Remember, you owe me, young bro. You owe me dearly."

"I know, and I won't let you down, man. That's a promise from me to you."

They stared at each other for a moment, knowing they would never see each other again.

"Take care of yourself, young bro," Mustafa said. "Yar-Hamok-Allah." In other words, *May God have mercy on you.*

"I will."

"Rand," the CO yelled. "Let's go."

Sirron didn't bother looking back as he left the cell for the last time.

✗   ✗   ✗

After Sirron stepped off the plane at KCI, he walked to the front gate and began searching for Nekole. He was excited and nervous about seeing a woman that he'd been sleeping with for years.

She wasn't at the front entrance, so he stepped outside. If she was late, he'd see her when she drove up.

Parked to the right of him was a stretched H2. A frail young white man in a black suit and chauffeur's hat stood on the sidewalk, holding a sign that read: Rand.

He smiled. "No she didn't," he said on his way over to the man who held the sign.

"You Rand?" the chauffeur asked.

"Yep."

"And your first name is?"

"Sirron. Sirron Rand."

The chauffeur took off his hat and opened the door.

Nekole soaked her body in a hot tub of vinegar and water. She wanted to tighten up before Sirron went up in it. The last thing she wanted was for him to think that she'd been out there fucking everybody while he was locked down. She expected a good ass whooping before they made love. Hopefully, he would be too excited about seeing her to trip about the past. At least for now.

By the time the stretched H2 pulled up to the hotel, Sirron had already downed three glasses of cognac. He was a little tipsy when he got upstairs to her room door.

He knocked three times.

"Come in," Nekole hollered.

She was sitting in the Jacuzzi sipping on a glass of champagne when he walked in. He smiled at her and she smiled back. He licked his lips and she licked hers.

Slowly, she rose up out of the water, revealing her naked body. Setting her glass down, she stepped out and walked over to him. He just stood there, looking down at her.

"Hey, daddy," she said in a soft, sweet voice. "Why don't you—OW!" He slapped her across her face. Rubbing her cheek, she looked up at him timidly. "I guess I had that com—OW!" He slapped her again.

Grabbing hold of her arms, he pulled her close and began kissing her roughly. She followed suit, helping him out of his clothes while he bit her neck.

"Ohh, I missed you baby," she said, unzipping his pants. She pulled them down to his ankles. "Let me suck it, daddy."

"Fuck that shit," he said as he turned her around roughly and bent her over the table. Spreading her ass cheeks far apart, he ran up in her before she had a chance to get wet.

"Ahh!" she bellowed.

With his hand gripped tight around the back of her neck, he began to pound her viciously. During the whole painful episode, she couldn't help but wonder why he chose that position. She hoped, for her health's sake, that he hadn't been fucking dudes in the ass while he was on lock down.

x   x   x

Since Geno was away in California, Freak called Maurice to see if he wanted to go out. He said, "Cool," and they agreed to meet up at the club they called "6902."

Maurice was already there, and had gotten a table by the time Freak showed up. They shook hands, said their hellos, then ordered a round of drinks.

"So what's been up?" Freak asked.

"I been chillin', man. I'm trying to get my stable of hoes built back up. I fucked up with a lot of bitches." The waitress came and set their drinks on the table.

"I ain't been doing shit either. Trying to make something out of my company. You know what I'm sayin'?"

Maurice had his glass turned up when he murmured, "Mm

hm." He set the drink down after he finished. "I heard they found Geno shot inside a storage room. What's up with that?" he asked. He knew damn well that Nekole was behind the whole thing.

"He told me something about it, but he didn't go into detail." Freak sipped on his drink. "So what's up with you and Michelle? I know she ain't cut out on you. Bitch loves your dirty socks and drawers."

Maurice frowned. "I don't know, I haven't been able to catch up with her lately."

Freak smiled. "I know you hate you ever met wha's her name, huh?"

He shook his head. "Nah. It was a good experience. I mean, shid, I wanted my game tested and she done just that." He took a quick sip of his drink. "Truthfully, I miss the shit out of her."

"What?" Freak said unbelievingly. "What's so special about that bitch that you can't let go of?"

"Well, for one, the bitch sucked my dick and balls at the same time. Not to mention, swallowed a fat-ass nut. You ever had a bitch put yo' dick and balls in her mouth, simultaneously?"

"Hell naw," Freak admitted. He imagined what it would feel like.

"It hurt for a minute," Maurice went on explaining. "But after her warm saliva hit my balls ... whew, that shit felt good."

When Freak laughed, his mouth opened so wide that the light reflected off of his diamonds and could be seen sparkling across the room. "No wonder you fell in love so quick."

"That bitch was a monster, man," he said seriously. "That bitch was a monster."

Chapter 28

Geno and Toni were driving east on Interstate 70 on their way back from LA. She was wearing a Minnie Mouse hat, and he had on a Donald Duck hat. If you were driving on the side of them, you wouldn't have suspected that they had forty-one kilos of cocaine loaded in the back of the RV.

Off at a distance, Geno could see two unmarked police cars and one Highway Patrol car coming their way, headed west. He straightened up at the wheel, looking straight ahead until they passed. Just as he was about to relax, he heard a helicopter hovering above them.

At about that same time, the two unmarked cars and the Highway Patrol made U-turns and began speeding in their direction. Geno remained calm, looking straight ahead. Then he heard the sirens wailing behind him.

Instantly, his stomach knotted up and his heart rate began to accelerate. For the last two years, he had been making this trip faithfully and the cops had never paid him any attention. Now he was about to get busted.

Geno kept driving like he didn't see or hear them trying to pull him over. The Highway Patrol car sped past the RV, getting in front of them. Then it slowed down, causing Geno to pull over. He put the RV in park, then shut off the engine. *Damn*, he thought. *I should've just laid low for a while.*

"Just be cool," he said, "and let me do all the talking."

Toni looked over at him. "I'm sorry, Geno," she said softly.

It didn't take him long to figure out why she apologized to him. Guilt was written all over her face. Before he could respond, the Feds rushed the vehicle and snatched him out of the driver's seat.

While he was face down on the ground being cuffed, Toni was escorted to the back seat of the Highway Patrolman's car. She avoided looking at him.

"You and Freak set me up, bitch!" he yelled.

A big, tall, red-headed agent stepped out of the RV holding one of the bricks of cocaine in the air.

"We got 'em," he informed his fellow agents.

While they clapped, high-fived and congratulated each other, Geno was trying to figure a way out of this.

x   x   x

After Nekole found out the news about Geno being busted with all that dope, she moved back into her house. Sirron couldn't believe the amount of money she had accumulated while he was locked up. She had damn near a million in cash, and she was sharing it with him.

She took him all the way to New York to get clothes for his new wardrobe. Once back in Kansas City, she took him to the Lexus dealership and bought him a new LS430. Fresh out of jail, Sirron was already on top of the world.

There was one thing that bothered Nekole. Why hadn't she heard anything yet about the police finding Joker's body? The only reasonable answer that she could come up with was that it must've still been at Geno's spot. If so, she had to get rid of it before the Feds got to it. If the Feds found the gun in Joker's hand that shot Geno, it would raise questions. And with Geno in the situation he was in, he would provide all of the answers.

Nekole snuck out of bed while Sirron was asleep. After she slipped into a pair of sweats and a T-shirt, she crept out to the garage. She picked up the gas can and shook it to make sure that it was at least half full. Then she put it on the bed of her truck.

Joker's car was still parked in front of Geno's house on 68ᵗʰ Street when she drove down the block. It was a little after midnight, so the neighborhood was quiet. Not wanting to be seen, she drove around the block and parked in front of the house that was directly behind Geno's.

Toting the gas can, she cut through the yard of the house, then climbed the fence over to Geno's backyard. The front door was still unlocked. A foul odor hit her in the face the moment she stepped inside. Her nose wrinkled up as she began to cough.

Stepping over the body, she went to the kitchen to find a trash bag. She returned to the body and carefully kneeled down and pried the gun out of his stiff hand. She put it inside the bag and set it aside for a moment. There wasn't enough gas in the can to douse the whole house, so she drenched the body and everything that was flammable.

She picked up the bag, set fire to Joker's shirt and the curtains, then walked out of the house.

× × ×

Toni fixed a pot roast dinner and set out a bottle of wine. Freak would be over any minute, and she wanted everything ready when he got there. She put on some Luther and dimmed the lights to set the mood. The table was just about set when the doorbell rang.

"Just a minute," she said on her way to the door. When she opened it, Freak was standing there, looking at her suspiciously. "What's wrong, baby?"

He walked in without saying a word. She watched as he cut the lights back up and turned off the stereo. Then he picked up the wine, opened it and took a long swig.

"So." He stopped to wipe his mouth with the back of his hand. "Geno got busted, huh?"

"Yep," she said with excitement in her voice. "Now we can be together." She tried to put her arms around him, but he stopped her. "What's wrong, baby?" She was confused about the strange way that he was acting.

"How did you get out so fast?" he quizzed.

She sat down on the couch and put her head down. "I snitched on him," she said in a low voice. Then she looked up at him. "But I only did it so you and I could be together. You said that we would if something were to happen to him, remember?"

In a swift motion he knocked everything off the coffee table. "Damn!" he yelled. "Bitch, do you realize what could happen to me now?" She just sat there with her mouth open, speechless. "You done fucked up a whole third of my income. Not only that, now I have to worry about Geno bringing me down with him."

Standing up, she walked over to him. "Baby, I—"

He pushed her into the wall. "Don't ever touch me again!" he yelled angrily.

Her eyes were full of fear when she looked up at him, hoping that he wasn't about to beat her up. She peeled herself out of the hole that was now in the wall.

"I'm sorry!" she cried. "I didn't mean to fuck up again, all I wanted was for us to be together. I thought you wanted me to get rid of him."

He wore a disgusted look on his face while he stared at her. "Me and my dick," he said to himself, then turned and walked away.

"Don't go, baby," she said to his back. Quickly, she got on the floor, reached under the couch and pulled out a sack. "Look, baby," she said, dumping stacks of money onto the coffee table. "That's twenty thousand dollars. You can have it all, just don't walk out on me. Please, not now. I need you."

Pointing a crooked finger at her he said, "Stay away from me, Toni." Then he opened up the front door.

She ran after him. "I'm begging you to stay, baby!" she cried, grabbing hold of his arm.

"Get off me!" he yelled, snatching away from her.

He got into his Cadillac and locked the doors. For a quick minute he watched her cry and bang on his window. Then he drove off.

✗   ✗   ✗

The next day, Maurice stood in his office window with a cup of coffee in his hand, praying that his headache would go away. A tall, blond, white girl, who looked like a model out of *Stuff Magazine*, was circling a blood-red Dodge Viper. Just looking at her made his dick stiffen.

Throwing the coffee into the trash, he left his office trying to get to her before Derrick or Roger could. Derrick was coming out of the restroom while Maurice was walking by. He bumped into Maurice, damn near knocking him down.

"Excuse me," Derrick said sarcastically.

"Bitch-ass nigga," Maurice said, loud enough to be heard. Derrick laughed but kept on walking.

The blonde turned around at the sound of Maurice's footsteps coming in her direction. Up close he could see that she was the athletic type, with muscle tone in her arms and chest.

She smiled, staring at him with her big, blue, almond-shaped eyes.

"How are you today?" he said in a professional tone. He shook her hand, noticing her firm grip. "I'm Maurice Jones. Is there something I can help you with?"

"I'm sure there is," she said, flirting. "How much is this?" She pointed at the Viper.

He whistled. "I'm not for sure, but I believe that it's somewhere in the neighborhood of sixty-five thousand dollars." She flinched when she heard that. Then he said his three favorite words. "How's your credit?"

"Excellent," she replied. "But my bank won't loan me more than sixty."

He rubbed his palms together. "Why don't we step inside my office to negotiate? I'm the head salesman around here, and I may be able to work with you."

"Okay," she said cheerfully.

Inside his office he asked her to have a seat while he pulled the file on the Viper.

"Umm ... I should tell you ahead of time that I already know about your personal loan program. In fact, that's why I came here ... pantiless."

He shifted in his chair. "May I ask where you obtained that information?"

"You know a girl named Nekole? Long hair and chinky eyes?"

"Uh huh."

"She told me about it," she lied. "She also said that you would help me out, for a small interest fee." She stood up, walking around his desk. "You like my titties?"

He turned his chair, facing her. "They aw'ight."

"How 'bout I pay you now and we can do the paperwork later?" She reached for his zipper.

"Please do." He slipped his hands up under her skirt and traveled up to her stomach. That's when he felt the wire. "What tha fuck—"

She put a gun up to the side of his head. "FBI, you're under arrest." She snatched him up and pushed him into the desk. "Turn around."

Now he knew why she was so fit. The bitch was a goddamn federal agent.

From his office doorway, Derrick saw two huge white men walk into the building wearing FBI windbreakers. Without knocking, they walked into Maurice's office. That's when he knew that someone had blown the top off of their scheme.

He jumped up out of his seat, opened up the file cabinet and grabbed every file that could incriminate him. Then he threw them into a briefcase and left his office. Everybody's attention was on Maurice's office, so no one saw Derrick when he slipped out the back door.

They took Maurice down to police headquarters where he was searched, booked and thrown in jail. He asked about bond but was told that he had to wait until tomorrow morning. Then he would be transferred to the federal courthouse. If the judge didn't grant him bond, then he would be detained until his trial date.

Maurice found the cleanest spot that he could and took a seat. He put his face inside the palms of his hands and shook his head. Since the agent had known Nekole's name, she had to have been the one who set him up. He told himself a long time ago that Nekole was headed down the path to hell or jail. That's why he left her alone. So how did he end up in this situation?

He glanced around the room to get a good look at where he was. Crack heads and winos were lying on the floor, and others were standing under the TV. It smelled like piss and throw up, and the one toilet was out in the open. He could never get used to this type of environment.

The loud clinging sound of the cell door sliding open got his attention. It shocked the hell out of him when he saw two guards bring Freak in.

"What the hell?" Maurice said, getting up.

Freak was just as shocked to see Maurice. "What you doin' in here?"

"Geno snitched on me," Freak said. "Told them muthafuckas everything."

Maurice was confused. He had no idea how Freak could've gotten mixed up in with what Geno was doing. "How did he tell on you?" Maurice quizzed.

Freak ran down everything to him about how he washed Geno's money for a hefty price. Then he told him about Toni and the affair they were having behind Geno's back. Finally, he got to the part about Toni setting Geno up so they could be together.

"Damn," Maurice said, not believing what he'd just been told. He didn't know his friends like he thought he did. "Man, this whole thing sounds like a damn soap opera."

"Now, tell me what your square ass is doing up in here?" Freak asked.

Maurice sighed. "Man, I ain't even sure what happened."

Freak took a seat on the floor. "Well, tell me what you do know. Because we gon' be here all night."

Maurice sat down beside him. Then he told him everything that happened up until he saw Freak walk into the cell.

Freak shook his head. "I told you that you was gon' get busted doing that bullshit."

"You did. It's just too bad you didn't stop me."

Chapter 29

Nekole and Sirron drove down to city hall to pick up a list of all of the buildings that were being auctioned off in the inner city. Looking at the list, she came across a familiar address. Moving her finger to the left, she noticed it was number ten. To her surprise, it was Geno's shop. A huge grin crept across her face. It was the perfect spot for her to open up Hollywood Hairstyles. God had to have been on her side. With Geno in jail, there was nothing that could stop her.

She decided to drive to the shop so Sirron could see their future place of business. Without Geno, Big E, Tish and Lucki working there, the place looked abandoned.

Sirron parked in what used to be Geno's private parking spot. When they walked up to the front door, they saw that it was boarded up and locked to keep anyone from getting in.

"Ain't it beautiful, baby?" Nekole said, looking at the building. Geno had it built from the ground up less than a year ago, so there wasn't much that needed to be done. All she had to do was change the name and hire a new crew.

He reached out and hugged her. "You did it, baby. I'm proud of you. I left you alone out here and you still made a way for both of us to live comfortably." He kissed her.

"Next we're gonna fly back to LA and hire you the best damn appeal lawyer there is," she promised him. "Then we're gonna get married and have lots of kids and—"

"Shhhh," he said. "One thing at a time."

"You the man, baby." She kissed him. "Now let's go home and play some fuck games."

"Aw'ight, but you driving." He jetted to the passenger side and hopped in. "Stop and pick up something fruity to drink."

On the way home she stopped at Good-to-Go and bought some lemonade for Sirron and an iced tea and newspaper for herself. On her way back to the car, she glanced at the front page and saw something that stole her attention: *Dealership Employee Indicted for Embezzlement.*

She stopped to read the article because she had a bad feeling that it was Maurice. She was right. The article told the story about how Federal Agent Charles Tunnel was contacted by the girlfriend of the accused and informed about a scam that was being run at the Midwestern Chrysler and Dodge dealership. Then it went on, saying how they sent in an undercover officer as a decoy and busted him in the act.

As of that morning, they had frozen $106,007.09 that was in his savings account, and over two thousand dollars in personal checks were seized from his house. No records of any illegal activity were found in his home or at his office. Mr. Jones was due to appear at a bond hearing at eleven o'clock that morning.

Nekole checked the time on her watch. It was almost nine o'clock. Good. She had time to drop Sirron off, stop by a lawyer's office and make it down to the courthouse before he was due to appear in court.

Even though Maurice didn't take part in helping her get the money, he was still considered a friend of hers. He helped her out when she needed it. So why not return the favor? Plus, she wanted to see him. She didn't know why, but some nights while Sirron was on top of her, she would look up and see Maurice's face on his body. Then she would have an instant orgasm. If she thought Sirron wouldn't get jealous, she'd ask him to let Maurice join them for a threesome.

She tossed the newspaper into the trash, then continued on to the car. Sirron had become impatient with her standing there, reading the paper, while he was dying of thirst.

"Can I have my drink, please?" he said smartly.

"Here, boy." She gave it to him. "They had an article in there that I wanted to read."

Nekole pretended that she felt her phone vibrating on her hip. She unclipped it and flipped it up.

"Hello," she said to no one. "What you mean, you goin' into labor? When? No shit? I'm on my way." She hung up.

"Unt unh," Sirron said. "Take me to the crib first. I ain't 'bout to be trapped in no waiting room all day and night."

"You're not gonna ride with me?"

"Hell naw. Take me home," he insisted.

"I am, I am. Hush up with your whining."

After she dropped him off at home, she called Larry Smith, an attorney that used to come up to the shop to get his hair cut. She explained the situation to him and was told to meet him at the courthouse along with half of the twenty-thousand-dollar retainer fee.

Maurice's nerves were jumping while he sat next to his young, pimple-faced court appointed lawyer. *If this is who I have to depend on to save my life, then I might as well plead guilty now,* he thought.

The judge finished reviewing his case and was about to deny his bond when he heard a voice from the back of the courtroom. "Wait, Your Honor," Larry said, walking toward the front. Nekole took a seat in the back row.

"Mr. Smith," the judge said, recognizing Larry. "I hope that you have a good reason for interrupting my courtroom."

Maurice's mother and father both gave Larry their full attention, hoping that he was coming to perform a miracle.

"Yes, I do, Your Honor," Larry said. "First of all, I'd like to excuse the public defender. He is no longer representing my client, Mr. Maurice Jones."

"You're late," the judge commented. "Mr. Peterson, you may excuse yourself." He was referring to the public defender.

After Mr. Peterson excused himself from the courtroom, Larry sat down at the table next to Maurice. "Ah, Your Honor, if you don't mind, I would like to take a brief moment to have a word with my client."

"Go right ahead, Mr. Smith."

"Thank you, Your Honor." Larry faced Maurice. "I can get you out on bond and probably get your whole case thrown out." Maurice started to feel some relief. "But, you gotta do one thing for me."

"Anything," Maurice responded, sounding hopeful.

Larry took off his glasses and looked Maurice dead in the eyes. "Take a good look at me."

Maurice looked at him.

"Do you know me?"

Maurice shook his head no as he inhaled the familiar scent of the Kenneth Cole cologne that Larry wore.

"Let's do this another way," Larry suggested. "You know a woman named Michelle?" Maurice opened his mouth to answer but Larry stopped him. "You don't know *me*, but I know all about *you*. Michelle is my wife." Maurice's eyes became wide as saucers. "Now, I can get you out of this mess, or I can make sure you get the maximum sentence that you can get. Stop fucking my wife, son." Larry extended his hand. "We got a deal?"

"Yes," Maurice said, shaking it. If he only knew, Maurice hadn't heard from Michelle in weeks.

Larry stood up, "Your Honor, may I approach the bench?"

"Step forward."

While Larry discussed the case with the judge, Maurice looked toward the back of the room at Nekole. She smiled and gave him an encouraging wink. He nodded at her, then faced the front of the room.

After a few minutes of conversation, Larry walked back to the defense table. He gave Nekole a thumbs up before he took a seat.

"Mr. Jones," the judge said. "I hereby grant you a signature bond in the amount of fifteen thousand dollars. In addition to this bond, you'll have to abide by the rules and regulations that are given to you by your pre-trial officer."

While the judge continued giving Maurice his speech, Nekole snuck out of the courtroom. When it was over, he looked for her to thank her, but she was gone.

x x x

Sirron was craving a Cherry Cola Slurpee from 7-Eleven. After he put on his jacket, he got into his car and drove around to the store. Just his luck, the Slurpee machine was out of order. A Cherry Coke with crushed ice was the closest thing he could get.

He was waiting in line to pay for it when he saw a newspaper sitting up on the stand. "Let me see what she was reading," he said to himself.

He picked it up, scanning the whole front page. The only thing that he found interesting was the article about an embezzlement case. He paid for the paper and took it out to the car with him. For the next few minutes, he sat reading the entire article. He wasn't certain, but he thought that Nekole was up to something. He could feel it.

Chapter 30

Sirron was sitting in front of the TV playing boxing on the Xbox when Nekole came in. He heard her set her keys on the table, then he felt her arms wrap around his neck from behind.

She kissed him on the cheek. "I'm back, booby. Did ya miss mommy?"

"Mm hm," he replied. "Your friend had her baby already?"

She had almost forgotten about that. "Nah, it was a false alarm." She let go of him and stood up. "Why do you ask?"

He shrugged. "Just wondering why you were back so soon, that's all."

"Sirron, please don't start," she pleaded. "We've been doing real good, so let's keep it that way." She headed for the bedroom, then stopped suddenly. A copy of the paper was sitting on the coffee table. *So that's why he's so suspicious,* she thought. All he had was a newspaper that couldn't prove anything, so she just let it go.

x x x

It was almost midnight and Maurice still hadn't gotten any sleep. The case that he was facing was on his mind, but that wasn't what was keeping him awake. He was thinking about Nekole. Like a superhero she had flown in, saved his life and then disappeared without a trace. His body was calling for hers and he couldn't rest until he had her.

Sitting up in the bed, he picked up the phone off the nightstand. Hesitantly, he dialed her number. He had no idea that Sirron was in town, and Sirron had no idea that he even existed. Sirron knew something was up; he just didn't have a name or a face to back up his suspicions.

Sirron had gone to bed hours earlier, and Nekole was kicked back on the couch, listening to the rain tap on the windows and watching "*The Mack*" for the hundredth time. She was just dozing off when the phone rang. It rang a total of five times before she finally woke up and answered it.

"Hello," she said in a sleepy voice.

"Wha' sup, love?" Maurice said. "Did I wake you?"

Instinctively, she looked down the hall toward the bedroom making sure Sirron wasn't around. "Nah, you didn't wake me. I just dozed off before you called," she said in a low voice. "I'm sorry about what happened to you. If I can help out in any way, just let me know."

"Actually, there is something that you can do."

"What's that, baby," she said, smiling. She loved that feeling she got when she was doing something sneaky. It set her hormones on fire.

"Get in your truck and come over here. I'm sick, and I need some tending to."

Knowing damn well that she should've just said no and taken her ass to bed, she heard herself say, "Alright, but I can't stay long."

"It don't take long to do what I'm trying to do."

"Give me a minute." She hung up.

Quietly, she tiptoed into the bedroom and picked up the clothes that she'd taken off earlier. Then she went into the bathroom to freshen up her coochie before she dressed.

Just in case Sirron woke up before she got back, she wrote a note telling him that Rolesha had gone into labor again, so she went to the hospital. She'd call when she could.

The rain was coming down hard when she arrived at Maurice's house. She pulled into the driveway. While she checked her face in the mirror, she saw a car that resembled Sirron's Lexus drive by.

Thinking that it was just paranoia, she ignored it and ran up to Maurice's door.

Avant's "*Separated*" could be heard playing through the door. She smiled to herself, knowing that he put the song on to make a statement. She rang the bell. He answered the door, wearing nothing but pajama bottoms.

Nekole stepped in out of the rain. "Let's not waste time," she said and began kissing him.

They took off their clothes right there in the doorway. He picked her up to carry her to his bedroom. Reaching back, she pushed the door closed before they both got carried too far away.

Maurice and Nekole fucked each other so hard that they passed out in each other's arms. He felt something hard and cold nudge him on the shoulder, but ignored it. Then he felt it again. He grunted and smacked his lips together as he opened his eyes. What he saw made him tense up.

A strange man, who favored him an awful lot, stood over him with a .357 pointed at his nose. He wanted to reach over and shake Nekole awake, but his arm wouldn't move. At least three times, he had dreamed about this moment. Now it was his reality.

"Do the best thing for you, homie," Sirron said in an angry but calm voice.

Carefully, Maurice sat up in the bed. Sirron grabbed him by his throat, pulling him up. "Get the fuck outta here!" he yelled, pushing him toward the door.

The commotion woke Nekole. Seeing Sirron with the gun in his hand made her want to scream, but nothing came out. Sirron gave her a cold stare. She knew right then that Maurice didn't have a chance.

Maurice remembered the gun that he had stashed under the couch. While Sirron had his eyes on Nekole, he took off down the hall. He was about two feet away from the couch when he felt the first shot enter his lower back. Before he fell face first, he felt another enter the middle of his back. Then the last shot struck him in the ass on the way down.

"Noooo!" Nekole cried, then lunged at Sirron. She pushed him into the closet door. He tried to grab her neck, but she was clawing and swinging wildly. He tried to step to the side and stumbled over one of Maurice's dumbbells. His reflexes caused him to grab Nekole's arm for safety, pulling her down with him. When his back hit the ground, his finger squeezed the trigger, sending a bullet through Nekole's gut.

Her face resembled a scary mask as her eyes widened and her mouth fell open. She collapsed on top of him. Quickly, he rolled her over on the floor and began to pump her stomach.

"Baby, wake up!" he said hysterically. Tears began to fill his eyes. "Baby, please." Pressing his lips up against hers, he began to blow. But it was no use. She was gone.

He laid his head on her chest and wept for a little while. Finally, he stood up, glanced down at her corpse one last time, then left the house.

In his car he threw a tantrum, banging his fist on the dashboard and the window. He was exhausted when he finished. After his breathing slowed, he calmly placed the gear into drive and pulled off.

At her home, he packed his trunk with all the money. By his calculations, he had over eight hundred thousand dollars left. In the back seat, he put all of the new clothes that Nekole bought him. Then he got behind the wheel and took off down the road. He took out his cell phone and dialed Christy's number.

"Hello," she said in a sleepy voice.

"Get up, sleepy head. This is Sirron."

"Sirron? Boy, what took you so long to call me?" she asked. "My daddy said that you been out."

"How is ole Mustafa?"

"He's fine. He's been waiting to hear from you."

"Yeah, I know. I had some business to take care of outta town first. But don't worry 'cause I'm on the highway headed your way as we speak. I got a new car and a trunk full of money so we can kick it. Pack your bags. I should be there in about thirty hours."

"Damn! Where you coming from?"

"Don't worry about all that. Worry about what you're gonna wear to Jamaica when I come get you. We're gonna bring in the New Year making love on an exotic island somewhere."

"Whatever you say, baby."

x   x   x

Feeling depressed, Pasha got into her car to take a drive. The rain stopped, so she figured the streets wouldn't be too slick for her to drive on. She cracked the windows so the cool breeze could blow through her hair. Finding herself with nowhere to go, she decided to drive out to Maurice's house. Hopefully, he wouldn't have company so she could tell him what was on her mind. That's if he would let her in.

Ever since he and Nekole had started fucking around, he had been acting like he couldn't stand Pasha. She hoped what she had to tell him would change his attitude toward her.

When she turned on his block, the first thing she saw was Nekole's truck parked in the driveway. Any other time she would have kept going, but tonight she had something to say to him, and she was about to say it. She was tired of playing cat and mouse.

She parked the car and stormed up to the house. To her surprise, the front door was wide open. That was strange. *He lives in a nice neighborhood and all, but this is ridiculous*, she thought.

"Hello," she called out, stepping inside. "Maurice?" All of the lights were out, so she couldn't see where she was going. As she walked through the living room, her foot got caught on something and she fell down.

At first she couldn't tell what it was. But once her eyes got in focus, she realized that she had tripped over Maurice. He was lying on the floor, face down, in a puddle of blood.

She took a deep breath and let out, "Ahhhhh! Ahhhh!" She screamed at the top of her lungs. Getting on her feet, she stepped over him and ran outside, yelling for help.

x   x   x

His eyes were open, but his vision was too blurry to make anything out. A bright light was in his face, causing his head to ache. He heard a bunch of different voices saying things like, "We're losing him. He's not gonna make it. He's lost too much blood." Then he heard what sounded like his mother crying. He passed out again.

Beep! Beep! Beep! The loud beeping sound of the heart monitor woke Maurice. His eyes opened much too quickly. The bright sun shone through his room window, causing him to squint.

Pasha was standing behind his mother, rubbing her back, and Steve was out in the hallway talking to the doctor. No one saw him when he opened his eyes.

It must have been a mother's instinct, because as soon as he got her into focus, she looked up. "He's awake!" she yelled, rising out of her chair. She ran out into the hallway to get the doctor and her husband. "My baby woke up! Come quick!"

The doctor rushed into the room with Steve and Mary in tow. Pasha walked to the side of the bed and held his hand.

"How ya feeling, son?" the doctor asked. He took a small flashlight from his pocket and got a good look at Maurice's pupils.

He tried to speak, but his mouth was too dry. He swallowed, then tried again. "I'm okay."

His eyes shifted down at his feet, then he saw something that scared him. His mother was massaging his ankle, but he couldn't feel her hand. He tried to move it, but it wouldn't budge. Then he tried the other leg with the same outcome. He could wiggle his fingers, but his toes refused to cooperate.

"Doc," he called out. "I can't move ... I can't ... feel my legs."

The doctor shot his mother a questioning look. Immediately tears began to roll down her face. Unable to look at her son, she turned and ran away. Steve ran after her. He didn't want to see his son's reaction after the doctor told him something that would change his whole life. He would never walk again.

Steve was halfway down the hall when he heard his son cry out. He embraced his wife. The two of them held each other because they could feel their son's pain inside their hearts.

* * *

When Sirron arrived in LA, the first thing he did was stop at Christy's house. It was a small, white stucco house with bars on every window. Seven or eight thugs were hanging out on the corner with blue rags hanging out of their back pockets. He ran his hand over the top of his head and licked his dry lips before he got out.

He knocked on the door two times.

When the door opened, he saw a light-skinned, short but shapely women with micro braids in her hair, standing there checking him out. She matched Nekole's beauty in every way. He thanked God that she didn't look like the typical jail hookup.

"You must be Sirron," she said in a childlike voice.

"And you must be Christy."

She stepped toward him and gave him a big hug. "It's good to see you again."

"Again?" he asked, confused. "Have we met before?"

"Nope," she said, stepping aside so he could come in. She closed the door behind him, locked it and took out the key. "Make yourself at home, I'll be right back." She disappeared into the back room.

There was a poster-sized picture of Mustafa taken in the county jail sitting on top of the fireplace. He glanced at all of the pictures of Mustafa on top of the TV. One picture caught his eye: a family portrait of Mustafa, his wife and their three kids. There was Christy. Next to her was some dude who looked familiar, but he couldn't put a name with the face. Then, kneeling down beside him, was a face that he could never forget. Not as long as he was alive on this earth.

Now it all made sense. Why Mustafa was so eager to work on his case. Why he insisted that Sirron go see his daughter. At first he didn't understand what Mustafa really meant when he said, "You owe me dearly." He wasn't talking about paying his debt with money. He wanted Sirron to pay with his life, for taking his son's. An eye for an eye.

Sirron ran to the door and tried to open it. But it was locked. Then he tried the windows. But they were barred. He had been set up and was trapped. Mustafa played his game by using Christy as bait to set him up, just as Sirron used Nekole to trap his son before they killed him. Sirron had become a victim of his own stratagem.

"Wha' sup, cuz?" he heard a familiar voice say. "Remember me?"

The voice was so cold that Sirron's body twitched.

Standing in the middle of the dining room floor with a .45 in his hand was the guy who stood up and yelled, "If my brother can't see his kids again, he shouldn't either!" during Sirron's plea hearing. Christopher Lamon's brother.

x   x   x

A week later, Mustafa stood in line at mail call, waiting for his daily paper. After he received it, he took it back to his cell and shut the door. He sat on his bunk and began to read. He found what he was looking for on the second page.

The body of Sirron D. Rand was found in a wooded area on the West Side of Los Angeles. Autopsy reports say that he had been beaten and sodomized before he was eventually killed. Police have few leads and no witnesses at this point.

Mustafa cut out the article and taped it up on the wall. After he shut off the light, he took off his shoes and climbed in the bed. Justice had been served. Now he could rest.

Epilogue

Four Years Later

Geno was convicted but sentenced to only seven years in federal prison after he gave up Freak and his Californian plug. Every now and then, I would receive a letter from him, talking about our lives before Nekole and how we allowed her to slither her way into our lives and spread her addictive but poisonous venom around, hooking us all like a contagious disease. That not only destroyed our lives, but the bond that we called "friendship." We both had our own version of how she'd done it, but would never admit it to the other.

Freak was released on bond shortly after he'd gotten picked up, and hadn't been seen since. Toni moved to Richmond, Virginia, and used the money that Geno gave her to invest in a book she wrote about her own life's experiences.

Last I heard, Derrick and Michelle were seen together leaving the Budgetel Inn during lunch hour. Even after seeing how I ended up, he still didn't take heed.

After Larry got my case thrown out of court due to lack of evidence, I tried to celebrate by proposing to Pasha, but she turned me down. I couldn't get mad because I put her through a lot. Even through all of the operations, rehabilitations and courtroom battles, she was right there to hold my hand. She ended up marrying some music engineer and moving to St. Louis. Still, we remain friends for our child's sake. She kept her promise by letting me keep him for two weekends a month, and I kept mine by being the best father that I possibly could.

Today I sit alone, looking out of my living room window. Maurice Jr., who is three years old, is bouncing his basketball in the driveway. I swear, each time I see him, he has grown an inch.

He dribbles to the left, then to the right. Finally he messes up after trying to bounce it between his legs. I want to run outside and help him, but I'm not physically able because I'm now confined to an electric powered wheelchair.

Luckily, my old and dear friend, Kim, the registered nurse, is still on my team to this day. She moved in about a year ago and we plan on being married by fall. I'm disabled, but I have a loving fiancée and I have a chance to be around to see my son grow up.

My mother told me a long time ago that every woman is a fool for a man in one way or another. Now I believe those words to be untrue. I take a good look at my current situation and find that everybody plays the fool at some point in their life.